Can I
STOP
NOW?

Cesar Acosta

Mike!
Brother-In-Arms,
And so forth. Take
care, dude. We'll
keep talkin'
later.
Cesar

ISBN: 1-4392-0760-7
ISBN-13: 9781439207604

Visit www.booksurge.com to order additional copies.

Acknowledgements

This is for the Acosta and Mendez families, bringing both names to greater aspirations and hopes.

A special thanks to my parents and siblings, and this includes those that came into the family through marriage, for their support.

A thanks to those brave men and women that chronicled their ordeals with criminal minds, and were able to share their insights.

A thanks to Dr. Robert Keppel, for giving me something to aspire for. I only hope I can save as many lives as you have, through your insights.

All of you have been able to give me the confidence to push forward and reach for my dreams.

.

Prologue

Streaks of yellow and an earthly copper flashed by the girl's eyes on either side of her thin shoulders, widening the breadth between the rows upon rows of cornstalks she used as cover. She thought only briefly of how she would run through these same rows in her younger years, laughing and smiling with her older brother. He was the older of the two of them, only by a few months, but he acted far beyond his years. She remembered him, even in her hour of darkness. She remembered the small tight-lipped smile he gave her after he would take a mild beating from their father, who used the same bloodied fist to pound their mother into a coma. He had demand that they believe his account, and tell all others accordingly that it had been an accident.

At the moment, though, Mina kept herself from letting her tears, build up into a wail of desperation. Her whole body had been sore since she left her father's den, as he was so fond of calling it. She remembered feeling her father's body cover her own as he spread her legs painfully wide, making the pelvic joint groan in protests. She tried to push him off, despite how much he outweighed her. His movement stopped for a moment. He lifted his upper body off of her, supporting himself on one hand. He pulled back the free hand, and brought it down hard on her small thigh. He did this with a smile and laughed as she yelped. She moaned as he shifted his waist to level with hers. Then she screamed as he penetrated her inner sanctum. He moaned loud, trying to drown out the shallow screams that peeled from her mouth. At times, they came out as not so much as gasps for air. He continued to motion himself into her, over and over. She yelled for him to stop once, getting another hard whack for that, on the same thigh he had scorched only moments before.

His jaw began to hit the top of her head in rhythmic thumps as he moved in and out of her. She started to sob as she felt herself widen painfully, her legs bending outward as her father pried them apart, plunging himself into her.

Suddenly, both heard the kitchen door fly inward and slammed against the counter top, breaking two of the bottom windowpanes. Mina found her voice, and started to scream as loud as she could. Her father started to repeatedly slap her thighs. Suddenly, he stopped and started to squeeze her small breasts so that she couldn't breathe in long enough to manage another scream.

Her brother came in kicking the locked door inward, splintering the wooden frame as the metal brace tore loose from its rotted mooring, flying to the floor, screws and all. Her brother stood there with a shotgun held within his thin arms. Len seethed, "Get off of her! Now!"

The old man looked back at her brother, almost smirking. She felt the part of him that was within her, shrink out of her. Much to her relief, he pulled out of her.

He pulled his jeans up, beginning to pull on his belt.

Len cocked both barrels, raising the shotgun to shoulder level, putting its butt to against his chest.

Len muttered, menacingly, "Buckle it, old man."

Then he risked a look at his sister, and asked coolly, "Can you stand?"

She choked out a grunt, her hand going to her mouth as she coughed violently.

"Don't talk. If you can, just run."

She did.

Now, here she was, running through the dead corn. She finally remembered that she had been happy that morning. Her brother, sickened by their father's perverse treatment of her, announced that they'd be leaving for the city. He had told her to pack because they'd be moving in with her mother's nurse friend.

Mina happily opened all of her drawers, and that was when her father came in, thereby beginning the cycle. She wanted it to end at that moment, maybe by killing him then and there. She had nothing to fight him with, and was defenseless as his massive frame consumed her vision. She could see nothing in those moments, and she would feel trapped as the smothering began.

Again, her brother's words echoed in her head as she brushed past the dead stalks of corn. She wanted to die with them, feeling that hot wind blow at her back as the moon slowly began to drift across the sky, while the sun painted the clouds with a deep shade of scarlet.

She thought longingly, *I want to be that sky...*

She finally let herself rest, getting to her knees and finally sitting on her lower legs. She realized then that the soles of her feet were quite sore. She looked back over her shoulder at them. She saw that they were not sweating, as she first believed, but bleeding. She wondered if she had been all along. The thought made her heart beat faster. She tried to keep from crying audibly, to stifle the moans of fear from getting past her throat. That got her coughing again. She tried to swallow each back down, but her tears made that impossible. She felt that she was drowning in her own tears.

She heard the unsteady thumps of her father's footsteps. She prayed for that to be her brother. Maybe, she hoped, he actually got out of fighting their father, and got off a shot. The other scene was not so pretty. He had actually gotten into a fistfight with their father, and managed to win, even though he took a few punches.

Still, even with these hopeful thoughts, she didn't dare call out for her brother. She noticed another sound as those stomping steps came closer. She risked a glance back seeing a hunched figure, lurching and dragging something behind them. She whipped her head to look forward, trying to tuck her chin into her breasts, praying deeply. She did this, still choking back the tears, and the acrid taste of her own blood. As she stumbled through the stalks, she had bitten her own tongue to keep from fainting.

The steps stopped right behind her.

She felt a moist thud next to her, as specks of dust and pebbles aggravated the pins and needles that crawled around in her lower legs. She silently cursed herself for letting her limbs fall asleep. She hit them over and over now; even pounding at them flat handed just so she could get moving again.

She saw something fall onto the ground beside her. Also, the nerves that awakened were not the ones in her legs. Instead, those in her scalp flared with pain. She felt her hair being pulled up. She looked down at the corpse of her brother; face down, though his head was slightly raised from the ground. She squinted trying to focus, seeing the thick wooded handle protruding out from under his head, the puddle of blood growing larger, sinking into the dry dusty sun beaten ground. Watching the blood sink into those dry cracks, she wondered how anything could grow here at all. Then she remembered that the crops were rotted stalks infested with termites, their eggs and whatever other vermin decided to settle.

She felt her father lick her neck, still holding her by up her long red hair. He kicked the corpse so it would face up, showing her his idea of power. Her brother, whom had protected her, made her smile, and held her when she cried for the first fourteen years of her life, was gone leaving only the husk. Those gentle gray eyes would give her those assuring winks and wrinkled at their corners when he smiled. Now, they were also gone. The right eye was a glazed marble of shock. The prying end of her father's stainless steel hammer destroyed the other.

He whispered into her ear, "You're stayin' here. If you try to run, I'll kill you the same way."

Despite the pain she felt from her scalp, or from all over her body for that matter, she rasped, "I'll take you with me."

She ignored the pain in her scalp as she turned to face him, and spat the gob of blood that had settled at the bottom of her throat; with it came some of her bloodied vomit. It landed squarely on his cheek just below his irritated right eye.

He threw her down, landing her atop her brother's corpse.

He yelled down at her, "You little bitch!" It sounded muffled, though, since he was wiping his face with his sleeve. In his utter rage, he kicked her in the stomach with his steel toe workman's boot.

She only grunted wanting to cry out, but not quite daring to. She didn't want him to have that satisfaction.

"I got a little job for ya... You love him so much, you bury him. Then you come to my room tonight."

With that, he limped away.

In those silent hours of sleep she dreamed, not of being smothered as she usually dreamt when her father would sit her in his lap after a long day at work out with his fellow drunks. His breath would smell of booze as he tightly wrapped his arms around her. One around her waist, holding her close to his lap, making her feel discomfort as the lump between his own legs grew larger and narrower. It was a trapped snake that tried to slither between her inner thighs. Before she knew it, that snake seemed to freeze, making her feel as if she were sitting flush to the horn of a horseback saddle, a worn one at that. She could smell the stale beer, mixed with tasteless corn chips. All this was drowning her, but it wasn't nearly as bad as the thick arm that covered her mouth. The hairy limb was a soft rotting tree that had been skinned raw and dowsed with after shave balm, and sweat that could've been shed a week before. The drowning was bad, but the smothering was the worst.

She would sleep uneasily on nights like that, if at all. She would dream of drowning in a dense stinking ocean permeated of sweat and after-shave balm that had gone sour. The stink filled her mouth, her nose, and her ears. Still she didn't want to swim up to the surface because of the logs floating on the surface. On this ocean, they were logs of flesh covered with hair, and callused skin. She began to kick upward because she didn't want to hang on the arms of her much-hated father.   She stopped trying to regulate her breath in this dream, though. She would've gladly died with her brother. She wanted to drown already, in that ocean of sweat, and week-old musk. This time, though, that ocean drained away. Then she felt her blood fill this ocean. She finally closed her eyes, letting the darkness consume her.

Mina woke up, looking over at her brother's corpse. The blood had long since dried, having doused the hammer in a coat of scarlet.

In that moment, her horror and revulsion had faded as she thought of her brother's last words to her, "Go on, move." He had been protecting her. That came with a wave of the fierce love she had for her brother.

There, growing in the lifeless ground between them was a single red rose. It was supple, fresh, and adorned with plentiful petals.

She plucked it, knowing it was for her alone, and went into the house, making note in her mind to bring out Len's best clothes so that she could bury him.

She was so tired after burying Len in the hole she had made. After filling in most of it, she stopped before filling in the last foot of dirt. She threw on seeds of rose. She felt it wasn't a waste. Her brother would tend to those roses even in death.

She had not been wrong about that. Indeed, that bush had grown up and out, choking the wilting stalks of corn. It did, however, give life to peas, and carrots allowing her to feed the rabbits in the hutch, as her brother had. Her brother had been good to her, always.

Her father had all too often picked roses from there for the women he would bring to the house. She laughed, though, because his callused hands were covered with sores from having been stuck with the thorns the several times he plucked a rose from that bush marking her brother's grave.

<u>Anonymous Martyr</u>
Will you shed a tear of blood?
While I Spill out all my hate and love,

Can I do this while you soil my home, Burn it down to the ground,
Telling me more and more, That my words are nothing to you

Is all this for your honor, Your glory,
So that you know you're king

Well then, Why don't we start to kill each other?
Then you can rule your kingdom of ashes, Building bridges over rivers of blood

So come and take me
Make me fight your war, Torture, Kill me,
Hide my death from all so I can't be a martyr, though,
Lest it be for your cause.

Am I a pawn, Or less than that.
If I am, don't tell me what to think.
Stop lying to my face, saying what you do is for my future.

If you are so worried 'bout my fate, Then come with me to fight.

Not even that, You fight your own fucking war.
Fight with your own hands; Stain them, cut them,
Grind them through the bitter soil.

Until you do all this, You are nothing to me.
Stop spilling my blood, killing me for your glory.

If you want to fight so badly, fight me, fight your child,
Kill each other; Spill my blood as I spill yours,
Then go home, Spill more blood there, If you like.

If you want to kill so badly,
It shouldn't matter who the target is.
Take your children, Take your mother, and Take your brother,
Take your sister; Take your father,
Just don't take mine!

What's that? You can't do it? Why can't you kill them?
They are your treasures?

Didn't you want war? To fight and kill and burn?
If you don't, someone else will.

You still can't? Then shut up about Justice, About Glory, and Loyalty.
None of that matters in the chaos you made, in the world you wanted

If you can't kill in my name, why should I kill in yours?
Still want to fight? Want to kill me?

>   -   Songs of Lester,
>   Coffee, No Sugar Album.

When Ryan Sandler got home his father was on the couch, passed out. He took a thin army blanket from the floor, and used it to cover his father. Then Ryan went to his room to begin the long tedious process of studying.

He had just finished setting up his books for easy access, having it all laid out on the bed. He heard a pounding on the door. He decided to open the door before his father broke the lock again.

He was surprised the flimsy wood survived the drunken pounding, even.

"What the hell are you doing in there that you got to lock the door?"

"I'm studying, sir."

Before Ryan could think of moving, his cheek flared painfully as he tried to keep his balance. He cursed at himself for not preparing, although he was ready for the next blow. It swung past him, back and forth, missing him. He knew that if it connected, he'd be in the hospital. The other fist went swinging and he was able to dodge. There was an opening in his movements, but he hoped his father didn't notice it.

An older boy reached for the old man, grabbing him by the shirt collar, and shook him, "What are you doing, old man?"

"Trying to knock some sense into your brother."

Eric shook him again. "He's not the one who needs it. You do, though. Go sleep it off."

He let the old man go, glaring at him until he left the room.

Ryan helped himself up, trying to settle into the wooden chair for his desk. Once he did, he pulled out the center drawer, which had plastic baggies and handed an empty one to his brother. Eric already knew the routine, and went to the kitchen.

He came back with the ice only minutes later. Handing the ice pack to Ryan, He asked, "What is it this time?"

"I never know with that guy."

"You know I'm at practice until five-thirty. Why don't you hang out there?"

"And face a whole bunch of guys who can't stand me, all fully aware as opposed to a drunken old man with a mean left? Great choices."

"Well, I keep telling you to stick with me."

"I know, I know."

"Then why don't you?"

"I guess because I don't want to mess things up for you."

"Now why would you say a thing like that?"

"I was with mom when she died, you know?"

Eric's mouth became a thin line. "It wasn't your fault."

Ryan hit his fist on the desktop. "Yes it was. Mom got killed trying to save me."

"That's what parents do."

"Not Dad. I'll bet he wishes I'd been killed."

"Now don't say that."

"Because it's true?"

Eric slowly inclined his head, unable to really answer.

Their father made it totally clear he didn't want Ryan around. Eric wondered why that was, but couldn't really go deeper than that. Ryan kept his place, now standing at the desk, and went on, "You know what mom told me?"

Eric shook his head.

"She told me to be careful. In fact she told me not to stumble on the dark star. That was in the ambulance."

Eric sighed, "Well, mom was into all that psychic friends stuff."

Ryan nodded, "I thought about that too. I don't think she would start going off about all that at the last moment, though."

"Ryan, it wasn't your fault. I don't think mom could stand to see you get hurt. She went with her instincts."

"If something that bad happened, I don't want you to get that kind of bad luck because I happen to be with you."

"That's crap."

"You think I'm messing around?"

"You're not thinking straight, of course. You're not. The old man hit you pretty hard."

"You're not listening."

"Yes, I am. When people at school tell me you hang out alone, I feel bad. Ryan, you're not alone, ok?"

The two brothers let the moment pass, and went to a movie that night. Their father was asleep when they left. When they got home, they watched some TV and fell asleep shortly after. It had been a good day for them.

It's so odd how the littlest thing brings a rift into the parent and child relationship. Dara Fanning felt she was closer to her mom, closer than most girls, in fact. Dara could confide in her the way she would an older sister. Her mom loved this; even bragged about how hip she was to the other moms that went to casino night at the Saffire Falls community center. "Oh, my daughter thinks I'm the bomb." while wearing a tacky pink shirt with a heart around the words, "HIP MOM!"

If Dara asked her mom to help her with homework for math, she'd get a response like, "What hell would I know?"

Sometimes, Pam would be a total airhead, and say, "What am I? Your mom?"

Dara forgave her, but she would never forget how it felt when her mother uttered such thoughtless words. Dara couldn't help feeling unimportant to her.

Melissa Thompson came up behind Dara, and covered her eyes, playfully whispering, "Guess who?"

"That candy peppermint perfume is way over the top, Melissa. I could smell you from down the hall."

Melissa pouted as Dara turned to face her. She dropped the frown in a second, though. She'd remembered what she wanted to ask Dara. "Are you going to Debbie's for the sleepover?"

"Like, hell yeah."

"Awesome. Now, for the tough question; who's going to drop you off?"

"My dad."

Melissa let out a huge sigh of relief.

Giggling, between breathes, Dara managed, "Why do you ask?"

"Your dad acts normal. That's why."

"I know my mom is kind of weird."

"Kind of? Oh my god. If she were driving you there, she'd be packing her own pajamas and toothbrush."

Dara nodded with embarrassment, "I know, I know."

"Allison nearly freaked when your mom brought over a six pack of beer. That almost got us kicked out for good."

Dara looked down for a moment, making Melissa reach out to hold her friend's shoulders, squeezing them gently. "Hey, it's not you, Dara. It's your mom. She's been trying to be in our group since that first Valentine's dance in the second grade. Don't you remember how she joked about spiking the punch? Hell, she was trying to fix me up with Bobby Shermer, and I was only nine. After that little event, she thought she did me a favor. She had lunch with us everyday, after that. I think she told me once, that she would be checking up on us. Now, if she wanted to have lunch with you, that would've been different. Nope. Not this lady, because she stood with us in the cafeteria line, and bitched with us about the food. She asked us about where we got our sneakers. I saw the guy serving up lunch that day, because he kept giving her that kind of look." Melissa tried to imitate a lurid gaze. "Then, she came up to the counter, grabbing a tray, and a milk. He thought she was nuts."

Dara looked at Melissa seriously, "Like the look your brother gives you?"

"Don't say it. It creeps me out enough, having to go home to that."

"Oh my god, Melissa. How long has that been going on?"

"Look. Never mind that. I'll deal with it when it becomes a big problem."

"It's looking pretty big right now, I'll tell you that."

"I'll deal with it."

"When? How?"

"I'll see. Right now, we're talking about you, and your mom."

"Like I said, I know my mom is kind of out there."

"Dara, she wanted to teach us out to French kiss at that last bash. She called it a rite of passage. I don't know what the hell that means, but I want to be a kid for a few more years, myself, actually. She's been trying to bring us into her world, seems like."

"How do you know that?"

"I overheard her talking to the cafeteria guy at our high school. She called us her girl friends. You know how that sounds?"

"Like she needs help, I know. Listen, my step-dad's been good for her. Ian's brought her down to earth, pretty well."

"I guess. . .She's calm in front of him, probably. With us, she's pretty wild, though."

"You can say it."

"She's nuts. I'm your friend, so I'm telling you up front what I think."

"Yeah, she is."

"That whole thing with her wanting you to call her big sister, and insisting that you call her by her name. Has she always been like that?"

"Not always. I mean, when I was really little, she used to be like a real mommy type. When I got old enough to go to school, and all that, she got bitter. So much that I didn't want to go home. Then, she met Ian, and got happy again."

"Yeah, she's too happy now."

"I know she's a pain. If you'd just give her a chance."

"You know, Dara, I'm not shallow. I try to be cool with everyone. When your mom starts handing out beers, and tells us to keep quiet about it, I have a problem with that. When she hands out condoms, just in case we bump into some cute boy, I have a problem with that. With everyone rushing to grow up, I'd rather not. I mean, oh my god, we're fifteen and all that, but hell, we don't have to act like we're twenty. That's such bullshit."

"Well, if you're not shallow, why does that bug you? Are you like embarrassed of her?"

"She's not my mom, but I'm embarrassed for her, *for her*. I feel bad for you too, Dara. I know you don't want to tell her any of this because you think you might hurt her feelings. I think she can take it, though. In fact, if you tell her, she might just curse you out, and bitch about having spent time all that with you.

She'll make it all about her, Dara. It's not all about her. It's about you, Dara. You're her daughter, and she's supposed to be looking out for you, and telling you what's right and what's wrong. She shouldn't be worried about what's cool, and all that shit."

"I know. You're a good friend. If she comes along, just bear with it, ok?"

"I won't promise anything."

"Please?"

"If she breaks out the condoms, I'm all over her, ok?"

"Thanks, Melissa."

Dara had only been home a few minutes, having dropped her backpack off in her room. She was thinking about how loose her mother was. The only thing Pam Fanning drew the line at was her suede jacket, which she kept for nights when she had a "business" meeting. Ian, her husband, knew nothing about the meetings, either. He was her dad, though, Mr. lay-down-the-rules and such. At least, Dara could go to him and tell him when she felt bad, and he would comfort her, but not cajole or patronize her. She was about to ask her dad where the frozen lasagna was when she heard her dad hitch back a breath before trying to talk. He found out about the meetings when one of Pam's gentleman callers showed up at the front door with roses and champagne. Ian told him that he had the wrong place, but Dara could tell he was hurt.

He cleared his throat, and looked over at Dara. He took a deep breath, and then gave her a sad smile.

"These salesmen can't take no for an answer. I told him I didn't want to subscribe to Daily Gents."

"Um, dad..."

"What, Dar?"

"Well...um,"

"I hate that stuff, anyway. But hey, I bet your mom would be..."

"Dad..."

She heard his breath hitch again.

"Yeah, she'd be real impressed if she knew I was..."

She said no more words and walked up to him.

"Trying to be...cool."

She hugged him. There he stood, looking away, hissing through his grit teeth as he tried to talk, and blink away the tears that formed at the corners of his eyes.

"Aww, dad....." She hugged him, closer still, and for the first time in a long time, she felt better about herself. For that moment, though, she hated her mom. She was fifteen now, and had known Ian since she was nine or ten. Her mother and been a real mess then, and a little older than Ian by five years. He had been twenty-three, a fledgling law student working his way as a law clerk, Pam would go to work in halter tops and go-go skirts. She rather liked, or pretended to be into Ian. She even brought him home a month just after their first date.

He had left his pursuit on a hold period. Pam introduced Dara as her niece and later as her daughter. Only, it was after the honeymoon in Vegas with Elvis as a witness. He realized only then that Pam had somehow tricked him into marrying her. So, for her mom she felt an almost intense hate.

He reached down and held her at arm's length, and told her that he would be going out for a walk. She watched him leave but never got to see him come home. For the last five years she called him her dad. This was mostly because he took care of her school matters. Also, he adeptly handled himself as her Guardian. In the short five years he became the one that lay down the grounding and punishments. It was during all that when her mom started becoming the hero of the day and would help her sneak out to parties and sleepovers. For a while and Dara was happy that her mom wanted to get close. When Pam started cheating on her dad she felt at a loss. It felt like Pam married him to do a lot of the parent role, and take the role of bad cop in her little game.

Without any help from her mother, Dara snuck out of the house. She was hoping to get to the Million-Dollar district. She was going to buy her dad a briefcase so he could go back to school and pick up his law career. She never made it. When she got to the corner of 8th, and Nash, she took a ride from a young driver. He'd approached her, claiming he was new in town. Dara wasn't sure what to think of that. She was only fifteen or so, and she felt odd about being asked for directions. He seemed to be leering at her body, his eyes moving up and down her legs, which were covered only by a short skirt her mother had given her for her last birthday. The outfit had gotten her suspended from school for a day since the skirt was far too high for any other junior high girl's skirt.

"Hi. Do you know this area? I'm kind of lost?"

"Well. I wouldn't know. I'm heading somewhere, myself."

"Well, hop in. I can give you a ride if you like. You'll have to give me directions, though. I'm such a dork."

She gushed and got into his car, "Thanks for the ride."

He tried to seem friendly but his eyes seemed to shift in their sockets rapidly. As he went in circles, she saw that Melissa was going to the corner market on her block. She was with her brother, Dave, but she still noticed that Dara was with a stranger. However, the events of that day were so terrible for Melissa that she would want to forget that night. Melissa did remember that she saw Dara a second time that night, but unconcious.

"Where are you heading?"

"I'm going to the Million Dollar District."

"Oh, I know where that is."

"Wait just a sec. Didn't you say you were new here?"

The driver motioned to a sign on her side, to which Dara looked and saw nothing interesting. When she turned to face him again he was armed with a long black crowbar which consumed her vision as it struck her forehead.

Hours later, after being beaten is enough times she did not fight it or bite when he forced her to perform oral sex. After choking up semen for half an hour she was anally raped for two hours. Then she was knocked out, and woke up in the dark. Then her kidnapper opened the door to his walk-in freezer. The green fluorescent lighting did nothing to clarify what he looked like. In fact, her eyes were too swollen to open. The light bothered her eyes and so she only caught a glimpse of him before she closed them again.

"Aww, fuck. You're all ugly now...I'll wait til your face gets all better, and then we'll have some more fun."

She reached out to touch his face gently holding his cheek in her hand.

Then she moved it all over his lips then up to his nose. Then her hand moved up to his eyes, and he closed them reflexively, and then opened them slowly. When he did, he realized that she was on her knees in front of him. She clawed her hands, and brought them down on either side of his face. He screamed as he knocked her away, and then she stood back up and calculated a moment. After which she kicked him in the balls.

He had a cup on, but made himself fall on his side breathless, lying across the entrance to the freezer thereby blocking it. She kicked him again, this time in the stomach. He had already pulled out his switchblade and his grip only tightened when she kicked him.

Before she could kick him again he pulled his right arm free from under his body weight and grabbed her ankle tightly. His left arm came up and stabbed her thigh. She fell back losing her balance. As he got up and crawled over to her she had little breath left.

He seethed, "You little bitch!" driving his blade into the center of her chest.

She coughed up blood, spattering it across his face, and using her last breath to choke out, "lil bish you cat fuh!" and then, died. He got to his feet, left the fridge and came back with a hook. He put it aside, and had his way with her. He then used the hook to boar a hole into each foot then he hoisted her whole body up to the meat line held by the thick hook.

By the time Ian got home Pam was back but she was sleeping on the couch, smelling of wine and roses. Her non-perfume seemed to permeate their little apartment He thought she might have gone out to drink with a few friends. He knelt on one knee by the couch to pick her up, leaning in close so he could squeeze his arm under her. She turned on her side so she could face him. That's when he found that she had not been drinking at all. It was her neck as well as her breasts that had the strong odor of alcohol, and it wasn't so much her breath tasted of wine but her lips. He found himself confused, still deciding whether or not he should leave her there. He softly called her name, to which she answered, "Hmm...Harry... no more tonight."

Then he asked, "Where's Dara?"

She slowly opened her eyes and realized where she was. He looked at her for one long moment. After he made eye contact and broke it, he stood up he made his way to Dara's room in the dark and found it empty. . He ran out to the living room, and demanded of Pam what didn't come naturally to her.

"Where's Dara? No lies."

She looked at him wide eyed and trying to piece together what he was saying.

He knelt by the couch holding her by the shoulders and asked as calmly as he could manage "Where's Dara? Did you take her to a friend's house for a sleep over or something like that?

"I don't know."

"Pamela!" He tried to calm himself and then slowly drew out. "Ok, this is important, none of this sisters' oath bullshit or any of this cool mom bit. Your- Our daughter is missing."

She still looked wide-eyed and bewildered. He thought it was like talking to a child who had lost their retainer.

After a while he let go of her shoulders, and heaved an exasperated sigh as he stood. He went over to the desk he used to study for midterms on. He looked in the top left drawer and pulled out the phone book he had bought when he first moved in. Now instead of friends' numbers it had the numbers for a bunch of his daughter's friends. Under each one was the number for their parents as well, mixed in with all those numbers were those for a couple of Pam's boyfriends as well. They weren't all ex-boyfriends, either. So the long tedious process of checking each one began. By the time he had finished it was a quarter of five. The last number he called was the police. This was the number for one of Pam's boyfriends and he was younger than Ian himself. Pam must have used the number dozens of times because he seemed over friendly in answering the phone drawling, "Hey... Couldn't get enough of me?"

To this, Ian answered, "I'm sorry. Have the local police gotten disturbingly friendly, or have I dialed the wrong number?"

That prompted the officer to clear his throat, his words spewing out in a confused jumble before he could finally manage something coherent. "I'm sorry. I thought this was Pam."

"Oh, she's around...I didn't call to talk about her though. Could you transfer me to the missing persons' department?"

"Right away, sir."

He heard some elevator music chime in for a good five to ten minutes. Then another voice came on the line. It was a lot older and somewhat tired sounding.

"Missing persons. Lieutenant Quartz speaking."

"I'd like to report my daughter missing. She's been gone since 8pm last night."

"Name and age?"

"Dara Fanning, approximately fifteen years of age. She has blue eyes, dirty blonde hair, slender build and is about five-seven."

"That'll be fine. This is some description, son. How old are you?"

"Twenty-eight."

"Sure you haven't tapped that for yourself?"

"I beg your pardon."

"Well, I mean...How do I know she wasn't running away from you?"

"That's preposterous. The very suggestion is inappropriate, as well. Besides, I'm only her step-father, but I do take care of her as if she were my own."

"I highly doubt that."

"Excuse me?"

"What's her favorite color? What rock band does she like? Who's her newest schoolyard crush? Don't you think a father should know these things?"

"If they're obsessed, maybe."

"Well, that's-"

"All I know is that my daughter is missing and we're wasting time. I'm faxing over her picture right now. Once you find her, I'll have a word with you."

"If we find her, what If I were to take her in for questioning at child services? See just how daddy dearest runs things."

"Go ahead. Then maybe I might be able to speak to your supervisor about you. By the way, your doubt over finding her sounds very discomforting. You're asking me about whether or not, If you find my daughter? What does that tell me about you?"

"Listen, I was only..."

"Doing your job?"

"Yes."

"Listen. Once you find her, I'll be glad to answer any questions you might have. In fact, you can ask both of us. Right now, though, I want to be clear on the fact that we both know the boundaries of a parent and child relationship."

"Look, pal!"

"Please find my daughter! I tried calling the parents of all her friends. The nightclubs all know whom to look for, but I want to be sure that the police are out looking as well. In the meantime, I will go out and look for her, myself."

"No, look. You need to be home in case we do bring her home."

Ian looked over to Pam, his eyes creased, while into the phone, "One moment, please." He placed his hand on the mouthpiece.

Pam was about to go to her room when Ian told her, "You're staying home, right?"

"I have to go to work."

"What work? You were fired two weeks ago."

"Well, I-"

"Stay home. Wait for Dara."

He took his hand off the phone and let Lt. Quartz know he'd be searching as well.

"No, wait. Listen to me. You're still a suspect as well."

"When she gets home safely, you can arrest me then, k? In the meantime, let me speak to your station chief."

"What for?"

"So I can let him know where to get all my information when the need for it comes up."

"I'll dig that up."

"All the same, I'd like that number. I'd also like to lodge a formal complaint."

"You don't want to find your daughter, do you?"

"Yes I do. If you're going to help, then, find her. Please!" with that, he hung up, only to pick up the phone moments later to lodge a complaint. He was given the cold shoulder, and the courtesy officer simply hung up on him when he finished reporting Quartz.

--2--

Hateful Reasoning
Let's set the world aflame, Let's kill everyone,
Let's make war, Let's destroy each other. Let's destroy our homes.

I'll light the torch, You burn my house, and I'll. burn yours, 'Til we stand in the ashes,
Then you can dance on them.

Don't cry over the graves, Not for your family. Why should you?
They are necessary sacrifices, Like mine will be, And you'll dance over their ashes.

Let's spill blood, Make futile rebellion. Grind my bones, using the flakes and fragments to
make mosaics of tragedy.

We'll make the sky rain Tears of blood. Though we cry out for more, we'll hate it
all the while.

You want war, Let's fight one, So bloody horrible, You'll remember always
The death you brought.

Show our wounds to all, Make them watch our blood flow out, rip off our scabs,
and Tear open our scars.

Let the blood shower them all, So all those who cry for war will be bathed 'Til they
cry for no more.

Let them all drown, In the rivers of martyred of blood; Make them swallow it all, Till
they cry no more war, when all are one.

Until then, Kill you, Kill me, and Kill us all.
Tear my scars open, Cauterize my mouth. Then you'll know you did your job.

When I'm buried and gone with all the others who died, All in your name, All in your
Royal name.

My Epitaph, If you let me have one, Will be, "In his majesty's name, Hail the Fuehrer."
- Songs of Lester,
  <u>Coffee, No Sugar</u> Album.

Mina looked at her brother's picture now, feeling older than she actually was. She marked her calendar, marking every day with each sunset that filled the skies with that deep red, which she wanted her father to spill. It had been a year since her brother had been killed.

She kept his picture in a box under her bed. Her father rarely looked since then. He had his shotgun blown knee to worry about. She supposed he had used his own blown-torch to cauterize it. He hadn't dared try her again after that night of her brother's murder; she didn't go to her father's room. She didn't bother following her father's request to join him. He went to hers. She opened her tired eyes seeing him lean over her. Only she saw he had trouble adjusting his waist so that it was close to hers. She lifted her head slightly, catching a glimpse of his bleeding knees. He was trying to keep them from touching the wooden frame of her bed, especially the rounded footer. She then let her head fall back on the pillow.

"Oh, daddy," she moaned, "You came to me . . ." She whispered these last words, trying to keep the revulsion out of her voice. She slowly opened her legs. He looked very confused for a moment. She put her arms on his shoulders, linking her hands behind his neck. She smiled, her eyes gleaming unreadable.

"What're you doing'?" he asked stupidly, breathing hard.

"All the other kids on TV do it, daddy. They call it foreplay."

He bent down, leaning closer so he could put his head on her shoulder, his hands reaching for his belt.

"Not yet, daddy," she giggled, "So impatient . . ."

He grinned then, placing his hands on the bed, spreading them evenly as she grabbed him under his arms, and pulled him off his feet. He tried to get his balance back, but the unyielding wood met his sore knees before then.

She wrapped her legs around his thighs, bringing his knees down on the footer over and over. She kept her arms around his middle, on hand keeping his head down in the pillow, despite his groans.

She screamed into his ear, "Yes, daddy! Yes!" still bringing his knees down on the footer over and over. He pushed himself up forcefully. Her legs unwrapped, as he breathed out.

"You little . . ." She pushed him off, letting him fall onto the floor hard. She rolled off of her bed and straddled him, one clawed hand resting its palm on his throat. She dragged his reddened hammer from under her bed, and raised it into the air. She brought it down next to his head, missing him by a breadth of three centimeters.

"If you try to touch me again, I will kill you. Do you understand?"

He croaked.

"I'll take that as a yes. Now, leave."

He did. After that, he stayed away from her for a time.

She returned to her house one night. She went into her room, feeling restless, even energized with the thought that she would run away tonight. She knew that he wouldn't stay away for long, so she felt she needed to leave. She began to breathe deeply, finding herself asleep moments later.

The loud slam of the front door awakened her. She managed to keep her eyes closed, though.

Her father's shuffling steps came closer. He turned the knob of her door, his shallow breath hitching. She could feel his tension. He apparently wanted to catch her by surprise. She allowed him to believe that for the moment.

He shuffled over to her bed, his steps betraying his intentions. This time, he began to undress her. Still she kept her eyes closed; though he just about tore off her nightgown.

She heard the jingling of his belt as he unbuckled his pants. Then he moved to climb over her. He opened her legs, and got ready to enter her. She slowly opened her eyes, keeping her eyelids drawn down in a dreamy gaze.

"Yes, daddy." She raised one hand up, touching his face. And he moaned, "You make me so hot, baby."

"Yes," she left her right arm to lay still by her body as her left rubbed across his chest. Her hand glided from his face, then down, finally coming to rest on his back.

"Make me a woman, daddy . . . I can't wait anymore." She moaned loudly. She supposed that in some way, that was true.

He groaned as he drove his member into her. This time, he felt that she had accepted him. She even held on to him, and huskily demanded to be on top. He shifted so she could do so. He reached up, and grabbed her small breasts. She leaned closer to him, even kissing him and caressing his face with one hand. Her other hand went under the mattress, and pulled a large buck knife out. She pulled it out, and held it behind her back. She sat back up, and moved more rhythmically. He began to breathe hard, and ragged. So his face took on a look of surprise when he saw her pull one hand from behind her back while the one that caresses his face began to squeeze his throat.

"Do you like penetrating me? Do you like driving yourself into me?"

She raised the blade high into the air and drove it into his chest, piercing the heart of the beast, at last. She felt his blood splash onto her, baptizing her into adulthood.

She pushed her father's body onto the floor; his eyes still etched with shock.

She walked over to the dresser, looking at herself in the mirror, and saw her brother looking back at her.

"I am fucking revenge itself."

"Oh yeah . . ."

She reached forward, to touch her brother's hand. He did the same. She cried for that moment, her tears rolling down her cheeks. She saw herself in the mirror, again. She didn't look away this time. She pulled a male three-piece suit from her closet. It had been her brother's. It was a full black. She put it on, along with his long black coat. She didn't bother to take a shower; this had been her baptism.

Doing his best to wash his face, Quartz's son, Lester, rubbed over the scratches with rubbing alcohol. At the same time, he was cursing himself for letting that last girl get so close. He was pretty sure he'd broken her. Then again, it was his first time. So he expected some bumps or even scratches.

Looking at his face in the mirror, he thought, *This is too much, though.*

His father might do more than just comment on it. This would earn Lester a beating. The very thought seemed to have summoned his father, who was now beating on the bathroom door.

"Get outta there, would you?"

Holy shit! When did he get home?

It didn't matter that the door was locked since the lock had been long broken. In fact, his father forbade him from changing it. So, it didn't surprise him much when the old man broke in. He tried to swipe up the bottles of peroxide and alcohol so he could put them away in his room. Instead, he knocked them into the sink. His father grabbed them up before they were completely empty. He slammed them down by the faucet, and quickly reached up to grab his son's face.

The cop demanded, "What's this?"

"Just a bunch of stupid kids, pop."

"How'd they get that close?"

"One of 'em tripped me, and the rest of them just fell on me."

"You gotta stop playing with kids, Les. It doesn't look good on me."

"Nothing ever does, pop."

Les felt the wind knocked out of him, doubling over on his knees as he tried to breathe. This was shortly after feeling his father's fist bury itself in his belly.

"What did you do, Lester?"

"Nothing. I swear to God."

"Cut that shit out! You don't fucking believe in God or anything for that matter!

"What did you do? Drowning a bunch of alley kittens is one thing. You better not lay one finger on any of the kids in this town, though! You Get Me?"

Under his breath, Lester muttered, "Too late for that."

His father had heard him, and pulled him up by the ear, making Les cry out in pain.

"What did you do?"

"There was this girl, and-"

"Oh shit, Les..." The cop was breathless now, trying to keep the shock from his voice.

"C'mon, dad. She was jailbait! Tell me you wouldn't have tapped her. I know you have with some of the girls in this town."

The cop pulled Dara's picture, the one Ian had faxed, from his coat pocket, and demanded, "Tell me you weren't playing with this girl."

"I never saw her."

He twisted the boy's ear, and growled, "No Bullshit, Goddammit! Because if you did play with her, I'll have to help you get rid of her like those fucking kittens."

Doing his best to wash his face, Quartz's son, Lester, rubbed over the scratches with rubbing alcohol. At the same time, he was cursing himself for letting that last girl get so close.

"I'm not believing you, son."

"Old man, she's the last one! Fuck!"

He let go of his son's ear and asked him, "Where?"

"The ice cream and deli, old man."

The lieutenant heaved a sigh, and kicked the boy in the gut, dropping him to the bathroom floor. He left soon after and joined the rest of his squad in the search for Dara Fanning. He felt even worse when he saw Ian show up for role call. In fact, Ian had asked the chief to set up a coordinated neighborhood search for his daughter. If something happened to him, no one in the squad would say it was Quartz, but the chief might, or so Ian hoped.

Quartz started barking orders, "Alright. Three teams for the north end of town. Fanning, you're going to check the Million Dollar District."

"Where are you going?" Ian asked him, trying to keep the iciness out of his voice.

"I'm on the south end. That's all you need to know." That said, He yelled out, "Let's move!"

Then he got into his car, and broke off from the rest of his party as soon as Ian was pretty well out of range, although he did seem to notice this despite Quartz's efforts.

ↂ

Harry went to meet his son in a deserted deli his wife had tried to make into her dream come true.

It was all paid for, since the owner of the building owed Quartz for keeping a muzzle on the real story behind his wife's accident. Good old Bob Trent was able to collect the insurance on her. It was all thanks to a bunch of blues that put the fear into a certain insurance investigator.

ↂ

As a thank you, Trent had sold the property to him for a song. Quartz gave the storefront property to his wife as an anniversary present. When she asked him how he had gotten the place, he answered, "Friends make everything possible." She was happy for the first year, and did her best to make the place into a deli

38

until Lester was announced in the fall of that year. She had him on the summer of the following year, and went back to trying to bring the deli back up when Lester was two, but Lester kept going into the cooler and ate a lot of the ice cream. Still, Mrs. Quartz threw herself into the project just as hard. She gathered a large amount of money and told her husband that she had the money to pay for a second year on the lease.

When he told her not to worry about it, she asked him what he meant. So, he told her a short, fictional version of how he had gotten the property. She took it all in, trying to figure out what he was hiding. After even going to the city hall to find out what the matter was on the property, she felt like something was wrong. He caught up to her on one of those little expeditions and told her to leave it alone. Perhaps she'd gotten closer than he would've liked and that made him desperate enough to threaten her. By then, Les was walking and talking.

Now, in all the ten years they'd been married, he'd never raised a hand to hurt her, let alone strike her. Apparently, this one and only threat was enough to get her packing. She left Lester with him because she didn't want to give him a reason to go after her.

As he looked over the storefront of the deli, he wondered just how badly he had scared her. Lester had too. She had been horrified with him when she saw the boy drowning kittens a year before she left.

She had been hanging linens on a clothesline by the side of their house. She heard laughing and splashing. She guessed Les was playing in his mini-pool, which he was.

Nothing, however, could have prepared her for the next moment. When she saw a large gray spotted cat with patches of white around its eyes, it was prowling, and looking over at her son. He was splashing and laughing. She joined its gaze and saw that he was drowning the kits, two at a time. He had them all in a take out box with holes near the bottom. The kittens were squealing as he plucked them from the box.

She walked over to the garden hose, pulling three yards from the coil, and turned on the water. She started splashing the area around the mini-pool and yelled, "Get your hands off those filthy things this instant!"

Lester began to cry, and she still she gave him a light shower with the hose, and yelled again, "Now, young man! Get in the house and to the bath with you! Go on!"

Once he left, Mrs. Quartz tipped the take out box on its side, allowing the rest of the kittens to go. The remaining two scrambled to their mother, who scooped one up with her head so she could carry the kit on her back, and the other she took with her mouth.

Sergeant Harry Quartz, having watched the whole thing, saw his wife splash water close to the mother, making the big cat run off and down the street with the survivors of her litter. His wife had come into the house and told him she was going to give Les a bath. When she asked him to take care of the mini-pool, and clean it up, Harry saw that his son had drowned six of the litter.

Later that week, she had wanted Lester to go to a psychologist, but Harry wouldn't hear of it. That had also been the year that Harry had been trying to get a hit and run off of his record. He had hit a local woman, walking home at the time with her son. The boy had been about six at the time. He remembered that the father had tried to raise a case against him. That fell through because his friends had managed to pull up some dirt on the old man, and made it seem like he was just about crazy. Harry wondered now if the boy might recognize him on sight, even now. He hoped not, because he had enough problems trying to attend to his son, who was showing definite signs of psychosis, and even the likelihood that the he was a sociopath. How Harry hated the medical classifications, and how his wife seemed to swallow every bit of the psychological crap that they used to put names to his son. She made it pretty clear what she thought of their son.

❂

He knew what she thought, and that echoed in his mind right now. He saw Dara's body dangling from the hook, and willed himself not to throw up. That didn't quite work, since he had to make a run for the exit, and made it just in time.

As dinner from last night, and the scant breakfast he'd attempted came up, he thought, *My son is fucking crazy...No, it's worse than that. Oh my fucking god, my son is a murderer...a murderer.*

After gathering his wits, he made some calls to a few friends that were only too happy to help. He managed to get an ice cream truck, a few butcher friends, and a couple of street vendors. By later that day, Dara was nowhere to be found, and Harry Quartz announced that he suspected foul play, implicating Ian as a homicide suspect. The charge fell through, though. Ian had already felt that there was something wrong with the whole case, and even after the search was called off, Ian continued on.

By noon of that long day, five of the hot dog vendors had a new brand of sausage and foot long hot dogs. The slum diners were serving up a new brand of Spam patties with a barbecue sauce. "Down Home World" had a limited time only slab of the best ribs in town. The organs were sold to the black market in the name of the deli property's former owner, which was fine since he was two years into his grave by now. Harry had made a good profit. No body left for an autopsy, or examination. Lester was clear for now.

❧

Melissa Thompson had asked her mother if they could report the incident involving her friend, Dara. However, the report seemed to fall on deaf ears. Despite the extremely accurate description Melissa had given, the missing persons department had said that they had too many cases on their roster, but they would get back to her as soon as they decided to take the case. Also, the report could only be filed by a family member, and with that, Quartz hung up on them.

❧

It was three in the morning when Ian got the call. He had only slept two hours, on account of the search ending about then. One of the younger officers had told him to go home, and get some rest. Even now, despite how tired he was the phone had to sound only once.

"This is Ian."

"Sir, we've found your daughter."

Ian sighed heavily. Then his breath quickened, "What's wrong?"

"Sir?"

"If she were alright, you would have brought her home by now. What's wrong?"

"I can't tell you that over the phone, sir. It's best of one of us were to-"

"Look! You've called…Just tell me what it is."

"I can't tell you how sorry I am to inform you…"

Ian's breath hitched, but he bit back a sob, "Don't give me that! Just tell me. Is she dead?"

"Yes sir, I'm afraid, so. We were only able to find her head, and even that has to be kept in the event the killer is caught."

Another officer in the background yelled out, "Give me that!"

Ian took the few seconds to compose himself, and then heard the gruffer voice, though Ian guessed that this other officer was mustering his softest tone.

"Sir, let me just say that we offer our deepest condolences, and although we may not understand the shock and outrage you must be feeling, we —"

Before hanging up, Ian muttered, "No, you don't."

Kicking the door of the freezer in the parlor, Lester opened it for a moment, as if expecting to find something. Of course, there was nothing since his father and his contacts had cleaned out everything, even the girl's head, which he'd kept in the walk-in freezer. He had such high hopes for the head. Although, he supposed his father knew. Had he been so obvious? The last thing he expected was a visit from the old man, now walking in and proceeding to grab him by the hair, and hit his head against the counter where the cash register used to be. Lester had pulled it off, and sold it to a local pawnshop. They didn't give him much, as far as antiques went. It was enough, though, to buy a large volume bottle of chloroform, another crowbar, a box of latex gloves, and a length of barbed wire. He had used the last item so close around the girl's neck and lopped off her head. He kept all of this from his father, of course, since that knowledge would lead to an all too familiar ritual of father-son time.

Lester felt stars shoot straight up into his eyes. The only warning he got was the curses, punctuated by close up views of the bare spot where the register used to be.

His father rasped, "You sick shit!"

Then, grabbing him by the collar of his shirt, "Do you know what it would do to this town if her body was found here?"

"You're the one that didn't let me get rid of her."

"You were going to dump her in some fucking public park."

"Not all of her."

"After this, I am not going to cover your ass, got it?"

"You won't have to."

"What made you want to keep the head? Answer me that."

"Aww, dad. Don't."

"Why?"

"I wanted some blow. Damn, you're so fucking pushy."

"You get a fucking hooker, but quit this sick shit."

Lester didn't reply. He didn't know what to say. That made Harry nervous, and he grabbed his son again. He spat, "What? What is it?"

"I don't want to fuck some used up hag."

"Then, what is it you want?"

"Like the last girl. Young. Hot."

"Fuck no! Never again! What if you can't have that?"

"Then, I'll take 'em dead."

By the time Pam came back to Ian's place, he had been home since five in the morning of that day. It had been a long day for him. He had finally gotten to sleep at six or seven. She was getting in at two in the afternoon. This was two days after Dara was reported missing. Only yesterday had she been reportedly found dead. Pam was only hoping she would be able to get in and out quick enough. Ian was making himself dinner, although not too much, since he barely had an appetite.

"Hey, Pam."

"I was just..."

"I didn't ask."

"Yes, you did."

"No, I didn't. I just said hey. I didn't follow up with any questions since I'm afraid of what the answers might be."

"So, where were you last night? I was here around eight, and you were like nowhere."

"I was out looking for Dara."

"Ugh. You know how she is. She probably went to a friend's house."

Ian shook his head. "I'd called them all, and they hadn't seen her."

"Well, she probably went to the mall, you know? Blow off some steam, or make steam." She giggled at that last part.

"Actually, she won't be coming home, Pam. I wish I knew how to-"

"You're way too intense, Ian. That's why I started dating other guys."

He shook his head, and said, "I'm being serious, as usual. Someone has to be."

"Yeah, I'm not. Whatever, so can you go pick her up?"

"I can't."

"And why not? My boyfriend is picking me up so I have to wait here."

"Well, when he gets here, pack your stuff."

"What?"

"I think you heard me. Also, I'm tired of being dogged on a constant basis."

"Whiny bitch. Just pick her up already."

"Would you listen? She's dead." He felt horrible that it came out so coldly, if only for the memory of his lost stepdaughter. He wondered if it was because he hadn't watched her closely enough. At this point, though, he didn't care if he hurt Pam or not.

"I don't want to hear that!"

"Too bad. That's a fact you'll need to live with."

She started to cry. He thought he could finally see a human side to her, a part of her that wasn't self-centered and selfish.

He almost approached her, trying to say some words of comfort as he got closer, almost placing his hand on her quaking shoulders.

"I just wish I could've introduced her to my boyfriend."

He walked past her, going to the door.

She was sobbing, and demanded, "Where are you going?"

"To the market, and I hope you have a lot of your things out of here when I come back."

"What about Dara's funeral? Don't you have to pay for the arrangements and all that?"

"It'll be a memorial. There wasn't enough left of her to bury."

Lester drove his father's car along route 88, a desolate road that lead out of Saffire Falls. It was one of the less traveled roads.

He had a girl next to him. He had her lain back against the seat, wearing sunglasses. He had fancied that she got into the car willingly enough, scantily clothed, and wearing too much make-up.

She had been standing along Motor Way, a strip of motels along the out going road. Lester felt that these whores must've been in dire straits if they were working this strip. So, there was this cute frail blonde. Her breasts were nearly hanging out of her halter-top and her leather skirt that barely covered her crotch. This allowed him to see her black lace panties scrunched between her legs. He could tell she had just finished with someone. He could smell her as she leaned in close to talk to him. She reeked of overpowering perfume, and the mushy smell of bodily secre-tion. She looked tired, but seemed to be psyching herself up for another round.

He reached over to unlock the door, wrapping his arm around her as she closed the door behind her. She leaned in close, as his arm reached around her frail shoulders, his forearm hanging low enough to take one of her breasts in hand. She groaned at this, and leaned closer. She did not seem to notice the hungry look on his face as he glanced at her. The sun barely touched the horizon as he started on the road. He inhaled, taking in her scent, and the smell of sweat excited him.

He commanded her to play with herself, while he drove. At this, she sat up to look at him, and tried to read him. He kept driving, but spared her a menacing glance. She looked down.

"I can do it. It'll cost you extra, though."

"Dig in my pocket, and that's what you get now. The rest you'll get later."

"How much, now?"

"Fifty."

"How about later?"

He muttered, "We'll see," letting his hand fall to his lap. Then, it slithered down between his legs, so he could dig under his seat. She didn't notice any of this while she was digging in the pockets of his flannel.

She pulled out a bill, and ogled, "Twenty fucking dollars?"

His hand came up, a tire iron gripped semi-loosely, hitting the side of her head. She was out cold, and her head dropped onto his shoulder. With utter annoyance, he pushed her off, and let her fall onto the seat. The streaks of red deepened in her blonde hair as she lay there.

He reached a cluster of rocks, jutting out of the ground on the side of the desert road. The landmark made him realize he was sixty miles from the city. He pulled off to the side of the road. When she began to stir again, he found himself in ecstasy. He pulled her out of the car, slinging her over his shoulder, taking her behind the rocks. She woke up, blood falling from her ears. She saw him, felt him over her, holding her legs open as he thrust into her. She screamed as blood flowed from her head. He pulled out of her. Then he roughly handled her body so that she lay on her stomach. He began to violate her again, holding her face to the ground. As she tried to scream, dirt filled her mouth. This made her choke, and her attempted screams rendered her dry throat raw. He reached down to pull her cheap imitation leather belt from the loops of her skirt. He wrapped the belt around her neck, pulling on the loop at the buckle, and tightening it. As he straddled her, he felt himself climax as the last breath left her body. He was a god, a destroyer. He soiled his pants when his semen overflowed as he pulled out of her. She'd urinated herself, so he took her clothes off, and stuffed them into a supermarket bag he'd brought with him. He tied a knot on it, and dressed. He sat her naked body up, leaning upon a rock. Then he pushed her legs up so she could lean her head on her knees.

She was left there among the rocks, and Lester went back to his car, ripping the plastic bag open. He started driving, and threw the clothes out the window. Even in the darkness, he stopped to pull the plastic covering from his seats, and left the folded covers under another cluster of rocks.

He continued on, buying gas every so often. His paranoia escalating as he got further and further away. Then there were shorter intervals between the fuel stops. The night sky lightened, making him feel even more exposed, as if some great eye in the sky had been watching him as he did everything. He only tried to excel in increments. He wondered if he would pose anyone else, and thought of that, long after he crossed the state line.

Empty Our Minds

I love Random Violent acts, because they need no Rationale.
So give me what I need, To raise hell, Kill Peace, Make me your warlord.

Give me a reaper, So I can be justice, Let me swing it round, Cleaving the weak at the root.

So let's all bow our heads, giving homage to your preaching, Let's empty our minds,
Mien Fuehrer

Truth is irrelevant; your words are solid, right? All is based on your truth,
Our Despotic Messiah.

Let me help you then, I'll help sow the seeds of hatred, Spread the words of spite, Because
Ignorance is Strength, right? The Power is in Our Division!

Let's kill all outsiders, It's all right, come along, Don't it just feel right?

The traitors must all die, Even if unarmed; Peace is for the weak, right? So I'll wage war
on you.

I'll kill your family, Burn down your house, destroy everything you love, Laughing
as you mourn.

If War is what you want, Let it be everywhere, In your home too, It is my right, after all
To make you feel pain too.

You can burn my house, Send your armies, All your loyal followers, and Throw some books
into that fire… the ones that don't agree with you.
Make me your follower,

I'll empty my mind,
Abandon all logic, and just accept what you tell me,
because I know you would not lie to me, right?

Baptize me in the blood you spill, Even if it's my own,
Make me your avatar, Giving me a torch and rank, protecting your truth.

I want to wear your darkened crest, to annihilate those that will not submit to your will.

I'll make them vanish, Make them fiction, Like those that think you're right,
So you can turn the page, Mark them all traitors, Then move on, seeing you are right.

I'm your faceless martyr, I will say you rule, Plant your flag. Even if showered with bul-
lets, Buried in a foreign land.

If no one mourns me, and then you come kneel by my grave, If you can find it, It
was in your name.

I'm not the last, though. There's more like me, Believing death is right,
That knowing nothing is power, Questions are for traitors.

Don't question war, We need it. Peace is weakness, right?
The killing is in your name, Isn't that want you want?
Take vengeance then, On tears of those lost, In your honor, justify all hate.

Burn the hate into all, being so powerful.
Divide them all. You can do it. You have been.

I will rule my own destiny, Trust no one.
Separation is power. Knowledge is weakness.

We trust you, Hail you as the leader,
We know you care. You are truth, Mien Fuehrer

-    Songs of Lester,
     <u>Coffee, No Sugar</u> Album.

   The blazing sunset horizon was broken shortly as a lone shadow rose into view. A slender figure that cast the long shadow along the deserted stretch of road was lanky, yet graceful. The silence was overpowering as she walked. The only noise was the rustling of the road gravel as she dragged her large rolling suitcase along. The rubber wheels threatened to choke on the pebbles and bits of glass from broken beer bottles. It was still able to sputter behind her down the shoulder of the road.

   The suitcase, itself, held things that helped her survive - bits of clothes and keepsakes that kept the tortured soul of Mina alive. She had suffered through many years of her father's "special" attention; she who watched her brother die at the hands of her hated tormentor- but the money she had taken from the dresser. She supposed it would be of some use if she wanted some food or water. Part of her wondered why she went on. While her true self could not let herself die just yet. Nor could she let her innocence, her soul- that still believed in goodness of humanity- die; she could not allow herself to believe that all fathers were like hers. She had to believe that there was such a thing as a happy family.

   There was one thing that bothered her as she walked on. It wasn't the monotonous grinding of gravel, or that the road seemed to grow an extra mile every so often. It wasn't even her tired eyes, which teased with visions of nearby cities. It was the incessant voices that made her increasingly nervous. No, she was horrified. They were harsh whispers at first, these voices that she continually ignored, blaming her imagination or rather her desperation-gradually becoming louder. Finally, she resigned her-self to listening, becoming very still and attuning her hearing at will. When she heard the voices in the wind, she fought hard to stifle a shudder. It was her father's voice, and he was drunk and drawling, "Wake up, wake up, ya little bitch. You get your ass on my lap for breakfast, and don't make me come and get you . . . Wake up, I said. Wake up!"

"No!" she moaned as she sat up in her institutional bed.

"Don't make me sit on your lap, Daddy!" Now she was screaming as she gripped the sweat soaked sheets, her eyes shoot-ing open and widening in mad desperation. If not for the sheet, her mails would've been digging into her palms, possibly drawing blood.

She forced herself to calm down, taking in a deep breath, and letting it out slowly. After a moment, she pulled the sheet up to wipe the sweat from her face and neck. She supposed she needed a shower later, or the hose down they'd administer.

It didn't take a second for her to remember where she was. She looked around the plain white walls of her new home. Her bed was a simple foam futon over a crisscross wired frame, no higher than her knees. There was not even a mirror and the only windows were the barred ones facing the outside, and the small porthole leading to the hallway, layered with mesh and chicken wire. The justice system called it Axford Asylum. There were several names for it. The three most common were Hell, the Pit, and the least common, home. Perhaps it was the overpowering smell of vomit, feces, and urine. This, combined with the smell of bleach, made the air unbearable. Still, the more coherent inmates had the options of watching TV, lift-ing weights, as well as arts and crafts. This was all under supervi-sion of course.

The inmates her age didn't think of talking to her. She didn't care. At this point, communication meant nothing to her. Rather than bothering to talk to the other inmates, or any of the other activities, she preferred to lift weights. In moments when she was in a daze, she often wondered what brought her to this point, what she had done to deserve the horrible fate of being put in such a place. She felt that she had released her mother from a slow meandering death.

After traveling for so long, and finding her way to her mother, she finally got to see her. The sight was not what she hoped for. Her mother lay still, amidst the tubes and IV needles poked into every major artery. Her complexion was waxy and her eyelids encrusted shut. The smell of alcohol was the most dominant, other than the smell of death.

Mina sat next to her mother every day, hiding in the storerooms or the custodial closet when visiting hours were over, and they would ask her to leave. She thought that she must've seemed like a transient. The oversized parka she wore every day, as well as the same green sweats and dying pair of tennis shoes didn't help matters any. Still she kept going, hoping everyday that her mother would wake up, and after a month, her hope continued to fall apart. After a month, the doctors were talking about putting her to sleep in their crude terminology. However, they seemed more like they were trying to conserve resources, and couldn't think who to bill for the life support, as well as other services on her mother.

She had overheard a balding, small-framed man with a tweed suit, and glasses demanding with a high, needling voice, "So, what do you think, Dr. Wallace?"

"About what?"

"That Thorne lady. She's been taking up too much of our-"

"Quiet! Someone could hear you."

"It's just that the directors are on my ass about floor resources."

"What do you expect me to do about that? The insurance is paid up, even though the bum who left her never showed up again."

"It's not a matter of money, doctor. It's a matter of resources."

"It's always a matter of money. Being the next in line as director, you would do well to remember that."

"But-"

"You do your job, and I will do mine. Besides, as long as the nag is paid for, it shouldn't bother you."

With that, the doctor and the floor manager went on their own way. Mina watched them leave, ready to hide. After a long five minutes of being perfectly still, she relaxed and returned to her mother's bedside. Her mother's hair was dark, and matted. The thin, brittle strands seemed to be falling lax. Mina already knew her mother would never wake again. She would never know her mother, who had given birth to her despite taking a nasty spill down the stairs of their home. Her father was gone by her own hand, as well as their home. Her brother was also dead, and her mother would join him in heaven, if there were such a thing in this cruel, sadistic world. She pulled back her hand and was about to end her mother's life then and there. However, she shook her head, relaxing her hand. She reached over to the outlet, and pulled the plugs to all the machines keeping her alive. It might've tripped the alarm, because she heard the clacking of shoes on the shiny wooden tile. She hid; keeping herself tightly flattened behind the linen closet. She saw the doctor come in, the same one who was arguing with the floor manager. Before she knew what she was doing, her anger drove her forward, and she was standing right behind him in thirty seconds. Then she stabbed him repeatedly in the chest, driving her knife as deep as she could, obliterating the doctor's pounding heart. It didn't help that the ribs were broken inward. Then, there came the clacking of several heels, just outside the door. She already knew she could not leave, not with fresh warm blood drenching most of her arm, up past her elbow. By the time the resident officers entered the room, the doctor's corpse fell from her arm, blood drenching the floor and seeping into the cracks between the tiles.

Now though, after a long trial with counsel only a month out of law school- and not because he was specialized or anything- she was stuck. She felt it was such a waste, especially since she had let him take her to his den several times, and all for naught. The best he could do was to declare her a minor and the trial, reconvened when she was old enough to stand trial on the murder charges. The doctor's family would not accept those terms. So, she had to make a plea for insanity, since her crime was so brutal, so horrible, she was not given the option of going to a correctional facility for juveniles. No one cared that she'd euthanized her mother, or why her mother was there in the first place. All of that was irrelevant, and mentioning her was deemed a 'diversionary tactic,"

Some part of her wished they had condemned her for matricide. No one remembered her mother, and Mina began to hate everyone in that courtroom for simply dismissing the act of her killing her mother. They instead raged over the doctor, even glorifying him.

None of this mattered, though, as she lay in her institutional bed. She also felt eyes upon her, which belonged to an orderly with a habit of quoting Shakespeare, and the like. Harold Feldon was a pompous, bulky troll who liked to show off by talking incessantly about anything and everything. The one thing that dispelled his image - as a "distinguished gentleman" with class and education- was the fact that he was a pervert. He leered at all the girls, or women that crossed his path, even being bold enough to pinch or squeeze their ass. He would even go out of his way to cross paths with a group of high school or junior high girls so he could flip up their skirts or grab at them. He was a pasty faced bear, with large hands that could easily squeeze the life out of someone. His thick blonde hair was slicked back, but the gel would make it so stiff that he seemed to have a crop of straw for hair. Still, his lack of height - just five inches shy of six feet - made him a joke for the other orderlies. He was watching her now, and she guessed that he was also drooling. She looked up at the door that opened to the hall, and there he was, staring in at her in her tank top, a plain white one that was soaked thoroughly, her apple bud breasts glaring through. His eyes seemed dreamy as he stared at her, the porthole glass fogging up every so often. She focused her eyes on his, narrowing them. His own eyes widened, and he pulled away from the door. His cell keys jangling as he paced away quickly. If she didn't know any better, she would think that he was afraid of her. Wishing that, however, did nothing to make it reality. In truth, she feared something in him. His lecherous grin was maddeningly reminiscent of her father. Harold even gave her the kind of "special attention" that her father gave, she knew he'd return.

Sometimes, the sedatives he gave out, during his nightly rounds would be tampered. The ones for her would be made especially potent, and her body knew they'd been tampered with. She could feel the reduction of iron in her bloodstream, the shakiness of her legs and how they refused to support her when she tried to get herself moving. How she tried to keep herself moving, so she wouldn't have to feel his body over hers, his despicable breath of cheese chips and licorice soda coming out in heavy clouds on her neck. After having the meds for more than a couple of months, she trained her body to recognize the regular med, and the tampered med. She remembered such, and relaxed as she lay down on her bed. For once, she had complete control over where the foreign chemicals went. She'd finally been able to assimilate the sedative, and reduce its effect on her.

So, she let him come to her. Apparently he'd done this several times. He might've expected her legs to be easy to move, and so she willed the muscles in her legs to go slack. He put her arms to her sides, and made her forearms bend so that they were reaching out, her palms facing up. Then he opened her legs, and put his massive waist between them. After forcing himself into her for about five to ten minutes, he'd be spent. All the while, she was defenseless.

He didn't do this as often as he'd like though. He had to space out his adventures at intervals of five to ten days between "visits." Then there were times when he couldn't, during "activity day," while most of the other inmates did arts and crafts, She chose to lift weights, bench press, and even running. While some of the others were left exhausted after their workout, she felt absolutely exhilarated, even happy at times. It was one of the very few things in her life that she could think of as normal. She felt that it gave her mind something to focus on when Harold did his routine. She'd be spared thoughts of her past. After a while, though, the sedative he'd made for her stopped working. It hadn't worked the last two times. She realized she was immune to its affects, and that gave her an idea of how she would escape. For once, that perverse oaf would be of some use.

Tonight, not sixteen months since being thrown to these wolves, she'd liberate herself once more, as she freed herself from the incestuous hell. She had feigned having the sedative take affect, and knew well enough that he'd shut down the power at the third hour past midnight. She was guessing that he did this to keep from getting caught. She heard her door being unlocked, and made herself lay perfectly still. She heard him tromp over, not even bothering with strapping her down, as he usually did. She felt lucky that she hadn't taken the med he had given her, since he might've varied it today. He approached her, and positioned her legs so that they were slightly bent at the knees, heels planted on the bed. Once he was ready, he dropped his pants, and got on top of her. He positioned himself to get inside of her, and felt her legs strain to accept him as he entered her. He began to move into her, slow at first.

His eyes widened when he felt her arms wrapped around him. She looked up at him and smiled. He started to move off, but she held on to him.

"If you wanted me so badly, you should've asked."

"Uh . . ."

Her hands went down his back, waistline, and her fingers working to massage that part of his spine. She moaned loudly, whispering dirty words into his ear, and she reached under the bed for her makeshift blade. She had molded one from one of the loose metal planks under her bed. She had kept the tip sharp by rubbing it against the concrete corner. She now brought it out from within her mattress, and held it high over him. Then she worked her other hand so that she had both on either side, still moaning and goading him. She raised her head to kiss him, allowing him to shove his tongue into her mouth. She bit his tongue, and held the metal plank with both hands. She drove the plank downward into him. She screamed with him as she looked into the eye that was visible to her, widened in pain and shock.

"Before you take any woman, you must first ask."

She showed him her bloody hand.

"k . . ."

He could utter nothing, and moaned desperately.

"Where's your locker, lover?"

"It's the . . . 587." He croaked, falling on her, losing feeling in his legs. She let her knee drop to the bed, and pushed him to the floor, wincing only once, when his full dead weight nearly crushed her right side. Once he hit the floor, she stepped onto him, then towards the door, wide open.

She showered in the dark, and then took his suit, and long dress coat from his locker. She was gone before anyone noticed. Harold was in her bed, covered completely. She cut his wrists, so he looked suicidal, hoping no one would notice until morning.

She walked down another empty road. This time, though, she was making her way to Satin Falls, not five miles away. She left Axford Asylum behind at last.

A few hours later, she found herself at her lawyer's office. She knew that he'd be hesitant to forge legal documents. So, she went to an shadier alternative, which charged a lot to prepare fake documents. She gave them all of her information, and asked that they change the name on the birth certificate.

The guy across the counter looked at her oddly, and asked her, "What do you want to change it to?"

"Scarlette Thorne."

He gave her a cynical glance, taking his cigarette from his mouth for a moment to make sure he didn't start a fit of laughter. After deciding he'd be all right, he placed it back in his mouth, and chuckled, "You're serious?"

She pulled her bloody red hand from her pocket, taking the cigarette from his lips, and placing it between hers. He had everything ready for her within an hour.

She could've been Scarlette's older sister, this woman who let her have a free bowl of soup. Even if Scarlette told her she wasn't hungry, Jamey Ann Hawks insisted on it. Only the first name was on her tag, but Scarlette knew her name. She was tall, at least five-eleven, slender, and had a crop of long blonde hair with streaks of red. Despite the fact that she smelled of cigarettes and wore too much make-up, she was quite pretty. She was eighteen, although she looked much older, and found herself being hit on constantly. She felt that if she could leave here, she would be in Hollywood. That meant a lot out here in the Dust Bowl. Scarlette could see the beautiful young woman within. She felt it as Jamey pushed the bowl across the counter towards her.

"I'm not hungry."

"Then pretend you are."

Scarlette nodded, and bent her head to eat.

"So, how long have you been out on the road?"

"I can't remember."

"That long, huh?"

"Well, I don't want to talk about it."

"It's alright."

"How much do I-"

"Forget it. It's on me."

"Oh, well, um, thank you."

The diner seemed to shake as Brad Hurk, one of the regular truckers stomped in, yawning like a bear, and finally slammed his hand on the counter, and demanded, "When are you getting off work, Jamey?"

"I'll be doing some overtime right now, unless you're leaving at this moment."

"You know you want me."

He blocked the exit, and raised the swinging countertop, ready to walk around behind the counter.

Jamey backed away as he came towards her. She held her hands out before her so she could push him away.

"Get out of here, you prick!"

He reached out to grab her, but she backed away further.

"You fucking skank, why are you trying to act like a fucking saint now?"

"Fuck off."

"We'll do some fucking, alright."

Scarlette could hear no more, as her hand slammed onto the counter. Her body seemed blurred as she leapt over the counter. She stood before Brad, looking up at him through her sunglasses.

"Leave her alone."

"What the-" That was all he got out before the air left him for a moment as she hit his stomach with surprising strength. He forced himself forward, leaning hard on her shoulders, clutching them.

His face darkened when she refused to wince. She reached up, using her pointed right hand as a blunt weapon and poked at his adam's apple, and pushed it in. He choked as he tightened his grip on her shoulders. She used her other hand to squeeze his wrist at its pressure point. Even after the hand lost its grip, she continued to squeeze it until she crushed the wrist within her hand. He screamed through his teeth, sounding like a pig being slaughtered.

She pushed at him, knocking him against the countertop. With quick hand motions, she pulled one of the knives, given to her by the diner, out of her coat. She drove the large spoon between his legs, and then quickly upward as she shattered his scrotum. Even after the bones in that area shattered, her arm continued to lift him up and over the counter. He lay on the floor, blood frothing from his mouth.

She saw him lay there for a moment, and turned back to look at Jamey, who was shocked, yet amazed. No...Scarlette recognized that look. Jamey was horrified.

Scarlette went over to her, and kneeled by Jamey. She cringed and shrank away when Scarlette tried to touch her.

Of course she would. Scarlette thought, seeing what she could do. Scarlette settled for just smiling at Jamey, inclining her head slightly, a motion that she understood.

"I want to thank you. You will make someone very happy one day. However, you must leave here, first."

Then, Scarlette stood up, and left. She placed a bill on the counter, and was out the door. Jamey stood up, and then looked at the bill for a long time.

∞

Lester stood at the front of his car, waiting, trolling. He saw Scarlette walking towards the curb where he had parked, marked off only by where the sand splashed across the asphalt. His reaction was guarded as he walked towards the diner behind her.

At the last moment, he decided he didn't want to talk to her. There was something about her that made his hair stand on end.

As he walked past her, she regarded him over her shoulder, asking him, "Do we know each other?"

He could tell that she was straining from gagging, but she kept her voice from trembling. He realized he did not want to deal with someone with that much control. That would conflict too much with his domination. So he snarled, "No, we've never met."

She walked on, and then her steps could no longer be heard. Only a few mutters and the sound of a motorcycle engine revving up, and speeding down the road. He was almost afraid to turn around. He only managed to do this when he told himself he was thinking of killing her. When he did, she was gone.

Jamey relented. She had promised that the meal was on her. She took up the money that Scarleette had left behind, and went out the door. If she could've have seen what Scarlette had done to the biker who had given her a ride, she might not have rushed out into the night. Not too far from the restaurant, the biker fell off his bike and off onto the side of the road in the deep desert. He had a large hole in his gut from where Scarlette had pierced him. He had suggested that she repay him by letting him have her before dropping her off at her destination. He hadn't had the chance to look back at her, as her face twisted in anger. Jamey never saw this. Perhaps if she had, it might have saved her life. She wouldn't have gone out into the night, where the monsters roamed.

Lester saw her walking towards him, this other girl. She was looking past him, and how he hated that.

"Have you seen a girl go by here?"

He hid a scowl, and gave her a nod. "She went that way," pointing towards his car, and she ran over. She scooted around the front of his car, and looked around frantically. At which time, she did not notice him walking back to his car, as well, and opening the passenger door. He pulled out a flashlight, and his tire iron. He walked around the front and joined her as she looked out into the great expansive darkness of nowhere.

"Here, let me help." He turned on the flashlight, shining it in her face with his right hand. She turned away, blinking and trying to adjust her eyes to the light, and his other hand came up, gripping the iron. It cracked the back of her skull as it made contact.

He caught her as she crumpled to the gravelly road. Then he dragged her body over to the passenger side, and stuffed her in. He closed the door, her legs had been bent to fit under the passenger dash, and her arms tied behind her.

After an hour on the road, she woke up, and began to mutter a prayer.

"Shut up!"

She did, reduced to whimpers and moans. After a while, even those quieted.

She couldn't turn to face him, since it hurt to even move her neck. She tried to speak, but screaming would take too much out of her. She settled for a mantra, saying it over and over.

"I'm just dreaming, and I'm going to wake up. I could be at one of my community college classes. I try not to, but I always end up falling asleep in those."

"Shut up, I said."

"You're not real. None of this is. You might be my brother. He always telling me to shut up."

"Shut up, bitch...shut up."

"When I wake up, you're going to disappear. Or wait, you might actually be my brother, like I was saying."

Obviously annoyed, he shouted down at her, "No, I'm not! Now shut the fuck up!"

He looked up, just in time to swerve out of oncoming traffic. He shouted down at her again, "See what you made me do?"

She ignored him, and continued with her mantra. He saw a turn off that went into the woods, and swerved into it. Now he was seething at her, "Shut up, bitch."

He came into the clearing, and stopped the car. He got out, walked around to the passenger side, opening the door in a hurry.

He grabbed her by the hair, and the waistband of her skirt, and yanked her out of the car. This did make her scream, but he didn't care. He let her tumble to the ground, scraped knees and elbows on the ground as he dragged her away from the car.

She went into her mantra again, making her oblivious to the pain, and horror that surrounded her.

"You probably don't even exist."

He raised his iron high into the air, the prongs gleaming in the moonlight as they pointed downward. He struck her, yelling, "Shut the fuck up!"

The chanting stopped, as did the moaning and whimpering. She would come around shortly, but he didn't care. For now, he pulled off her skirt and work blouse. Then he pulled off her bra and panties. He knew what he wanted as he carried her naked body further into the woods.

He leaned over her, spreading her legs, and forcing his way into her. She could only moan and cry. He reached up, and choked her as he thrusts into her. She hadn't bled as he penetrated her, he observed. He looked into her eyes as she died, after catching his breath, he muttered, "You filthy whore."

Lester posed Jamey into a fetal position, like his last victim. Unlike his last victim, he actually buried her so that no one would see her, or know her. There would be no memory left for anyone. His ultimate revenge would be to make her non-existent to everyone. Unknown to even him, though, she had become important to him. However much he tried to rationalize burying her, he would never admit that she left an impact on him. That was later. For now, he screamed at her unmarked grave, "You disappeared, bitch! You're the one that doesn't exist now, you whore!" He kicked at the dirt he had just flattened as he ranted, "I'm real, bitch. Try waking up from that!" he looked around, when his flashlight lost power. The sky was completely black out here in the middle of nowhere.

He got to his knees, his hands frantically groping for the flashlight. When he found it, he hit it a few times, and got it to light up again. He scrambled out of the woods to his car, and slammed the door shut behind him. He muttered over and over, "I'm here. I'm real," Like a mantra. He went on until he fell asleep, and dreamed of being buried alive. After two more false starts, he finally managed to take a deep sound nap. When he woke up the next morning, he drove out of the woods, and never returned. He knew there would be more burial grounds he could visit, but this wasn't one of them.

--**4**--

Death Machine

Crawling through the grinding sand, I thought of all I left behind,

Charging into the fire, feeling your heavy hand, Resting on my back and keeping my face to the ground,

Can I go home now, Without the medal?

Or In your eyes, does loyalty mean Coming home in a coffin?

Will you let me leave, After making a few kills?

Burning some of the land, Or must I destroy it all?

I am Loyal to my family, Not to you, or your cause,

Stop telling me to fight for you, I know already what you want.

You want me to kill, To stain my hands,

Cut them as sand flows in, infecting the sores that you put there.

Still I crawl forward, Across the burning specks,

Sand flooding into my mouth, blinding me as it blows into my eyes,

Let the flying hot steel Shatter muscle and bone,

Reddish gray flakes dripping from my leg, splattering out onto the marooned sand,

Would you have me in your chariot, want me in your death machine,

So I can burn, making the ashes fly plunging me into the swirl of gray wind.

At least it's from a distance; Safely sheltered in your death machine,

Never mind my targets, since it's my job,

I'm Defending Freedom, right?

I only wish I could forget, That I ripped my targets to pieces,
Watching them holding their bloody stumps, Even as they stumble on shredded knees.

I block out the thought, Never mind that it could've been me,
The job is done, you say, Justice has prevailed, and freedom rules,

If that's all you can say, then screw you,
Since you marked me for that death,
You are now the reaper making my soul a hell bound creature,

So I'll keep charging forward,
Protected by your death machine,
Damning myself with each mile,
I know that means nothing to you.

So what if my targets are brothers, and sisters, fathers and mothers.
They're not my own.
Just targets for your death machine.

> \- Songs of Lester,
> <u>Coffee, No Sugar</u> Album.

The first day of school for Rebecca Stratsford was pretty odd in her book. She was approached by one of the jocks on the football team. He was easily a foot taller than she was. His hair was combed back and he was somewhat lanky.

"Listen, you're new around her, right?"

She nodded.

"I'm Eric Sandler."

She almost gave her old name, out of sheer force of habit, maybe. She cleared her throat, and offered her name, "Rebecca Stratsford."

"Cool. Listen I'm wondering if you could help me out a bit."

"You don't look like you need it."

"It's my brother, actually. He's a really shy dude."

She almost rolled her eyes. Then, she stopped herself, trying to think unlike herself. Her old way would just get her in trouble. So, she found herself nodding and smiling. He turned and started leading her to the courtyard just outside the locker room. She obliged and followed him to one of the trees, which lost its summer coat.

Sitting at the foot of the tree, Ryan hardly noticed their approach. He was too busy reading. Eric had to tap his shoulder to get his attention.

Ryan looked up and gave his brother thumbs up, smiling weakly.

Eric smiled back, and offered his hand. Ryan took his hand and helped himself up.

"Need a place to hang out?" Ryan asked, glancing at Rebecca.

Eric smiled nervous, "Actually, I wanted you to meet her."

Still smiling, Ryan shook his head at Eric. It was a sort of gesture that said he couldn't believe his brother thought him so truly desperate to need a matchmaker.

Then Ryan turned to her, "Well, the name's Ryan, but I'm guessing you got that part."

She chuckled at that.

After nudging Eric, he went on, "I don't know what my bro told you, but I am not one of the lonely wolves' clan."

She muttered, "You should brush up on your social skills."

"Oh," he grabbed his book bag, "Well, it was nice meeting you."

Eric chimed in, "Dude, we're going off campus for lunch."

Ryan looked at them over his shoulder, "Enjoy."

"Dude, come on." Eric barked.

Ryan narrowed his eyes, and snapped, "You two have done your good deed for the day. Treat yourselves to lunch." He walked off.

Eric groaned, "What am I going to do with him?"

"You're not his dad."

"I'm glad for that. Our dad is an ass to him. Nevermind, long story."

She looked at him, "Then, why don't you tell me about it?"

"Sorry, I guess I was talking too much."

"No. I mean, I want to know."

Ryan was pulling on his jacket as he grabbed his backpack and went out the door. As he went out the front door, he could see his father making a grab for his arm. Ryan dodged, and ran past him. Eric was right behind him, grabbing at his father's wrist, squeezing it, "Not now, old man."

Then they were out the door, and Eric was trying to catch up to Ryan.

"Wait up."

"Come on, then."

"Wait, I said. Why the rush?"

"Trying to meet a friend."

"So, you hit it off with that girl from the other day?"

"The one you introduced me to? No, I don't think so."

"She was pretty cute. Why not?"

"I just think that being friends doesn't start out of pity."

"Dude, that wasn't it. You misunderstood."

"I get it...You don't think I can make friends on my own, so you found one for me. That's great. Big brother comes through again."

"Ok. You don't need to be so bitter about it."

"Well what do you expect? Thanks? Should I drop to my knees and thank my lucky stars for you?"

"Ok, stop there."

"Stop what? You don't like hearing you're wrong?"

"I thought I was helping you out."

Ryan looked over at Eric, who now seemed somber. "I know you are. I know you meant well. Just let me do things on my own, you know?"

"Well it doesn't seem like you want to."

"It takes me a while."

"I'll bet."

"Thanks for the vote of confidence."

"Sorry. Just don't take so long to get yourself together."

"I won't....Why the worry, all of a sudden?"

They'd just run past the gates of the school. Out of the corner of his eye, Ryan saw that the image of a girl with long red hair, and a long black coat. She was there one moment, gone the next. He looked back to Eric, and he could've sworn he had seen a sort of fear mixed with acceptance. Eric finally said, "I won't always be around."

Before Ryan could ask what he meant, the school bell rang.

For a moment, Ryan thought he might like Becca. If only for an instant, he thought she looked pretty when she took the stage in their drama class.

When she got back, she demanded to know, "What are you looking at?"

Ryan stammered, suddenly caught off guard, "I was just…. Well, I was listening to you read, and you sounded great as Jul-"

She turned away from him, facing ahead again, and cut him off, "I know."

Ryan, somewhat perplexed, more at himself, than her, was even more surprised at what he said next, "If that sounded dumb, sorry about that."

Rebecca turned in her seat to face him, "It's not that. I'm just not into guys like you. You know?"

Ryan inclined his head slightly, "I guess I'm the shy type."

"No, you're just the untouchable type."

"What's that?" his voice reeked of iciness.

"You're the type that no girl in her right mind would date."

His voice dripped of sarcasm as he bit out, "You have a nice day too. I don't see a line of guys exactly hot to meet you, either."

He didn't notice the slight smile on her face as she turned back to face forward in her desk. She thought this just might be the beginning of something.

She found herself looking at the drama teacher's chest as he stood before her desk, angry as hell. His tone, however, was pleasant enough.

"Would you care to share the conversation with the class? It might be a good exercise for the class."

Ryan spoke up, "There's nothing to really share. I asked her something, and she needed to go all like an encyclopedia on me."

"I see. Don't let it happen again."

Rebecca turned back to look at Ryan, who gave her a shrug and a smile. She couldn't help doing the same.

Ryan found himself waking up rather late. In fact, his eyes told him it was half past nine. He freaked out, threw some clothes on, and was out the door in minutes.

He was down the corner from his house not too long after. He didn't bother waiting for a bus. He just ran. He found himself at another corner. He gave himself a few seconds to catch his breath. Then he was read to sprint yet again.

He had one foot off the curb when he felt a hand grab his shoulder, and pull him back. A few seconds later, a bus rushed past him, not even stopping.

"What the hell were you thinking? Were you thinking at all?"

He recognized the girl's voice from the other day. His brother had tried to fix them up.

He turned around, Rebecca stood there, furious. She was giving him a once over, and rolled her eyes. Then he realized Rebecca had no backpack on.

"What're you thinking? Do you know how late it is?"

She laughed when she saw the stricken look on his face.

"What's so funny?"

"Today's a school holiday, silly."

He muttered, forgetting himself, "Crap, I could've slept in."

"Your welcome."

"Of course. Sorry. Thank you."

"About damn time."

"Believe me. I meant to thank you."

"When? After you got home?"

"I said it, didn't I?"

"How long did that take you?"

"Ok. You're mad. I got it."

"I'm not mad. You're being a dork."

"Oh, well, thank you again."

"Shut up."

When Eric came upon them, he had a large grin on his face. "You two should get a room."

Both of them turned on him. "Shut up, dude."

He waved his hand in front of himself, in a gesture of defense. "Sorry, sorry."

Eric turned to Ryan, "I was wondering what you were doing rushing out the door."

"It's a holiday. I got it. I got it."

"You don't have to get so defensive about it."

"I am not!"

Rebecca chimed in, "Yes, you are."

He glanced at her for a moment, "Again. Thank you."

"For what?"

"For clamming up."

"What a charmer. I do hope you don't approach all the girls like this."

"I didn't."

"Not with that attitude."

Eric was still grinning, "Seriously. You two should have a sitcom or something like that. I swear to god."

"Would you shut up?" Ryan snapped angrily, his face was sardonic.

Eric began to laugh out loud; supporting himself on Ryan's should, to keep from falling over.

"I'm sorry . . . It's just that you have this funny look on your face when you're pissed. Do it, again."

Rebecca chimed in, "Leave him alone already."

"Did I strike a nerve?"

"No, you're just being annoying."

"You two make a good team. Look, you both want the same thing."

"Dude!"

Eric nodded, his laughter tapering off, "I get the message." He went his own way, to the corner market.

Ryan had his hand on his head, rubbing his temple, and turned to Rebecca and shrugged, "Sorry about that. He's a little too pushy on some things."

"Don't worry about it. He seems like a cool guy. He also worries about you a lot."

"Too much."

"That's not a bad thing. He just tries to help you out."

"He takes it to a whole new level of protectiveness."

"I guess you should be happy, though. Most people aren't that close, let alone siblings."

"I guess. We've always been pretty close. So much that I didn't think about it until now."

"No one does, until it's too late, or close to it."

He looked over at her a moment, wondering if she knew about his near-death experience, and shook it off.

He looked to the ground, trying to figure out if he wanted to tell this girl anything about himself.

Eric came back around, and suggested they go to the movies.

Rebecca shrugged. "Wish I could but I don't have the cash at the moment."

"Money is no object. Let me worry about that."

Ryan chimed in, "I guess I have some money. This'll be my treat."

Rebecca looked to him for a moment, expecting a sarcastic comment or something of that sort.

"What?"

"Nothing. Well, ok, if you're fine with it."

"I would've said something by now otherwise."

"It's settled then." Eric put his arms around their shoulders. He looked over to Ryan, "You alright?"

"Yeah, I guess I am. Sorry about that."

Rebecca wanted Ryan's attention, again, "Don't go all butter-fingers on us now."

∞

Ryan walked Rebecca home, still lugging his huge backpack, but keeping up.

"Thanks for the movie."

"No problem...Thanks to you, too."

"For?"

"For saving my life, and thanks for not going all queasy when we walked to the theatre."

"Now, you're just being silly. Still, your welcome."

They arrived at her house, sooner than she had hoped. He smiled at her, inclining his head, and began to walk off.

"Ryan?"

He was halfway down the walkway, so he turned to face her, "Yeah?"

"Try to watch where you're going ok?"

He smiled at that, a rarity, "Sure."

She walked up behind him, and hugged him from behind, just as he was about to walk off . . . That made him look at her, over his shoulder. Saying her name, his voice full of concern, "Becca?"

His voice just made her feel warm all over. She held him tight, and smiled when she felt his hand come up, and rested it on hers.

"Are you glad we went out?"

He was silent a moment, "Of course. I just didn't know how you felt. Most people who end up around me feel like they're stuck with me. Also, you seemed like more than I could handle."

She drew back somewhat, "What's that supposed to mean?"

"Well, you just seemed so together. I just didn't think you needed someone like me around." He stammered as he said it.

"Someone like you?"

"Well, I've got so many problems."

"Are you saying I don't have problems?" her voice was full of tears. "Well, you better believe I do. You think you've got the market cornered on problems or something? I've got a lot of shit in my life."

He turned in her arms, and held her. She was at once puzzled, yet feeling almost exhilarated. She didn't know what to do at that point.

"I'm sure you do. When you're ready to talk about it, I'll listen. I might even tell you what on my mind a lot of the time."

"Tell me now. What's on your mind right now?"

"I'm wondering what dumb thing I said to make you feel so bad."

"It's not you ... It's all this other shit I've been through. I've done some things I'm not proud of."

"We all have. It's ok. Look, I'm the last person to judge. In fact, if it weren't for me, my mother would still be alive."

"How'd she die?"

"She was hit by a car." He struggled to keep from choking up. "She was trying to save me, and got hit herself."

He shook his head fiercely, trying to shake off the grief he thought he had gotten through.

"Anyway, we've all got to live with something. It haunts us, and makes us crazy sometimes. Still, we have to push through it. That's the only way we can conquer that part of us, the ugly part."

"You sound like you've been doing it for a long time."

"I guess. It's because I have to fight myself on everything. So, I'm used to it."

"I don't see why you'd have to."

"There's a lot of ugliness."

She pulled back to look at him, making sure her eyes were on his. For a long time, as long as she could keep those eyes, they stood there.

"No, there isn't. You listen to me. There's nothing ugly about you. Hear me?"

"You don't know me yet."

"Maybe, I do." She leaned in to kiss him. He held her for a long time as he returned it. Her scent was sweet, and the taste of her was that of peppermint, and cinnamon gum.

When they pulled back, she looked at him, "Wow."

He smiled, "Wow, yourself. I guess I should let you go."

"Could we stay like this, just a moment longer?"

"If you like."

They stayed like that a few moments longer. He kissed her goodnight once more, and went home.

When he got home, his father was waiting for him. He was sitting on the steps of the small porch, sucking on a beer bottle.

"Where the fuck have you been?"

"Out." He stepped past the old man.

"Where?"

"Doesn't matter."

"Holy shit, were you out with a girl?" the old man grinned, showing a huge gap in his yellowed teeth.

"Yes, I was."

"Hallelujah, my son's not a fag!" He raised his bottle in a mock toast.

"Whatever you say old man."

"Did you do her?"

The old man didn't feel the last word come out. He was too busy gasping for air as Ryan's fist flew into his beer gut.

Ryan was through the door before the drunk could find the air to spit up the last few drops of his precious beer. The old man was on his knees, and gagging moments later, trying to breathe, and talk at the retreating figure of his son.

He found his voice, and although it tore his throat doing it, he yelled,

"Your mom shoulda let you die, boy. It's your fault she's dead, but I'm pretty sure it'll come around to you. Payback's a bitch."

Ryan did an about-face, and kneeled on one knee by the old man. He lifted the old man's face to his.

"I'm already being punished. I have you for a father. I know what happened to mom was my fault. Tell you what, though. When you're not drunk off your ass, deal with me then. Until then, don't say a damn thing to me or you'll be dealing with the police."

"They won't do shit."

"Without proof? Don't worry about that. There's plenty. In the meantime," He reached out, swept his hand through the old man's hair, and grabbed at it, using a tuft to pull back his head, "Leave me alone, you got it?"

He released the old man, and went to his room, trying to calm himself. That was the first time he had done anything besides dodge. He felt emotionally drained, sinking to the floor next to his bed.

He sat there for a moment, his head spinning as he looked around the room.

He didn't have many things. His only books were textbooks from school and those were on loan from the local library.

When he was a kid he had a ceramic miniature golden retriever, and a husky.

His mother had given them to him on his ninth birthday.

When his mother died, Ryan came home to find them shattered on the floor. He wanted to weep, but his father came in to yell at him for crying. He lay in bed later that night, bruised and crying.

He swore not to let himself collect things.

Now, he was sitting on the floor. He pulled a box from under the bed, and looked at the ceramic dogs lying in a blanket of tissue.

"I did it, mom. I stood up to him."

He looked at them for a moment longer. Then, he put the top back on the box, and placed it all back under the bed.

He crawled into bed, still in his jeans and his backpack stayed on the floor. He slept without dreams; he was too drained from dealing with his father.

It wasn't much of a fight, but it took all he had just to walk through that door while his father stood there.

He wouldn't be a victim, anymore, nor would he let his father destroy his soul, his courage, or even his very core, which was fragile enough.

As he fell to sleep, he whispered, "I finally. . . . stood up to . . . him."

Lester's first victim had been Dara Fanning. She was fifteen, a winsome blonde that had scratched his face that first time. He had been very careful since then about getting near them while they were conscious enough to move.

The second victim was seventeen year old Myra Landers. She had quit school two years before then, and had been kicked out of her house. Her only income was the money she would get from prostitution. She was nothing more now than a bleached skeleton under a cluster of rocks. A person who would be looking closely enough could find her there as they drove by. They would see that her torso had fallen over, and her legs and bottom half would still be sitting up. Her knees locked together, drawn up against a chest that was no longer there.

The waitress, Jamey, having just turned twenty-one, was a student at the local community college, months away from graduation, despite her waning grades. She had really wanted to go to the West Coast to be a movie star. Her brother used to tease her about it, but he could tease her no more. He was currently seeing a school-side counselor for his depression. At times he would drive home, and ask his sister how her day was. Remembering that she wouldn't be answering him would bring the tears every time. She left Lester so shaky; he took a lot of other girls after her. Destroying her hadn't been enough for him.

Dana Thorn, a nineteen-year-old hitchhiker caught a ride with Lester on his way to Dalian. She was a petite brunette who had colored her hair a golden brown. She had dark eyes, but her lips were a ruby red and her cheeks would color easily when one complimented her. She was actually a college freshman, and had been visiting her folks in the suburbs, and was returning to her fiancé, whom she lived with. He hadn't been able to let her have use of the car because he constantly had to take his father to visit his dying mother. Dana told Lester she had to be home soon, and told him she'd get home to him, no matter what. She never made it.

Stephanie Miller, twenty-five, was a winsome bleached blonde, slender in build, and yet her face seemed so full that she smiled and could light up a room. She was a nurse that had been working the midday shift at the hospital. She would stay until the late hours because she wanted to make sure that all her charges had gotten what they needed. How they loved her when she would go to their rooms and replaced the flowers with fresh ones, always remembering each patient's favorite. She had been worried about one of her charges that would be undergoing heart surgery at that moment. The doctor told her she should just go home. When she insisted on trying to work another shift, they told her she was done for the night. She stood there in the night, whispering her prayers and hopes for her charge. Lester hit her on the back of the head to kill her outright.

Tammy Good, eighteen, was a busty blonde with penetrating blue eyes. When she smiled, her dimples would compliment her smile as her slender cheeks colored. She had a southern accent, and laughed easily. She had been hoping to reach a friend's house, after being called from a party. Her friend was a recovering alcoholic, and he was having a hard time resisting the bottle. She walked to her car, not really intoxicated because she had been worried about her friend all night. Lester feigned being sick, and when she got close enough, he had knocked her out, and had taken her into the woods.

Sierra Davis, twenty-five had long locks of golden blonde hair that went to her waist. The working mother had clear blue eyes, as well. Her face was thin and severe. When one got her to smile, however, she was a beauty. She was trying to catch the last bus of the night. Her son was waiting at home with her live-in boyfriend. He wasn't very dependable either, so she was in a hurry to get home as soon as she could. Lester drove up, and offered her a ride. She began to ask questions when he drove into an alley, making him whack her forehead with a crowbar he had handy.

Maya Delaney, nineteen, the petite brunette, only stood at about five foot one. Her coworkers would joke about wanting to marry her then and there because she was so sweet. She was actually going home early from her night shift job. She was trying to figure out how to tell her boyfriend that she was expecting. She had been so eager to get home that when Lester had offered to give her a ride, she took the offer. He took her life.

Savannah Hazel, twenty-two, also brunette and petite with a shy smile, and small dark eyes ran home two blocks away from the drugstore, trying to get an asthma bottle for her teenaged brother. Lester asked what she was in a hurry for. She said she didn't have time to explain. He said she didn't have to explain anything. He knew what it was like to be in a hurry. He took her breath away . . . with her own blouse, tied around her neck. Her brother did find an extra bottle, and would've hugged his sister for getting the new one, either way. He waited all night.

Francine Holt, twenty-seven, had walked the head librarian to her home after work. She kept her hair tied back in a bun. When she let her auburn her loose, though, she was a beauty to behold. It would be a moment of magic when she would regard you with

her gray eyes, and smiled your way. She helped the elderly
Ms. Forester into her apartment. Her house had only been down
the block. The street lamps were flickering on and off, and the
winter breeze would toss the traveling dust into one's eyes. She
stopped and rubbed her eyes for a moment. Lester offered her a
handkerchief to help her rub her eyes. She hadn't even a chance to
thank him. He had hit her behind the head before she could say
anything. Dragged her into his car, and drove her out to the desert
beyond the suburbs to kill her, and have his way with the body.

Nancy Talbot, eighteen, had been visiting her ill nephew at
her sister's house. She had bought him new toys, as she always
did. Her sister had just told her that he wouldn't live the year. Her
great brown eyes filled with tears as she walked to her car. She
wore her hair in a long braid behind her back; Lester would use
this to strangle her after he got her into his car. He found that
the strangling hadn't killed her. So, he raped her as he choked her.
He dug into her bag for money, or anything valuable. He found a
waitress uniform, and stifled a scream as he kicked her dead body.
He couldn't get aroused, so he buried her.

Lester seemed in a better mood. The waitress left him so
shaky; he took eight others after her. His mood improved with the
passing week since there was no mention of the waitress. He felt
as if he were in the clear. No one would ever find her, he thought.
He sat in a booth, drinking very little. He looked about, trolling,
his eyes seeming to glaze over for a moment.

He watched her come in, with her long, golden blonde hair,
and pale skin. She was such a beautiful victim.

She opened her mouth, and that made her all the more enticing. A string of vulgarities spewed forth, seemingly flowing from her red lips. She was cursing into her cell phone.

"You're a fucking faggot. No! Don't fucking pick me up! Because, you're a pussy-whipped bastard . . . .Well, fuck you. I don't love you, asshole. I'm just going to get drunk and fuck the first guy that comes along. I don't care if I'm breaking your fucking heart. Fuck, no!" She closed her cell phone.

By this time, Lester had been creeping until he was sitting on the stool next to hers. This time around, he would only kill six, including the whore, whom he was sitting next to at the bar. For now, he muttered, "What an asshole."

"I know."

"He was giving you all that mushy shit."

"Yeah, what a faggot."

"Sounds like you'd be better off not having met him."

"No, no. Then I'd have to pay for my dad's funeral."

"So, he's throwing that shit in your face?"

"Nah, he just says he that he loves me, no matter what. What a dumb fuck."

"Is he coming for you?"

"I guess he would be. I'm fucking pregnant. You know what, though? I won't be here when he gets here."

"Does that mean you're coming home with me?"

"Sure. Want to do it doggy style?"

He took her hand, and led her out, "That'd be great."

She walked out of the bar with him and was never seen alive again.

He walked her to his car, offering to carry her purse for her. He thought he'd made a big mistake there. She was so drunk, though, she just tossed it to him. He caught it, walking over with her. Now that he was opening the passenger door, he feigned fumbling with her purse, dropping it.

"Oh my god, you dumb fuck." She bent to pick it up. He pulled out his iron from the space just above the tire, and whacked the back of her head with it.

He picked her up, and tumbled her into the car. He locked the door from the outside, since he'd disabled the handle mechanism on the inside. He placed her in so her head was on the floor. Her breasts were heaving, so he leaned the passenger seat back so she looked like she was just sleeping.

She awoke just as he stopped the car, and put it in park. He got out and walked around to her side, and opened the door. He let her fall out of the car, and grabbed her by the hair, dragging her towards the large oak.

She was whimpering, and moaning. "Oh my god."

He grabbed her face, and put his own in hers as he snapped, "That would be me, bitch."

"What do you want?"

"I wanted you."

"Wanted? Waitaminute . . . oh, god. Don't let me die." She started jibbering and started crying about how she didn't want to die.

"Shut up for a minute! Listen to me!"

"Don't let me-"

"Die?"

"I'm gonna have a baby. She's-"

"Gonna be a whore like you? Shut the fuck up, and listen."

She whispered curses, crying and whimpering.

"I'm god now, ok? You should be praying to me."

She screamed, and that made him laugh. He mimicked her scream, and yelled at her, "No one can hear you, bitch."

She whinnied, and he mimicked this as well, "oooh boo hoo hoo hoo!"

"I don't want to die."

"Well, guess what." He ripped her shirt off, making her scream again, using it to wrap around her neck, twice around. As he tightened the loop, she reached up, trying to grab at him. After a while she stopped struggling. When her hands dropped to her sides, he let go.

Once her body fell to the ground, she tried to crawl away from him. He caught her, and began to sodomize her, making her grunt out the last breaths of her life. He shoved her face against a patch of moss on the tree, his strength being so much that he drove her teeth into the bark. Then, she stopped moving. The fact that she was dead didn't stop him from moving into her. In fact, it spurred him on, even made him climax.

He didn't bother burying her, leaving her body under the brush surrounding the oak. He didn't even get her name.

Fiona Parks, seventeen, a petite girl with long blonde hair that went past her waist, was said to have dark yet thoughtful gaze. She walked around the shopping center of her town. Lester had stood by her, observing the CDs she was looking at. He said she had good taste, looking at her basket. He suggested listening to them in his car. When she looked into his car, and saw he had no CD player, he knocked her out cold, and took her into the mountains.

Catherine Greene, seventeen, and the only child of the widowed Henry Greene, was her father's pride and joy. She was also Detective Damien Greene's youngest niece. She was already preparing to go off to college. She was actually tall, at least five foot nine, and she had blonde streaks in her otherwise brown hair. She had seen Lester trying to walk around with a broken leg, simply leaning against the wall because he couldn't reach his crutches. She went over to him as he kept making attempts to reach down, and told him not to worry. As she bent to pick up his crutches, his crowbar hit the back of her neck. He dragged her into his car, and had her there. Then he went into the mountains, and strangled her. He climaxed twice before finishing with her. Then, he buried her.

Julia Daniels, twenty-five, was leaving her house at a late hour after having caught her husband with another woman. She had seen Lester feigning concern, and walked over to her. She let him hold her as she cried, and he took her to a bar. She didn't talk much, and Lester was grateful for that. He offered to drive her home, and she took him up on it. When she looked inside, she found that the passenger door had no handle on the inside. He was behind her before she could scream, and strangled her right there in the parking lot. He had her for a few hours before he buried her, and covered her burial mound with brush.

Misty Kline, as she was called when she danced, walked to her car. She was a buxom brunette with long legs, and a thin face that was pretty even without make-up. At that moment, she was trying to think about how to pay for her mother's hospital bill, and figured if she made enough, then her mother would be able to stay in the hospital for the month. She saw Lester lay on the hood of his car. When she approached him, he told her that he was locked out of his car, and if she had something he could use. He followed her to her car, and saw that she bent over to pick something that was pretty far in. This time he used the hood to slam down onto her back. When she was still screaming, he drove the crowbar into the back of her skull. He took her over to his trunk and dropped her in.

Sarah Preston, fifteen, drove home from her boyfriend's funeral, since he had been drunk out of his mind, and had gotten himself killed the week before. She was a natural golden blonde; her freckles were lightly sprinkled over her face. She could only cry now, and saw Lester sitting outside of the cemetery with a bottle of gin. He talked about having lost a sister. She stopped to talk to him, and suggested they go grab a bite to eat. He agreed, but he just needed to grab some money from his car. She followed him over, and saw that his car had a few odd stains on the tires. He hit her on the forehead hard enough for her to crumple into his arms. He only had her after he had killed her, and didn't bother burying her. Something made him feel that when these girls worried about others, they seemed to be feigning a shallow concern. To him, they were fake, almost unreal. Only after burying them did he feel like he'd had contact.

Kendra Harker was his next victim, whom he had picked up just outside of a dance club. She had actually managed to get away from him, and was able to flag down a patrol car before he could get to her. He ran from that encounter, and invaded the home of Amanda Thorne. He raped her, and left her for dead.

Scarlette had made her own trail of blood. She felt that she was somehow purifying the world. Yet she never quite grasped the nature of her acts, and in that way she seemed quite the sociopath.

Trevor Craig was an ex police officer with his own daughter waiting at home. He was all she had. He had picked up Scarlette because she reminded him of his daughter. She asked if he thought his daughter beautiful. He readily agreed, and felt Scarlette's fury before he could finish. He had meant to add that any father would think of his daughter as beautiful, and that he only hoped he could give her a better life than he'd had. He only felt Scarlette's dagger driven into his back. He was coming out of the bathroom of a gas station they had stopped at. She drove his car up until she heard about the checkpoints a mile up the road. She regretted leaving his police radio behind, but she felt that she could take nothing with her that would tie her to her prey.

Roland Haas was driving home when he saw her on the side of the road. She looked like she was meandering, and suffering from heat exhaustion. She accepted his ride, and killed him after he took her past the checkpoints. He had lied to the police about her being his daughter. For that she was grateful, but the act wasn't enough for her to spare his life. When he begged for his life, she was disgusted, and gave him a quick death. It was the most she felt she could do for him.

Ronald Salvine was a retired police officer. He saw her standing by Roland's car, and feigning that she was a damsel in distress. She asked if she could have a ride to the next town. He had told her that he was forced to leave the police force after an incident with a young girl. She was a witness to a crime, but had been raped and killed. Everyone had thought it was him, and had given him the full inquiry only to find out that he hadn't been responsible for her murder, but her ex-boyfriend had been. She felt that was his way of hiding something. In fact, she thought he was very capable of such a crime. For now, he wasn't a threat to her, so she allowed herself to doze for a moment, grateful that she could get some rest. When she awoke, he had told her they were a half-mile away from Dalian. She thanked him for his kindness, and killed him outright, driving her dagger into his neck. She had claimed that he might've been undressing her with his eyes, and might've even copped a feel while she was asleep. He hadn't, but she allowed herself to believe the lie she was telling herself.

Oliver Danes saw her standing by the road, again in a daze. He offered to take her to the hospital. That night, however, he was wearing a leather jacket, and leather pants with a chain belt. He had been going to a costume party, actually. She had thought he was a biker that was trying to take advantage of her. She had killed him for his bike, and left him on the side of the road.

When she got into Dalian, she found a girl being chased by a couple of punks. She scooped the girl up, and told her to hold on. She dropped the girl off by a security guard station, and rode on with the punks on her tail. Now there were three, and she saw she would need to take them in private. She drove into an alley, and abandoned the bike before she rounded the corner into a dead end. The punks had left their own bikes, and were stomping towards her now, drawing two switchblades each. She pulled out her own dagger, and killed the three of them. As she killed them, she thought of how the world seemed to be full of sinners.

--5--

Chaos Reigning in the Light
No one looks his way, not even to smile,
Silence was his shield, Or maybe just an escape

His peers spat on him, while destiny chose him to suffer endlessly.
Despite such, he would save the world that caused him pain.

The pain lingers in his air, like flames consumed his mother,
As the hot air that blew the day when death filled his life,

The Dark Star has risen, claiming what's left,
challenging him constantly to bring balance over chaos,

Despite the blood that flows between them, in rivers of rage, and mad pleasure,
Dark Star lets him live and suffer as they dance in the tears, laughing madly.

So rages on the battle, 'til death claims one or the other,
When judgement is passed, that day will see humanity dying, writhing as it bleeds

He is the savior, though self-damning, feeling himself to be nothing.
Would he save us all?
How could he, if even He doesn't want go on?
-       Songs of Demi
          Light of Hope Album

Allan Hollister went into the Coconut Room, the bar where Lester had left with Allan's wife on his arm not an hour ago.

Allan looked to the bartender, and asked, "Wasn't Sloane here a bit ago?"

"I'm new here, so . . ."

"Well she's blonde . . ."

"Dude, you know how many blondes I see here every night?"

"I'm trying to find my wife."

"Drove her to a bar? Nice man."

"Well, I didn't bring her here. Anyway, I have to get her home since she's-"

"Drunk? Well, no shit, buddy."

Allan turned to leave, "Thanks for your help, really."

"Don't mention it."

Allan muttered under his breath, "You dick."

"You say something?"

"No."

"I heard you, you little shit."

"I'm just looking for my wife. She's pregnant, so she shouldn't be drinking, but she came here anyway."

"Do I look like I give a shit?"

The manager came out, and asked what the problem was.

"It's my wife, Larry. She was here, but she was drunk. You know how she is when she's like that, not quite herself."

The manager nodded, "Sloane was here for a bit. I heard her ranting, but then I heard her leave. So I thought you came and took her home."

"No, it took me a while to get here from the station. This place is way too isolated."

"Yeah, I know. Sloane used to come here a lot. Once she met you, she quit coming for a while. I thought she quit drinking for a while."

"Yeah, so did I."

"So, you're a cop?"

"Yeah, I've been on that missing waitress case."

The bartender put on a nervous smile, and tried to be friendly now, "That must be tough."

Allan looked at him with a scowl, but kept his attention on the manager, who offered to help look for her.

"Look, dude . . . When I get off work, I could help you look."

"Well, thanks."

"There's a chance she might be with another guy."

"Yeah, I know that much, but I still want her home."

"Well, I'll be around."

The search started at six in the morning, and ended around sundown with no results.

Bobby Kennedy, the bartender, kept at it until midnight with a flashlight.

Neither he, nor the police found anything that night.

When Allan got home, Dinner was ready and waiting. He barely touched it,

Sloane's sister, Demi, asked him if he wanted to eat at all, her tone snide. Demi was Sloane's half-sister, their mother died at her birth. Her father had left her at the hospital so Sloane had to pick her up, but left with her own dad, even if he was retired. He had to go back to work at the steel mill. An accident at work had costs him two fingers. It was enough to leave him with a lifetime deal. Sloane started dating Allan a year before her dad died. When he did, Allan took Demi in, despite Sloane's protests. Even though, Demi was a bit of a smartass to him. He let it go, and after a while, Demi was his sister. She was a cute little girl, at fourteen. She had long brown hair, with a touch of auburn, and her skin was clear of any blemish. Most of all, her blue eyes were soft yet penetrating, and Allan knew that she would break many a hearts when she was older. For now, he was glad for the company.

He looked up now, barely eating.

"You didn't even touch your tuna sandwich."

"I'm sorry. I guess I wasn't hungry."

"Is it Sloane?"

"Well . . ."

"She said something to you, didn't she?"

"She did . . . A lot of things."

"Yeah. I could tell. It's in your voice, you know?"

"I hadn't noticed."

"She drives you nuts, you know?"

"That she does."

"Why do you put up with it, then?"

"She's my wife."

"You wish . . . She told you she didn't want to get married, remember?"

"She stayed with me, though."

"I hate to break it to you, but she only stayed because of me."

"Meaning?"

"Well, if she'd left, would you have let me stay?"

"You know I would."

"Yeah, I do. She didn't think so. She thought if she left, you'd send us both packing, and she'd have to look after me."

"That's what she really thought?"

"Yeah, when she told me about some other dude who caught her eye."

He swallowed hard, "I see."

"She did you wrong so many times, I'm surprised you hung in there as long as you did."

"That so?"

"C'mon, What'd she say to you?"

"She called me from a bar, talking about how old fashioned I am. I told her to come home. She refused, and hung up."

"K. Thank you for the PG-13 version of it. Now, tell me what she really said."

"She told me to leave her alone," he snapped, "Is that what you want to hear?"

"She told you that?"

"That, and I wasn't a man she'd want at all. She said she would find the first guy who would sleep with her, and go home with him."

"Did she sound drunk?"

"Yeah, she totally was."

"Ah, you know how she is when she's like that. She never means it. She just shoots off her mouth."

"Well, when I got there she was gone. I called an hour ago, remember?"

Demi nodded, "Yeah, but she stays out late."

"Well, I know that, but I was desperate. I mean, I put out a search for her."

"That was going over the top."

"I didn't think so."

"What if she came stumbling through that door any minute?"

"I doubt that. Besides, that's why I called in the first place, if that happened to be the case."

"Oh, ok."

"Besides, she wouldn't be doing that, unless she stopped going to her AA meetings."

"Phew, a while ago."

"When was someone going to tell me about this?"

"She asked me not to."

"Did she?"

"Yeah, she said if I told you, she'd slap me upside the head."

"Nice."

"So, if she doesn't come home, tonight, what are you going to do?"

"I don't know."

"Well, she's easy to pick up. She's probably at some other guy's house all passed out, and shit."

He wrapped his knuckles on the table, and bit out, "Stop trying to comfort me."

"Don't yell at me, pal."

"Sorry."

"Yeah, I am too. I'm used to her bullshit by now, see? I just wish she were nicer to you."

"You make it sound like I'm her pet or something."

"Only if you let her do that to you."

"Too late."

"No, it's not. Let her know. Talk to her about it. You know . . . fix it."

He smiled, "Thanks, Demi. I will, then. When she comes home, I'll let her know that we have to talk."

"See? Everything will be fine."

"Yeah." He pulled her over to him, hugging her, "I think so."

When Sloane didn't come home for the next three days, Demi started to worry about Allan, very much so. It was bad enough that he had been working on the missing waitress case, but Sloane joining the roster of the missing did nothing to ease their minds.

There were no leads. The waitress had been taken from her workplace. Sloane, if she was taken, had been in the bar. For that reason, it was treated as two separate cases.

He asked the bar for surveillance footage, and Bobby Kennedy got him a copy of the video for the night Sloane had disappeared. He also gave a description of the guy Sloane left with. He was a young man in his early twenties, late teens.

He'd had longish dark hair, not nearly shoulder-length, and hardly any blemish on his skin. At least, the guy who'd been with Sloane, had been seen by the camera. No one else had a clue what had happened to her, let alone having seen someone like that. One exception was an old couple came forward with some story about a young man, of the same description, waiting for someone in front of the local diner. Only then did Allan make the connection. When he did, some part of him knew that Sloane was dead.

❦

Lester was out of town before the first alert went out. He felt they might find his latest victim, which would be a given. Still, he had concealed her enough to keep a hiker from stumbling over a ribcage or something that gruesome. It had been almost a week, so he thought the forest critters would find her, and split the goods. She could keep them fed for a week, at the most. He was glad that he had only left one body there. When he thought of the waitress, he almost chuckled, "No one's finding her. She's way dead"

Then his moods shifted from laughing glee to utter depression. He began to pound at the steering wheel in a sort of tantrum. He muttered, "She doesn't exist. I mean, I'm still here, and she isn't, right?" He extended his arm, slamming his fist on the passenger seat.

In that instant, he saw her standing before his car, her torn uniform falling apart as she rotted before him, and moaning, "You're god. Why won't you let me in?"

He had to restrain himself from breaking hard. It was all he could do to keep from pulling over to the side of the road. He took the next highway, and went into the interstate flow, leaving this town with at least fifteen or so under his belt, in a manner of speaking.

Rebecca remembered how she had come into this town. She had been Kendra Harker back then, so long ago. Also, she had been a real bitch. Even though she longed for those simple days, she was glad she'd met Ryan and wouldn't have traded that for her old days.

Her brother, Matt Harker sat in the library, waiting for his sister, Kendra to finish up her detention. They'd been late again, thanks to her boyfriend who was supposedly giving them a ride to school. Instead, they took a detour to the mall, and Kendra gave Matt a fifty.

"Here. If you don't tell, it's a gift."

"Right. Everything's closed so I'll just grab a bite, and head to school."

"Um, I didn't ask."

"Sorry."

"Don't be sorry, be quiet. Now, be a good boy, and don't tell. ."

"I won't, I said."

Derek Hall chimed in, "Now get lost, you little shit."

Matt ignored him. "See you later, sis." He hurried away, knowing they'd start getting hot and heavy sooner or later. What bugged him was that all her boyfriends were like that.

Kendra and her Neanderthal pet had gotten there later, and were busted of course. It wasn't through any fault of Matt's own, though. It was just bad luck.

There she was now, stomping towards him. Once she reached him, his right ear exploded in pain as she pulled at and twisted it.

"You didn't fucking spend all my money, did you?"

In spite of his pain, he managed, "That's odd. I thought it was my money."

"Only if you didn't snitch."

"I didn't!" He swiped her hand away.

"Fucking little liar. Derek told me he saw you waiting around for us so you could tell the dean."

He calmly dismissed it, "That guy is a liar."

"What'd you call him?"

"He lied to you too." He pulled the money out of his pocket. "You know what. Here! I didn't spend a penny of it."

"Did you eat?"

"What do you care?" He grabbed his bag, and walked out.

The librarian coming out of the stacks called out, "What's going on out there?"

"Shut the fuck up." Kendra snapped, trying to catch up to her brother. When she found him, he was chatting with Amanda Thorne. She rather liked Matt as the younger brother she never had. Amy had lost her mother as well, just as she was trying to bring him into the world.

As he saw Kendra approaching, he politely excused himself, and walked on.

"Okay. What'd that little shit tell you?"

"Not much, Kay. Would you look at him though?"

"He told you about me and Derek, didn't he?"

"Um, no. I mean his ear, did you do that?"

Kendra nodded, looking at her brother getting further, "He can take it."

"You should be good to him, you know?"

"What're you, his mother?"

"I wish. Then, I'd keep him away from you."

"Hey, fuck you, Orphan Annie." Then, Kendra realized she said too much, watching Amy's tears build up. "Aww, come on. Don't cry now, jeez."

"You know, I don't care what you say anymore. I will tell you this, though. Love the ones you're with, otherwise, you'll just lose them."

Kendra rolled her eyes, "Spare me."

"Not just lose them. Everything you're doing now is going to come back to you in the worst possible way."

"We still meeting at the club tonight?"

"You got a lot of nerve."

"Yes or no. Real simple."

"Okay, but I won't stay there too long. That area's bad news."

"You're such a priss, but cool. I'll tell Derek to pick you up." To which Amy shook her head.

"Too good to catch a ride with us?"

"At least we're going. Don't push me now."

"Fine, fine."

When she caught up, her brother was listening to his head-set, having calmed down a little. For that moment, watching her brother walk serenely, she felt a wave of affection for him. So much, she wanted to hug him. So, she was very sad when he flinched at her touch.

"I won't say anything. I promise. Just don't touch me." His voice cracked in desperation. Then he ran home before she could say anymore.

She muttered under her breath, "He's scared of me." She almost felt like crying, but she swallowed that as much as she could. She tried to tell herself that she wasn't hurting, but she knew if she did, she would be lying.

Derek drove up next to her, and yelled, "Bitch, where'd you go? I was waiting for you at the school."

"Your caring brings tears to my eyes."

"Shut up, and get in here."

She did, but they went to his place first. They had sex, and she went home.

She tried to talk to her brother, but he wasn't home. She looked all over his room, and found he had a few pictures he kept in his desk drawer. They were taken only a few years before, when she was still a bookworm. She was hugging him as he sat at the dinner table, about to put a chunk of garlic bread in his mouth.

Another picture had them dressed in Halloween costumes. He was dressed as a ninja and she as a princess.

She heard the horn from Derek's car, so she threw something on, and went out to him. They sped to the club.

When they got to the place, Derek snarled, "I'm not going in there. It's a dump."

"How would you know?"

"Because I've been there before."

"How? This place opened just tonight."

"No, it didn't, I was here last night."

"With who?"

"None of your damn business."

"Drop me off at the end of the block."

She got out of his car on the corner, slamming his door closed.

"Hey bitch, watch the door."

She flicked him off, and walked down the wide sidewalk.

The area had been cleaned up, but not by much. She guessed the club was one of the firsts to open and might end up being the only one.

She saw Amy waiting in line with her boyfriend, and rolled her eyes. She looked around, and saw an older guy, though he didn't seem too much older. She almost walked past him, but he squeaked out, "Excuse me."

When she heard the desperation in his voice, her resolve to ignore him cracked. She went up to the car, and they started talking.

Watching from his car, he spotted a winsome blonde strolling down the sidewalk, which was bathed in neon blue. Her long blonde hair hung over one shoulder, covering part of her tiny black top. When she walked, her tiny leather skirt rode up, showing off her bare crack.

Lester sat in the shadows, satisfying himself. He needed only to imagine her dead, and that made him climax. Once he was done, he fixed himself up, slicking his hair back, and scooted to the passenger seat so he could lean out the window and get a view of her bobbing breasts, enticing him. He called out, but not lewdly. For once, his voice seemed to crack with the only emotion he could feel.

She seemed to have heard desperation in his voice as he called out, "Excuse me?"

She seemed to pity him, her eyes almost creasing with an affectionate regard reserved for a lost puppy. How he hated that, yet he successfully kept a scowl from spreading over his face.

"What can I do for you?"

"Well, you see my friend brought me here for a boys' night out. He found a date, and now I'm stranded. This is his car, too."

"Aww. You're not making this up so you can get into my panties, are you?"

"I just want to get out of here, you know."

"I say fuck him. Take the car, that'll teach him to ditch you."

"I can't really drive."

"It's easy. I'll tell you how for a small price."

He grinned widely, "Name it."

"A night out on the town. Spot me for dinner, and I'll be dessert."

"You got a deal." He scooted back to the driver's seat after unlocking the passenger door.

"Hey, Kendra," one of her friends called out. She was waiting in line to get into a club, her boyfriend standing next to her.

Kendra rolled her eyes, got into the car and gave her friend the bird as Lester's car sped off.

In Lester's mind something was terribly wrong. This girl couldn't possibly be fighting him off, couldn't possibly have awakened so soon after having been knocked out. He didn't even have a chance to tie her up since he'd assumed her down for the count. He found himself panicking when she came out of her daze and bit his hand. Only a few moments before, he'd been stroking her fine blonde hair.

When she bit his hand, he snatched it back so forcefully, hitting his other hand, and forcing him to swerve left. Oncoming traffic had slowed and come to stop for him.

He was committed and forced to make a left.

Kendra was setting herself right side up, even as the car made a sharp turn.

It coasted through the woods. He managed to break before hitting a tree. He tried grabbing her again, snatching a grip of hair as she tried to open the door.

It must've hurt, but she whipped her head back and bit his wrist. It was hard enough to draw blood. Then she was out the door, and making a run for it.

Lester's anger only grew, even as he was surprised by her escape. He got out of the car, and gave chase. He almost tripped over her shoes, her having left them behind.

Kendra was running hard, tripping only once. After that, she was sprinting and jumping over tree stumps and dead fall like they were hurdles. No one had been able to keep up with her when she ran. It didn't seem this guy could either. He was a good five meters behind, but she kept at it, running through thorn bushes and dying branches that scraped at her arms.

Finally, she was back on the highway, and she made for the middle of the road, screaming for help.

A highway patrol car stopped for her and let her in. Lester ran back the way he came.

She couldn't have gotten away, he thought as he got in his car. He drove around the residential area, slowly, but not so much anyone would take notice. He saw another girl being dropped off. It was the other girl's friend from earlier. He parked some ways down, and waited behind the bush with his crowbar.

As soon as he heard the door clack unlocked, he moved in. He hit Amanda in the back of the head, and caught her before she fell to the floor. He took her inside and closed the door. He looked around, seeing no one was home. He dragged her up the stairs as she moaned.

Once he got her into the master bedroom, he locked it. He looked through her closet, taking a wire hanger. As soon as he untangled the coil, he wrapped it around her neck twice, and turned her on her belly. Then hey lay on top of her, just rubbing against her until he was fully erect. He raped her, and pulled at the hanger. He became aroused as she choked with each thrust. Then he began to stab her with his pocket-knife. He finally carved "bitch" on her back. She screamed the whole time. So he turned her so she could face him as he choked the life from her. He climaxed when he saw her eyes roll up in their sockets.

Satisfied, he got up and left. He was down the stairs, a little unsure if she was dead. He went back to look at his handiwork, and he was sure.

He was out of the neighborhood before the first police car arrived at the house. He had left two living witnesses. The one he hadn't known about would be in the hospital for months to come. Amanda had survived her ordeal despite the odds.

When Lester first heard newscasts of a night stalker on the loose, he was out of town that day. On his way out, he hit a bicyclist almost killing him. Oncoming traffic forced the cyclist to limp to the curb as fast as he could. If asked, he wouldn't be able to remember the make or model, let alone the license place. The devil's luck helped Lester thrive.

Scarlette could feel the blood shower her as she did away with Alex Fanta, a college kid that had been kicked out of the university for raping his girlfriend. Scarlette had seen the girl crying as she tried to hold herself together. How Scarlette felt for the girl, and how angry it made her when girls were taken advantage of. She needed to punish them all, somehow.

She had taken to the kids at Dalian University, and had tried to be their friend for the time she was there. She found herself especially fond of Chris Bailey, a boy who tried to befriend her. She felt she could not get close to him. There were too many shadows haunting her past, and she did not want to hurt him. She had killed one of his friends, and her boyfriend, who had been a very vindictive abusive on the psychological level. The girl had been weak, too. The one known as Diane was such a shallow girl that her loss was considered acceptable. She wondered at that point, had she lost sight of what she was trying to protect?

Shortly after she disappeared from the university, she killed three fraternity boys who had hit an old woman as she walked home in the evening. Their SUV never even stopped as they wandered through the night in a drunken stupor. They didn't last the night. Scarlette used the bike she had gotten from a previous encounter, to ride right beside them, and drove them off the road. They crashed into a large tree, and the two in the front seat were thrown through the windshield as the last tried to scramble out of the truck. Scarlette caught up with him, and cut off his head. Then she placed the head between the bodies of the other two, and wrote in blood, *Acceptable Losses.*

--6--

Let the Games Begin

Let's play war now. Drop your load on homes like mine,
Wait, aren't they like me? Nothing like me, actually, that's the point.

I can kill them all because they are different,
They would have me gone, So, I'll hit them, before they hit me.

We must strike now, right?
Or risk death at their blade; Light their fires,
Before they light ours.

Come along, let's light their fires, and Let's do them before they do us.
It's so easy to think all this so easy to say it can be done.

Angry voices scream for Justice,
Some yell for freedom,
But what's that mean to those who sit on high?
Sending our own into death.

For Every One casualty of theirs,
We lose four or five to their holy fire,
The blaze of glory lights up for a moment,
Leaving chunks of everyone littering the ground in its wake

So let's burn the holy fires,
The tower of fire reaching the sky,
Let the whole World Watch
Cheering until that fire rain on us.

What do you care, though?
Since you seem to scream for more,
Wanting our fathers, and our brothers,
To charge willingly into that fire,
While you would not.

This is your Ideal;
Your cup is overflowing with blood,
Mine will be spilling from that cup, as well, if I Let you,
Even as I bleed, you won't let me die.

Your words are still raining on me,
Hate must prevail you say,
Though you call it freedom, is that then what we kill for?

I'll tell you this then, Let's not deceive ourselves.
What you want is death, Not just for the enemy, but for our own.

Let the games begin, Your sick concept of them,
Where the losers are victims and the winners are sadists.

Let's build your empire high, All hailing your despotic Wisdom,
Changing the world to your vision, All united in hateful desire,

Watch over us, oh despotic messiah, even when we didn't want it.
Keep us in line; make us your puppets, With your psycho lobotomy.

> \- Songs of Lester,
> <u>Coffee, No Sugar</u> Album.

Detective Damien Greene called Allan Hollister after seeing the fax that'd been sent to him a few months back. It was an enhanced still capture of the video from the Coconut Room. The two girls, who survived an attack from the same guy, came forward. One of them could only point at it emphatically since she'd just come out of throat surgery. The girl that was brought in the CHP car was able to give a full description. In fact, she almost lost it when she saw the still. She yelled out, "That's the son of a bitch, right there!"

After they managed to calm her down, they asked if they could interview her.

She agreed. In a moment, they were in a lounge of sorts. The seats were sitting in the floor, sunken a good three feet down. They wanted her to feel as calm as she could manage.

Detective Greene handed her a bottle of iced tea, and suggested, "Shall we start with your name?"

"Kendra," She'd already put it on the report, but she didn't have the strength to argue that point.

"How old are you?"

"I'm fifteen, but most people think I'm older." She smiled at that.

Damien smiled back, "And here I thought you were a college girl."

Kendra flared red at that, but she seemed to pale when Damien's smile thinned.

"Now, I'm going to ask you something hard. Can you deal with that?"

"Depends. Ask away."

"You said it was five nights ago. The incident, that is."

"Yeah."

"How did you bump into him?"

"Well, I was waiting to get into a club. I ended up not going in, though."

"Was that when he approached you?"

"Sort of. He called out with a squeaky voice like a lost tourist or something."

"So you went to him?"

Kendra hung her head, "Yeah."

Damien sat next to her, and put a hand on her shoulder, "Listen. Don't beat yourself up. He sounds like he's done pick-ups like that before."

"Yeah, but I fell for it."

"You're still here, right? I'd like to find out how. Now go on with it. You approached him, and . . . ?"

"He gave me some bullshit story about his friend ditching him. So, I told him I knew the area well enough to show him a good time."

"Alright. Now I know this is hard for you, but in some cases, rapists get the wrong idea when an unsuspecting victim flirts with them. I hate to ask. Did you flirt with him?"

"A little."

"Did he force you into the car?"

"No, I got in myself."

"After flirting with him?"

She hung her head again, tearing up this time, "I totally told him he'd get lucky."

She sobbed for a bit.

Damien looked over at his partner, totally at a loss.

Kendra moaned, "That's gonna mess you up, isn't it? You won't be able to put him away because of my dumbass."

"Yes, we will. Listen, consented sex isn't a crime, but statutory rape is. So is kidnapping and assault. Now, clearly you've been victimized. We need to know what he did, though. Where he took you, and what he was planning to do. Most of all, how did you get out of it?"

She calmed herself, and began again. She started from when her ex-boyfriend left her at the corner. Then hearing that squeaky voice, the bullshit story, and getting into the car. She paused a moment to drink some more ice tea.

"So he asked me where we could be alone for a while. I was thinking he was just some horn dog since that's what he wanted to do first."

"And you told him?"

"That's what was so weird. He seemed to know his way. When I suggested the pizza parlor, he gave me a really mean look."

"What made you suggest that?"

"Well, it's usually pretty dead. That and I didn't want to be totally alone with this guy."

"Why?"

"That nasty look he gave me. It didn't look normal. He wasn't the shy guy I saw in front of the nightclub. He was different."

"Did you try to talk to him again during that ride?"

"I just wanted him to stop at a gas station, or something. You know, give him a quickie so he could go his own way."

"Did he talk to you?"

"He didn't seem like he wanted to talk. He just kept driving towards the mountains and I got scared. He looked over at me, and grinned. He was pointing at a sign with some graffiti on it."

"Did it get your attention?"

"Well, yeah. Like a dork, I turned away from him to look at it. I could've sworn I saw dried blood on it."

"Why do you say you're a dork?"

"Because the guy knocked me out."

"Do you know what he hit you with?"

"His fist, I think. He was wearing gloves though."

"What woke you up?"

"Head rush. I guess he stopped for a bit to put me in the seat upside down."

"Hence, the head rush."

"That and he was playing with my hair. So I tried to turn on my side so I could face him."

"He didn't notice?"

"I guess he did because he looked over at me. Just a glance."

"What did you do then?"

"I bit him . . . really hard too. I didn't know if it mattered since he was wearing gloves. He snatched it back really hard too."

"Did it seem like he was getting ready to get a weapon or something?"

"If he were, he didn't have time to make a grab for it."

"Why not?"

"Well he hit his other hand."

"The one on the wheel?"

"Yeah, he had to catch the wheel with both hands, but it was too late already."

"How so?"

"He'd swerved left, and I heard a few cars brake hard."

"So he had to make a left?"

"Right, heading straight into a wooded road. While he was doing that, I got myself into a better position. You know."

"Right side up. Go on."

"As soon as I sat up, though, he took a grip of my hair and smashed my head on the dash."

"How'd you snap out of that?"

"No, wait- I was grabbing at the door handle, which didn't work. So I had to reach outside to open the door. That's why he grabbed my hair. It hurt like hell, but I whipped my head back, and bit his wrist this time. I dug in until he let go. Then I ran."

"Did you know the area?"

"Actually, I did. I used to go there with my ex."

"For what purpose? If you don't mind my asking." The partner wanted to know.

She grew red again, and muttered, "Have a little fun. Get high."

Damien nodded at her, "Go on, then. You knew the area, and ran through the woods."

"I was like the wind. The sonofabitch could barely keep up."

"Did he take time to grab a blunt object or even a gun?"

"If he had, those cops that helped me would've gone after him. He would've shot me, and they'd see me all fucked up, and go after him."

"He didn't have a gun then?"

"I don't know. I didn't look back."

"You knew which way to go through. How?"

"I was all numb before, but while I ran, I could hear everything, Every fucking thing. I heard the traffic so I went that way. He couldn't yell at me either. You know, like say shit to make me nervous."

"So you found the road."

"Yeah. I jumped the rail guard like a hurdle. Then I was all screaming, and highway patrol picked me up. Never thought I'd be so happy to ride in a cop car."

Dana Emerson, Damien's partner, spoke up, "I have a journalist friend who is going to make this interview public."

Kendra looked very worried, making Emerson pat her shoulder. He told her, "Don't worry about that. Your identity will be protected, Kendra. My thinking is that if we publish this, other girls might come forward and tell their story. We would get a better chance at catching him."

"If you can find him. He's probably ditched his car and shit."

"I don't think so. This guy is a creature of habit. He has his routines and a big part of that is his car. Also, the car has too many traces of himself to just leave on the road."

Kendra's voice was a nervous whisper. "So he's still out there."

"Even though the article will have you listed under a pseudonym, you and your family will be placed into witness protection."

"Like where we all have to change our names?"

"That's right."

"I always wanted the name, Rebecca. Is that cool?"

Damien smiled, "We'll see what we can do."

CICO

When Hollister answered, he sounded very tired, "I'm told you have a lead on this barhopper."

"He's not just a barhopper. I heard your boys found a few things on your end."

"Just bones, mostly. A boys youth pack went into the local woods over the past weekend. When they tried to pull some kindling from a dying bush, a skull tumbled out and came to rest by the kid's foot."

"Holy. Did you find out who it was?"

"It was my wife, or she would've been anyway."

"What else?"

"About her? She was five months pregnant."

"Oh my god, I'm sorry."

"Anyway, there were at least seven other sets of remains, matching some of missing persons for the same month. He had been really busy."

"Still is, seemingly."

"You're serious?"

"Unfortunately. However, there is a light at the end of this tunnel. We have two living witnesses."

"Make sure you have them-"

"Placed into witness protection? Yes, that's all being processed as we speak."

"Did you get a name?"

"None. We'll have to deal with some press nick name."

Hollister was not pleased, "Great."

"At least we've got a description, now."

"I hope that'll be enough."

"Me too, friend, me too. What will you do from here?"

"Gather all the case work from the finds we've gotten. Hopefully, when we get more information, we can connect him with all this. I'll leave the search to you. Find him, now. If I can, I'll try to start a portable lab and catch up with you."

"You got it, Hollister. With your info, we might be able to make a federal case against him."

"Catch him first, or all the evidence in the world won't matter."

"If it comes right down to it, I'll help the manhunt myself."

"Understood. Until then, take care of yourself, I'll keep you fully posted."

"Thanks. I'll set up a care package for you, then."

"Much appreciated. Take care." With that, Damien hung up.

Damien felt bad for Allan, losing his wife the way he had. He supposed Hollister had already gone through most of the grief stages. Even if he had, he did, he didn't show it.

Emerson had already sent the interview tape with explicit instructions for the press to never approach Kendra for any reason, or risk having their network or paper barred from any information on this particular case. Before joining the force, Emerson had studied law extensively. So, he knew how to keep the press on a leash of sorts.

When Damien looked up at his office clock, he got up hurriedly. He had to pick up Kendra's family and drop them off at the airport soon. He slung his coat over his shoulder, and hurried to his civilian vehicle. It was an old fashioned family wagon he had bought at a police auction.

When Damien got to Kendra's place, the movers were just about done. He knocked on the door, and announced himself.

One of the other officers let him into the house. Kendra actually went up to him and hugged him.

"So did your boss say I was ok?"

"That they did. I'll tell you all the info once we're on the flight, though."

"Could you tell us where we're going?"

"You'll have to wait."

"Aww, alright."

So, all seemed to go as planned. Even Amanda got the same first class treatment.

For this one moment, Amanda smiled with her.

Kendra hugged her brother to her, and told him, I'm sorry for being such a bitch to you."

"No worries. I got used to it."

"Well things will be different from now on."

He gave her an askance glance, "Yeah?"

"You bet."

Amanda surprised them when she spoke up, "Does that mean I get a new best friend?"

"Sure."

"Well, put it in writing, then."

Detective Damien chimed in, "Well, she is turning over a new leaf, isn't that right, Rebecca?"

"Yup." She smiled broadly, and held her breath as she sat back and waited for the plane to lift off. She was Rebecca Stratsford now, and felt like new again. Just born, in fact. She hoped she knew what mistakes not to make.

❧

Later that night, she went to the lavatory, and when she looked in the mirror, Lester was standing behind her.

Before she could react, she felt a bolt of pain as her head was smashed into the mirror.

She saw him reach over and pull a shard of glass from the sink, and his breath was upon her now, hot and desperate, as he seethed, "Try running from me now, bitch. You think it'd that easy?"

Then she felt the area between her legs being penetrated with the shard.

When she screamed, it was an empty hiss. He had slit her throat, and she screamed into the silence.

She felt herself being shaken awake, and opened her eyes. Her brother was standing over her, looking a little worried. She told him she would be fine. Then she looked outside and could see nothing but the inky black night.

Damien called everyone into the onboard meeting room for a briefing. He was relieved to see everyone handling relocation so calmly. He figured Kendra, or rather Rebecca, was just glad to be alive. Amanda was also one of the lucky ones. He hoped for the best for both of them. Also, now that the flight was in the air, and they were given an all clear, he began.

He handed them all folders, with their new dossier, and a newspaper clipping of their former local paper.

"Now, as far as everyone's concerned, you're on vacation, until we catch him. According to another department, he might've killed seven other girls that we know of. He's very adept at being invisible, having been able to stay at large for over a year now. He's also been moving around a lot."

Claudia Raven, formerly Amanda, chimed in, "So, he's a serial rapist, upgrading to murderer?"

Not missing a beat, he answered, "Actually, he's a full fledged serial killer. He's extremely dangerous, and that's obvious enough. He'll be looking for you. That's why you're here. Try to blend in as much as possible. Also, do not contact any of your old friends for any reason. If you want a message sent, use us to forward it. Emergencies only, understood?"

They all nodded.

"When we find him, all you'll need to do is point him out. We've gone ahead and published your interview. Becca, that was done with a pseudonym, as promised. The press won't lay a finger on you just to get a lead before we do. If even one of those sleazy tabloid types approach you and try to talk to you, just report him to us." He handed each one his business card.

"That's my private line. If you have any problems, concerns, do not hesitate to call me."

Then, they were on the ground. A car was waiting for them when they did. It was only a mile away from Saffire Falls, their new location. Becca looked at the airport a moment, and watched it shrink from view. Her old life faded away, only taking a few seconds for it to disappear.

The local force was briefing them on all the arrangements for living quarters, as well as school and work.

It was all done like a behavior class, teaching them what to say, what not to say. Then it was over, each one of them were brought to their new homes, and Introduced to the special agents, who would be watching over them.

--7--

Can I Stop Killing Now?
I'll never wash the blood off, The blood you made spill.
It sickens but excites me, making me want more.

I did not think that I could, Ever feel the high of killing.
It fills my head with passion. It only makes me want more.

I guess I can doubt myself later, Though right now I just see red,
I want more on my hands; it makes me feel alive, like a god.

Yes, I am a God, Deciding who lives and who dies,
That should include you, Don't beg for mercy, for you gave me this urge,

When I'm done breaking them all here, I should come and break you too,
Don't you dare cry for your life; you taught me that was weakness,

When I have you at my mercy, I'm your local god,
Don't ask for compassion ever, You killed that when you made me fight,

I'm the god of War; you made me what I am,
Always wanting to crush and break, I thrive on and love the sickening crack.

I am your plague, The Angel of death incarnate,
Swinging round the reaper, With a mad smile on my face.

My lips are drawn back in a sneer, While I kill, gut and Maim,
Then I can gold plate the enemy heart. Make others drink from it, worshipping my power,

When I kill again, That will be for me alone,
I no longer need your orders. You're nothing to me.

I rule this stained soil, Saying I'm loyal all the while,
Smiling as I watch your blood boil, You put me here, so I'll make you march single file,

I'll send you into the fire, set your living treasures aflame,
Hating you for giving me the Death Desire. For you only take the freedom you claim.

The real traitor is you, For making me damn my soul.
I'm now your tool of madness incarnated anew, Since that urge to kill, I can't control.

My only freedom now is death, On this last act I've made my vow, to fight to my last
breath, Are you happy now?

> \- Songs of Lester,
> Coffee, No Sugar Album.

When Derek went to the police, he was already pretty sure what they were going to say. They were going to tell him Kendra was either dead or holed up somewhere. As it turned out, they told him nothing.

Two days before, he had found an article in the local paper about a girl's narrow escape from a rapist. Now they were looking at something worse. Newspapers listed very few victims. They were a waitress from a roadside stand, a pregnant barfly and a fifteen- year old school girl. Only the last one was more based on speculation. Also, the father wasn't really her father, and the mother was a kind of flake. He wasn't too surprised on that, his own mother was the same, being so worldly. To put it plainly, she married some new guy every four or five years, or so. In fact, his newest stepfather had gotten her the car he now drove.

At any rate, when he read the interview, he recognized the girl in the paper as Kendra. He figured they might extend him the same courtesy of press coverage, interviews, and all that. He figured he was entitled since he knew her. They might even give him certain benefits if he played his cards right.

He went into the station, sitting in the visitors' lounge, and looking over a copy of the paper he brought with him. When Detective Damien Greene came into the station, he recognized the young man from Kendra's description.

"Can I help you?"

"Where's my girlfriend?"

"Could you be a little more specific?"

"She's been missing a few days and I can't reach her."

"Maybe, she's avoiding you."

"She's been missing so I want to file a missing persons report. Unless one has been filed already."

"If you like."

Derek dropped his paper to the coffee table, Kendra's article facing up, and snapped, "You seem to have found her, I think." He did his best to hide the smarmy tone, but failed.

The cop kept a poker face, muttering, "I don't know what you mean by coming in here and insinuating something. You'd better leave."

Derek looked around, waiting for a crowd to gather, "Can't you do anything for my girlfriend?"

"We're doing our best."

"No, you're not. You're sitting on your ass, and waiting for her corpse to turn up. If you can't help me, I'll look for her myself."

Now, Damien was helping him out the door, "Do what you like."

Derek was a mere foot from the door when he yelled out, "I'm sure the press would like to help."

Damien stopped short, and then pulled Derek along as they went into his office.

"Have a seat."

"Right. Can we say Police Intimidation?"

"Whatever. What is it you're asking for?"

"I just need to know where she is."

"Why?"

"She owes me something for my trouble."

"What trouble is that?"

"Making me worry and all that shit."

"Right. Are you two close?"

"Very."

"Slept with her yet?"

"Hell yeah."

"I see, you've known her how long?"

"We go way back."

"Of course. You seem awfully broken up about all this."

"Well, yeah. I mean. I look to her side of our bed, and it's empty. Makes me all empty inside."

"Sounds pretty bad. Want me to get you a drink?"

"Got anything hard?"

"Now, waitaminute . . . Just how old are you?"

"I'm old enough. Twenty-three just this year in fact."

"Of course. So what is it I can do for you?"

"I just want to know where she is, and being that I'm one of her loved ones, you should be giving me the same courtesy."

"I can't say."

"I know she gave an interview to you guys. I know you published it to see if you could get people to come forward if they had the same kinda thing happened to 'em."

"Whatever you say."

"You can tell me where she is, or I can make the search for her go public, and you'd have all kinds of trouble keeping the media quiet."

"What are you asking for?"

"A few favors, and even privileges . . . You know, to keep me quiet."

"Can't tell you since I don't know what you're talking about."

"Fine, be that way. We'll see how the press likes it when I tell them about how police negligence that happens just because she happens to be a whore."

"How's that?"

"Oh, come on. If you knew her like I did, you'd know she sleeps around. I know some things that would kill your poster-girl's image. There goes any chance of using her to pull girls out into the limelight. There goes your case, all because you decided not to help me out."

"I'd been asking what you wanted from the onset."

"Visiting rights, driving kickbacks, your personal guarantee that you'll leave me alone if I'm going over sixty-five."

"How about you walk out of here without a damn thing?"

"So you want to play rough?"

"I won't play at all. If you have the sense to leave, I'll let it go at that."

"Been a pleasure doing business with you, dickwad. My lawyer will be on your ass with a shitload."

"Based on what?"

"Your attitude says 'pig' and your face says you want to beat the shit out of me."

Damien inclined his head for a moment, looking severe. After a moment, he looked up and smiled broadly, speaking evenly, "You do realize you've committed statutory rape, by your own admittance, as well as driving while intoxicated."

"I never said that."

"How do we know? Maybe this conversation never took place. Since you never came to me with those idiotic demands, how will I know that you've been taking a little girl to bed?"

"You're blackmailing me?"

"I couldn't have done it without your big mouth. Now you can go to the press if you like. However, the moment you do, I'll have you on charges so quick you'll never know what hit you."

Derek looked confused, "I have a lawyer, you know."

"Well, they should've come with you."

"I can still-"

"Walk out of here? Yes, you can, and if I see you with another underage girl, I'll have you in on rape charges, understood?"

Derek nodded. He walked out, turning back every so often, but unable to voice his thoughts. He shrugged and went home. He arrived there, and found out that his mother had gone ahead and enrolled him at Harcourt Academy for some technical classes. He shrugged at this, figuring that he had nothing better to do.

Not wanting to stay home alone with her brother, Mellissa Thompson asked her mother if she could sleep over at a friend's house. Her brother, Dave, seemed to glare at her as she asked this. It took all of her strength not to wince at him.

She even glared right back at him. It might cost her later on, but now she wanted desperately for her mother to say it was alright. Finally, her mother nodded and said she'd be glad to drop her off. Mellissa only needed to pack a few things for the night.

As soon as Mellissa went to her room, Dave grabbed his mother's arm, his grip closed on her arm like a vise.

"You're spoiling her, mom."

"It's just for the night, Dave."

"I don't care. Don't let her go."

Mrs. Thompson had gotten used to her son's rough treatment. He'd started that when Mr. Thompson had fallen ill, two years before.

The sicker Mr. Thompson got, the meaner Dave got, and the more possessive he got with Mellissa.

At first, Mrs. Thompson was afraid of him. After a year of threats, though, she was tired of his brutality. Not that he'd hit her directly. He would threaten to hurt his own father if he didn't get his way. Ultimately, the old man died some time after falling down the stairs of their old home. After he died, they had to give up the large house, in favor of the three bedroom apartment. She didn't care if she had to hold two jobs to keep the place.

She wasn't about to let Dave stay in the same room as his sister. There was something in the way he looked at his younger sister that bothered her. There was a seemingly obvious craving for her. It had started the month when hospital visits had become a constant for Mr. Thompson. Dave had to take care of his sister during that time.

Mrs. Thompson, Lorna, was tired of being intimidated by him. She knew what he wanted with Mellissa. She couldn't be home all the time, though. At that time, it got harder to be able to do much for her husband and her daughter.

David had been very attentive to his sister, more than necessary in her eyes. Mellissa would go to her bedroom, and sleep in the floor if she felt she needed to. She just didn't want to be in her room. Then, one night, after having placed a camera in her daughter's closet, she found out why.

She saw David creeping into the room. He stood over the bed, his eyes leering over her. He reached down, pulling the covers away, and exposing the girl in her extra fluffy nightgown. She looked up, sobbing quietly as he leaned over her. He pulled his leg up to lean on the bed. He leaned in close to kiss her, and whispered something to her. She nodded furiously, and made herself quiet down. David, then, moved in on her.

After that, she'd let Mellissa into her room every night, locking the door afterward. David, in turn, got more frustrated, and angry in the next few days. He would go to her empty room, and throw around everything that wasn't nailed down.

Then Mr. Thompson got worse, and Lorna knew she'd be out all night. She decided to take Melissa to the hospital, and would call for someone to pick her up from there, and be away from home for a few days.

"What the hell, mom?"

"I'm taking your father to the hospital."

"So? Leave Mellissa here."

"She's coming with me."

"You can't always watch her."

"You can bet I'll try."

Off they went, and Mr. Thompson died that night.

Now, here they were, three years later in yet another stalemate and trying to decide what happened to the youngest.

"Where is she going?"

"You don't need to worry about that."

"I'm her brother."

"Yes, and you know things a boyfriend would know."

"Meaning?"

"You know what I mean, you pervert."

"Are you trying to accuse me of something?"

"It's not an accusation. If you touch your sister again, you're moving into a friend's house."

"Are you kicking me out?"

"Not yet."

Lorna left, pulling Mellissa along with her. Dave watched them pull out of the driveway, his eyes creased in utter hatred as his mouth was drawn into a tight thin line. He waited a few minutes before picking up his own keys, and pulling out of the driveway, himself.

He managed to travel on parallel roads to avoid being seen. When he saw where his mother left his sister, he made his way to one of the nearby back roads. He sat there in his car, leaning the seat back and relaxing.

He thought about the first time he had taken her body, but not her virginity.

Their mother and father had been out, so long ago.

He'd gone into Mellissa's room, as she sat on her bed reading a magazine. He leaned his head forward so he could peer in, and then leaned on against the doorway.

"You could look like that too, you know."

"Like a supermodel? No way."

"Sure. You just need to have that professional look."

"How can I do that?"

He walked up to her slowly, almost slithering, and touched her face, "I'll teach you, if you like."

She smiled brightly, and chirped, "Sure." She had come home from bringing some groceries. Also, she remembered having seen her friend, Dara, riding with a stranger. She thought it was the oddest thing because the stranger was leering at her, and now, so was her brother.

His hands moved down to her neck, and down to the bow, which tied the front of her nightgown. He wedged his fingers into the loosed knot. He pulled his finger forward, undoing the bow. Her apple-bud breasts exposed to the room's cool air. He reached up, and squeezed her nipples, making her yelp. His eyes came back to her face, and he gave her a wolfish smile that frightened her. His head went to her breasts, licking the area between and this made her moan shakily. He bit her nipples; first her right, and then her left. Not leaving either alone until he had covered them with spit. He licked and sucked each one, thoroughly. He did this until he felt her whole body shaking violently. He reached down between her legs, and was satisfied when he felt she'd wet herself. He felt himself release. He helped her lay into bed, and leaned over her, whispering, "That's just the first part."

She looked up at him, her face damp with frightened tears. How that infuriated him, and enticed him at the same time.

He turned her over, and pulled her panties halfway down her legs. Then he let his own pants drop to the floor, as he got into bed beside her. He positioned himself so that he was hovering over her, and moved his member all over the area below her waist. He climaxed again, and continued to rub it between the cheeks of her buttocks. As soon as he was sure he was wet and slick enough, he pushed her head into the pillow so he could muffle her cries. He pushed himself into her butt, making her scream into her pillow. This only spurred him, on, and he began to move into her faster and harder. He climaxed inside her three times, and finally let off when he was exhausted. He got off her, and pulled her panties up, and leaned in to whisper, "You better fix yourself up before mom and dad come home. You'd better not tell either. Or I'll do much more than your ass."

He sat in his car, thinking of her small frightened face, and was able to climax. He relaxed a moment before collecting himself.

When he sat up, he looked around, seeing the streetlight blink off. He got out of his car quietly, trying to close the door gently so he wouldn't be heard.

He walked along the side of the dirt road, climbed over the fences and trampled through leaf piles until he reached the house where Mellissa was staying.

Now he knew that his mother already had another house lined up. He hadn't known where the money would come from, but he knew that Mellissa was alone.

He climbed the lattice, pulling out a thick winter glove so he could punch into the window without being heard.

He saw the light come on three windows down, and hid in the shadows as he saw the window being pulled up. He scrambled through the dark, and tumbled into the window.

Mellissa pulled away from the window, trying to stay as far away as she could.

She backed away too quickly, tripping over her own feet. He was on her before she could move. He was already breathing heavily, his shirt soaking up the sweat that seemed to permeate the whole room. She rolled herself into a ball, trying to keep him from grappling her. He grabbed her wrists, pulling them from her knees, which she had drawn to her chest. He squeezed them so hard so as to make them numb, his gloves leaving welts in her skin. He pulled back his hand, giving her a wide ranger backhand slap. She wasn't out cold, but she moaned numbly. Her legs went slack, allowing him to pull them down, spreading her body out.

"Happy sweet sixteen, sis." He grunted, almost out of breath. He unbuckled his pants, and let them drop to his knees, on which he was supporting himself. He then reached down between her legs, and ripped off the bottom of her panties.

She turned away from him, laying the side of her head on the carpeted floor.

He played with his member for a moment, getting himself aroused. After a few moments, of rubbing his member around her sex, he penetrated her virginity, making her cry miserably. Her hands came up again, to push off his huge waist. That made him slam into her faster and harder. Finally, he released into her, and she screamed into her hand through tears of shame.

He pulled out of her, and he sat up next to her. He watched her thriving as she tried to clamp her legs closed.

"Damn, you're beautiful."

He got up, pulled his clothes together, and went out the way he came.

He made his way down the lattice, and dropped into the garden. Then he made his way back to his car. He lost his footing in the woods, and hit his head on a thick branch, thereby knocking him out.

Once he got there, he found it covered with rose petals and dirt.

"What the fuck . . . ?"

He heard a sultry voice seethe, "Did you enjoy penetrating your own flesh and blood?"

"None of your fucking business."

"I thought you would say something like that. Would you like to be penetrated?"

He turned around, swinging his lumbering arms, and bit out every curse he could think of.

Scarlette caught his arm by the elbow, squeezing it hard enough to shatter it. He screamed as his arm dropped to his side, slack and broken.

She put one hand to his neck, and lifted him by the neck, her slender hand driving itself into his jaw. She pulled her other arm back, poising for a strike. Then she drove it home, through his chest. Blood poured from his moth in a torrent. She lowered her arm, allowing his corpse to slide off. He crumpled to the ground, his face etched with shock and hatred.

She walked off, leaving him by the side of his truck. He seemed to match the surrounding dirt and garbage.

His body convulsed, and the constant jab of smaller branches into his back had forced him awake. He lay in the woods, unable to tell what time it was. He got up and hurried back to his vehicle. There was no one there, but he was nervous all the same, and scrambled into the driver's seat. He looked around once more, trying to make sure he was alone. Indeed he was. So, he went ahead and shook himself again before the shakes caught up with him on the road.

8

Blood Legend

My hair is like silken fire, falling over my sneering face,
My eyes look out with hateful desire, The liquid fire flows within me at deadly pace,

The blood inside me causes rage, making me lose control,
My clawed fingers buried in your rib cage, having thrusts them forward; I've forced out your soul.

My vision plunges into crimson lead, While my blood boils, I'll make your pain so much worse. I'll pull my claws out when I'm sure you're dead, The deadly gift from a god, and then passed down, is my curse.

My father's brutality has made me obsessed, Driving me to finish my bloodline's holy war. I'll rip out the still beating heart from his chest, ending the life of that spoiled arrogant eyesore.

It's become my forced imperative; A lesson learned through my father's fist,
Only after silencing his voice in me, I'll try to just live, though even in dreams, I hear my father's screams in the mist.

He rants on, in dreams, of what he wants, killing, hating, driving me into my rage.
It's as if I cannot block out his overcritical taunts, Yet my rival can wield his flames, like some damn mage.

I wield my flames and my hands throb in pain, So I must learn to use my skill,
My intense drive making me seem insane, I'm completely self-aware, though, so I know I'll laugh after this kill

I feel my hate will not be silenced, Not while my father screams in my mind,
Only until, in my rival's blood, I am cleansed, my own peace settling in once his death
warrant is signed.

When I finally kill him, make his blood erupt; I will bathe in its crimson rain.
So what if I sound corrupt, If you hate me, I'll make you feel my pain.

So stay out of my path. Don't challenge me, Unless you want me to assist your suicide.
I'll now give you my decree; I have no problem with homicide.

I choose to live what life I have left, At least succeeding in outliving my rival,
Although my death will leave none bereft. It doesn't matter; such to me is trivial.

At least I can laugh over his grave, I will know that I ended his bloodline's legacy,
It will fill my mind with the silence I long crave, I bet that most regard all this as heresy,

My Blood is my curse, bringing the reaper ever so close,
Staining my hands as the rage gets worse, My victims fall, as their insides I expose.

So when I Utterly defeat you, Hate not me, hate your weakness, you pathetic wretch,
You are nothing to me, you see? So here now, take this remnant femur, and go Fetch.

  -    Songs of Lester,
       <u>Coffee, No Sugar</u> Album.

Lester was taking a walk in Country Court, the local park. He had been doing this same routine for a week now, but no one seemed to want to come near him. He felt as if he had come to a slump in his hunting career, especially since his car was being fixed by Big Lou, who hadn't recognized him. Lester had stolen enough to pawn so he could pay for the car. He'd also left a different address at each one he had gone to. One thing that gave him an advantage was what he knew about good ol' Lou, who had impregnated his own daughter. Les could tell Lou would not want to deal with any cops, or he'd have to explain his daughter's condition to them. More than likely, they would use DNA testing to figure out whose child she was bearing. Word of mouth was mighty powerful in these parts, and Lester wanted to make certain that he had the advantage. He looked around slowly, trying not to attract attention, and his sights came upon a young woman, who was fixing her own car. He happened upon her, and began by introducing himself.

"Hi, I'm Lester. I'm kinda new here, but I can tell that's probably a little problem compared to yours."

The young girl was at least nineteen, and she had a power suit on. She had the hood up, but was afraid to do anything for fear of dirtying her suit. She looked up at him, and bit out, "Fuck, yeah, and I have to go to an interview in the city."

"Tell you what, why don't you let me help? I'll even drive you over there when I fix your car."

"What's in it for you?"

"Let me buy you dinner, and I'll be your chauffeur for the week."

"You have got yourself a deal . . . Now fix my fucking car."

So he did. As promised, he took her to the nearest city, Cainland, for her interview, and did the next best thing to bringing her home. She was sitting in the car a moment, and looking over at him, as he smiled back at her, "Well thanks for letting me buy you dinner, Alley."

She looked over at him as he got out of the car, "Where are you going?"

He went over to her side, standing over the passenger door. His eyes seemed to glaze over for a moment as he bent to open her door for her.

"Everything ok?"

"Everything's fine. I just figured I should get out, since it's your car."

"Oh my god, you're right."

"It's ok. Even I forgot all about that. I just figured I should go the whole nine yards, and help you out of your car."

"Walk me to the door for a goodnight kiss?"

"If you'll let me."

She dropped her head for a moment, and stood up and out into his arms. He was surprised for a moment, and then gratefully accepted her kiss. For once in his pathetic excuse for a life, Lester felt human, or as close as he possibly could. It was a feeling he never achieved when he was out hunting. It might've been that part of him wanted to stop, but he couldn't be sure. He supposed he was just feeling a temporary high, and that the feeling wouldn't last as long as he wanted it to. He forced himself to let her go, and she released him from her kiss.

"What's wrong?"

"Nothing. I'm just trying to get used to letting you go."

"And what does that mean?"

"Just now, I was thinking how much I wanted to hold you. I was thinking, in fact, that I didn't want to let you go."

"That's ok."

"No . . . It's not."

He took a few steps away from her, and muttered, "I can't stay. I've gotta go, and like right now."

"Well, wait. At least give me your number."

"I can't. I won't be in town long enough to get one."

"What about your cell?"

"I'm sorry I don't have one."

"Well, how the hell am I supposed to talk to you again?"

He went back to her abruptly, and gave her a deep kiss that left her breathless. He held her for a moment, and again he had to force himself to let her go.

"I'll write you and tell you how I'm doing. Just do me one favor, alright?"

"What's that?"

"Remember me the way I am now, ok? Please . . . Just remember me this way, and I'll remember you. I'll remember everything about you, your face, your hair, your eyes-"

"Lester, you're scaring me."

"Good. You should be scared. Listen. Just do me that favor, alright?"

She inclined her head slowly, not really knowing what to say anymore. It was as if he had taken everything she had to say, and put it back into her head, letting it bubble and amass. Most of all, she wanted to know who this guy was, but he wouldn't let her into himself. She wanted to say something else, but he placed his hand gently over her mouth, and shook his head.

He began to back away from her, and smiled, "Let me remember you the way you are now."

"Will I see you again?"

"Probably not. I'll have to fix some things. Let me get everything settled, and then I'll come back to you. I'm not sure you'll want me back, though."

"What do you mean?"

"Nothing. Nevermind it, ok?" Off he ran, not looking back. He wasn't sure he wanted to because he didn't want to see her face as he would the others. He didn't want to see those dead eyes looking at him, not from her face. He couldn't bare it. So, he ran for blocks. He ran endlessly until he couldn't breathe. He was back in the park, and he almost wanted to throw up. His hands flung to his head as he ran into the area surrounded by the tall bushes, and gave up his three course dinner. He wanted to forget he ever met this girl, and part of him wanted to go back to her. He wanted to forget himself, and just live with her as a small town boy. He didn't even want to remember what he was doing before he arrived in town. He wanted to forget about his car, and then the memories that went with it became strong enough to knock him to the ground.

He looked up, and saw that waitress from long ago and my god if she didn't look so lonely. She looked down at him, her eyes pleading, and he knew that she wanted him to kill more so that she wouldn't feel like she'd have to suffer that hell alone. He got to his knees, and looked up at her, "I can't. I can't give you anymore."

She simply looked at him, her eyes still burning into him. He wanted to bury her again, but she was out of reach.

He found himself in the middle of the park on all fours. He looked around, and saw that no one was watching him. He stood up, and straightened the thin flannel he was wearing. He wanted to forget that any of this had happened. It was as if all of his nerve was beginning to diminish. What made it worse was the fact that he started to see his victims again. If he could put them out of his mind, he knew he would be alright.

However, with this last girl he had actually felt somewhat normal, even flirtatious and bold. Something inside him was yearning for a sort of reaching out. He began a slow walk to the garage where his car was, and then a jog to a sprint. He just wanted out of this town all of a sudden. He didn't care about blackmailing Lou anymore. He didn't even care if Lou was planning to overcharge him. He would pay whatever it cost to get his car out of the shop and moving.

When he arrived, he saw Lou's daughter sitting in the office, her eyes puffed with tears, and her lips puckered into a grimace. He peeked into the office, and introduced himself to her.

"So, where's Lou?"

"He's actually on the phone in our apartment. He saw some wanted poster, and wanted to cash in on it."

He fought hard to keep from scowling at her, and looked out into the garage area so he could look for his own car. He found it, well repaired, but something was amiss, and he realized it when he saw his hubcaps were gone. He didn't really care, though, as long as Lou had repainted his car a tanned color. It had to be enough.

He looked to Lou's daughter, and asked, "So what got him so excited?"

"He said that he saw someone in town that looked like the guy on Nation's Most Wanted. He figured he could get some cash if he reported the bounty."

"Well, I'm going to leave your dad's cash here on his desk. Do you know where my keys are?"

She stood up, and Lester thought that she didn't look pregnant. He supposed if Lou was calling the police, all the stories about him were just rumors. What really worried him was that Lou was talking to the police after all. He looked to the daughter, and noticed that she had a bruise on her wrist when she reached in to get the keys to his car. She handed them to him, and he took them gratefully. It was all he could do to keep from asking her to come with him. The last thing he wanted was to attract attention his way. Also, now that Lou was in contact with the police, she was untouchable. He said his goodbyes, and left a couple of hundreds on the desk.

He was almost out of the town limits when one of the road troopers pulled him over, and asked to see his identification.

"May I ask what your business in town was?"

"Well, I'm doin a cross-country tour so I can meet my missus in California." He added a twang to his voice,

"You tryin to be a smart ass? Don't make fun of me, boy. I could throw you in the tank for drunk and disorderly if I wanted."

"Sorry about that. I really am meeting my wife, though."

"You're a bit young, aren't you?"

"Well, she moved out there to live with her folks so they could help her take care of the baby. They thought I was too young."

"Aww, well, you look like you could handle a family now."

"I'm hoping so."

"Well, I'll let you off with a warning this time. Watch your speed, a lot of other guys with speed radar out there, and they ain't half as nice as I am."

He hadn't even realized that he was speeding. It made him furious that he had been so obvious. He was starting to slip, and he was hoping he could get out of this town before he felt himself fill with something he never had to deal with, some sense of remorse, and he hated it. He wanted to take what he wanted, and not care who would miss them. Once he met his victims, they were his alone. The hick trooper continued to go on about how different all the road cops were. He could only offer a nervous smile, and nod when the officer asked for him to agree.

"Well, I'll be careful then."

"You better. You're no good to that kid if you're wrapped around a tree on some godforsaken road."

"Thanks, I'll keep that in mind."

Lester was gone before the trooper heard his radio. When he finally did pick it up, he got the all-points alert about Lester, but the trooper couldn't remember what color the car was. He shrugged, and reported back that he hadn't seen anyone like that.

Lester, himself, was trying to keep himself calm as he passed troop cars every five miles. He felt lucky that he hadn't taken Lou's daughter.

When he got to a roadside stop, he heard the police were also looking for a girl with long red hair. She had been responsible for at least one murder at a roadside stop, and then she disappeared.

That made Lester nervous, because he remembered having a close encounter with a similar girl, only she was blonde. Also, he was hoping that they didn't connect him with the waitress he had taken that night. God, he hated that damned waitress for making him remember her. He wanted to forget she ever existed, but she seemed to come back in his dreams, and he felt himself slowly slipping over the edge.

He fought to keep himself from shaking his head nervously. How strong was the denial that he seemed to act reflexively whenever thinking about it? He didn't want to even see himself doing what he had done to that girl. He wished he had never met her at all. It wasn't out of sympathy that he wished for this. Rather, he wanted to keep killing without having to see the faces of the lives he destroyed. He tried to remain calm, no matter how many troop cars he passed by. Finally, he went on to another highway, and the road was clear for miles. He allowed himself to breathe a sigh of relief.

"Allan, I've got two pieces of news; one good item, one bad item."

"Give me the bad news first, Damien."

"I will, all in due course."

"I understand. I guess I could use some good news first."

"We finally got a lead, Allen?"

"Excellent. When and where?"

"Apparently, some mechanic had been watching Nation's Most Wanted, and saw our man in his humble abode. He was pretty sure it was our guy."

"Did he get a license plate number?"

"He got everything, even the color he had it refinished with, sly creep."

"Well, let's get over there then."

"That's part of the bad news. The creep must've found out that he was being reported and slipped out of town."

"How'd he do that? We told everyone about this, even the state troopers."

"Well, one of the older guys with a speed gun thinks he might've seen him. He's a bit of an old-timer, though. So he doesn't quite remember what he saw."

"He just let him go? Oh my god, how the- Can we talk to him?"

"They already grilled him when he came in. According to the local office in that area, he went in and muttered that he had seen the guy in our pictures. One of the heads heard him, and pulled him in to talk about it."

"What'd he say?"

"He didn't get that much because the old timer said he had to get home before dark. Also, at the last moment, he started complaining about his memory failing when put under pressure. So they just told him to call if he remembers anything."

"What route was he on?"

"Route 79."

"Which lane was he speed-scanning?"

"West bound."

"That's it. Get everyone to converge along the roadside stands and drive through towns. I don't care if they have to dig in the garbage for something he ate. I want everyone along those towns screened."

"I'll let them know. If they find him, what then?"

"I hope they drag that son of a bitch in here, so I can get a good look at him before prison does its work."

"Do you think the old guy blew it?"

"If he had kept quiet about it, he most definitely did. He blew it by not stopping him and bringing him in."

❧❧

The Midnight Butcher was playing at a five and dime theatre. Lester chose to pay for a show with cash, but ended up staying there for two showings. When he sensed that the manager was approaching him, he stood up, and left.

The Butcher had been played by Christopher Karloff, one of his all-time favorite horror show regulars. He remembered how Karloff played a well to do butcher that sold the best meat in a small town. However, every now and then, children would disappear, and no remains were ever found. It was found, later in the movie, Karloff had been feeding his clients their own children, and they never suspected until the end. The last failed attempt at taking a child had gotten him public attention. In the last scene, he was being lynched by a mob as a whole crew of police specialists were breaking into his butcher shop. The last three scenes of the movie were his hanging body, one of his victims on a hook, and the last was both images superimposed over one another.

The whole movie had been enjoyable, but it had given him a bad turn. He could only think of what mistakes he had made. He decided that the only way to cut any risk of being lynched would be to kill the girl who survived. The only problem was that he couldn't find her, even when he returned to the club at which he picked her up. He then realized he was making a mistake by returning. He couldn't help it, though. He wanted to silence anyone that could identify him. If it meant nearly being exposed, he didn't care much, as long as it wasn't the town's people that didn't find him first. He went outside of the theatre, trying to figure out what Karloff's mistake had been, and couldn't help feeling that he had made a similar error by not killing his victim outright, instead of keeping them alive until he could rape them. He wanted them to at least suffer first, and then he would kill them, as they begged him not to. It was the pleading, and the streaming tears that excited him. What power he felt when their eyes widened as he choked the life out of them. However, with the one that got away, there was a chance that he could find a mob waiting around the corners of every small town. He was relieved that he hadn't buried a whole bunch of them at one site. He had actually buried them at least a two or three miles apart, and not always on the same side of the road. He figured if the cops didn't find anything buried within 2 miles of the first site, they might stop digging.

He sat in his car, and trembled with glee as he giggled. He remembered how easily they came to him, wanting to help him with attaching a surfboard to his car. He didn't actually have one. So, when his intended victim arrived at the car and asked about the board, he was already behind them, with a tire iron in hand. In one instance, he had the sharp end of the tool facing outward. In that incident, he had killed the high school girl immediately. Her white sweater stained a deep red, and the green darkened almost immediately. He had shoved her into the car right away. As he was driving, he realized he had been dripping. Rather, she had been dripping. He couldn't even do anything with her, except to bury her. As he dug her hole, he looked longingly at her body. Her bleach blonde hair was already caked with blood. He dropped her into the hole, and left her there for a moment. Then he crawled back into the hole, and crossed her arms over her breasts, and brought her knees up to cover them. Only then, did he fill the whole.

Later that same night, he went into Dalian City. He entered through the red light district, and looked around. He paid for one of the hookers, and took her to bed. He had her for a good two hours, and paid her what she asked for. He did his best not to ask her for anything. He, in fact, put on the shy boy veneer, which made her feel in control. What she didn't know was that as he watched her, he needed only to imagine her dying, and was able to climax. He was gone before she awoke the next morning. Only, he was actually watching her from a distance, and pondering whether or not he should kill her.

He watched as she took another john, and followed them to the same motel he'd gone to. He looked into the window, and saw that he was wearing a leather mask, and had her wearing a mask. She was tied up with a leather strap, as the john spread her legs wide, pulling a spiked play toy from his bag. With that, Lester pulled back from the window, and figured she wouldn't really remember him, or anything else but the weirdo she was serving at the moment. Satisfied, he got into his car, and left Dalian behind. Only two college girls had disappeared, but both had an abusive, father, or an abusive boyfriend that gave them visible scars. After that last girl had escaped him, as humiliating as it was, it taught him to make sure the following victims were vulnerable, emotionally and physically.

He had found one crying on a park bench, and he took a seat next to her, holding her as she cried. He asked her what was wrong, and took her to his car. He offered to take her to the police to file a report, and instead took her into the north hills of Dalian, along lovers' lane. He knocked her out on the way, and choked the life out of her, with her own belt. This time, he sexually ravaged the body for a few hours, and left her buried her deep under the tender soil. He gave her a traditional six-foot grave, and placed her in fetal position. Then, he pulled himself out of the hole with a rope he had tied around a tree. He fervently shoveled dirt onto her face, and worked slowly and steadily as he covered the rest of her. As soon as he could pat the sods flat, he threw wet leaves, and twigs onto the grave. The other girl, he had seen at the amusement park. He posed as a manager when he heard her complain about one of the rides. He took her behind one of the booths, and punched her in the stomach to keep her from screaming out loud. He took her a few miles from the carnival, just on the outskirts of Dalian, and strangled her as he took her in missionary position. He then took a rock from the area, and brought it down on her head. He buried her under a cluster of rocks, but the grave was shallow, only four feet deep. He hadn't bothered to take her clothes off, he was too tired to remove them at this point.

Her name had been Lillian Bond. She was petite, at five feet. She wore her golden blonde hair in a bun, tied behind her. She was also very slender, and she had thin face, which made her look almost like a little girl. She was a high school senior with an abusive boyfriend. He drank, she didn't. Still, she wanted to give him a chance, and she did. She was very patient with him, and even tried to get him to go to AA meetings. He had finally taken her one night, drunk out of his mind. She begged him to stop, but he never heard her when he was in that state. He had raped her that night, and had threatened to kill her if she had told anyone. She was sitting on the benches by the field the next morning, crying and wondering what to do. That was how Lester had found her, promising to help her with her problem.

Sandra Halt had been the girl at the carnival. She had been there with her younger brother so she could make up for a fight they had gotten into. He had wanted to go see a movie the week before and she said she had things to do. He hadn't been very happy with her, but his face lit up when she mentioned taking him to the carnival. He spent the whole night at the carnival looking for his sister.

Karen Chastener had finally been able to make the cheerleading squad. She had been working to get in for the past year. She had actually been shy for the first three years of high school. She had promised herself that she would try to be more outgoing for the coming year.

Lester had managed to drive into the outer area of Saffire Falls, and had gone to the local high school, trolling for a victim there. He had managed to find someone and felt much better after that. He was relaxed and satisfied as he drove out of town. This time, there was a younger cop with a speed gun. He stopped Lester a good five miles out of Saffire Falls.

"May I see your License and Registration?"

"Of course, officer. I just wanted to let you know that I'm on the way to a family event, as we speak."

"Is that why you were going fifteen miles over the speed limit?"

"I assure you, I wasn't going that fast. As I said, I'm in a bit of a hurry."

"Well, I'll stay right here. You have five minutes to make your call, and tell your folks why you'll be late."

"Pardon?"

"Go ahead, and call them. I said. I'll even vouch for you being caught up."

"My cell phone is in the trunk."

The officer pulled out his own cell, and offered it to Lester. "You can use mine."

"Well, I don't think I should."

"Go ahead, and dial the number, sir." As he was saying this, he noticed that Lester was digging under his seat. He pulled out his pistol, and pointed it. "Sir, please step out of the car."

Lester hid the hateful scowl that was forming on his face, and opened the door slowly. "Sir, I assure you. I am going to a family affair."

"So, you've said. Why don't you call them?"

"Well, the number's on the phone's memory. I don't know it by heart."

"Open the trunk."

Lester did, having forgotten the one of the girl's jackets. He looked up at the officer, and explained, "It's my girlfriend's jacket."

"Call her too, if you like. Now pull that sweater up. I want to see what's under it."

Lester did, and the crowbar was still a shiny silver, brand-new and gleaming in the sun. Resting with the crowbar was a girl's pair of panties, soiled, and a torn skirt.

"You have the right to remain silent. Anything you do or say- Get back here!"

This because Lester began to run into the deep desert, and panting as he limped, having twisted his ankle as he turned to run. The officer easily overtook him, and had him handcuffed in his state trooper car shortly after.

⊙⊙

Ian Fanning decided to finish his law school career at Harcourt Academy. He was expected to graduate by the coming autumn. So, he decided to leave Pam behind, packed up his car, and moved to another apartment. There was enough food for him to last him the week, and enough coffee for the next three days. His last days with her were not so easy, however.

"Where are you going?"

"Why do you care?"

"I'm just asking. What about this place?"

"Look, it's paid up for the next month. After that, it's your deal."

"My other guy won't help me with the rent, though."

"Well. That's just tough."

"You're not being fair."

"Don't go there. Get me started, and I'll never be able to finish today."

"What the fuck is that supposed to mean?"

"You know damn well what it means."

"Can I call you?"

"No."

"Come on. Give me some way to contact you."

"Why don't you ask your new boyfriend to take care of you?"

"He's only good at one thing. What if I get tired of that, though?"

"You? Tired of that? I doubt it. Seems to be one of the only things you can do right."

"What's the other thing?"

"Having Dara. She was great. Just wish I could've done more for her."

"Oh yeah? Like what?"

"Take her far away from you."

"You know, I could tell the police about that."

"I'm really sure the police will listen to some negligent mother."

"That's not fair."

"Oh, yeah. I forgot, you were more of a sister, weren't you?"

She started to sob, "You're really hurting me."

"Crocodile tears. Now you know how I feel a lot of the time. Don't like that feeling much, do you?"

"You bastard! Get the fuck outta here, then! Get Lost, you fucking Loser!"

"With pleasure." He slammed the door behind him.

He never thought he would ever feel so relieved to be away from Pam. He couldn't imagine what made him stay so long. He was unpacking to his new place, just as Allan Hollister was packing his own belongings.

Having all of their stuff packed, Allan Hollister and Demi were ready to let the U-load truck people do their job, and start driving towards Saffire Falls. Allan had heard that Harcourt Academy was one of the best in the country, and he was willing to pay out the tuition if it meant giving Demi a good school.

She walked up behind him, as he finished taping the last box, "Doesn't seem like much when it's all packed, huh?"

"Don't worry. I'm sure we'll be able to clutter the new space we're going to. I actually think we should just move your stuff in since it might take up the whole place, you know?"

"I don't have that much shit."

"I didn't say that. I was just saying that you might need your stuff to get its own room."

"You're so funny. You should be doing stand up."

"I was for a while. It didn't work out."

"Oh, yeah? You never told me."

"Well, it worked out, but then I worked it back in."

"Oh my god, that is so old."

"I told you. That's why I stopped doing stand up."

"Yeah, that was really smart."

"I thought so. Ready?"

"Yeah. I gave my friends the new address. Is that cool?"

"It's fine. I left my new number with Bobby Kennedy in case he came up with something."

"Aww, why?"

"Well, he asked for it. He also said that he might be going to work at his uncle's English Pub, which is in our new town."

"Well, ok. I've seen him around. He's always asking if I'm ok."

"Does that bother you?"

"Naw. I guess it's weird having two big brother types always asking if I'm doing ok. Sis never really cared."

"I'm sure she did, in her own way."

"I really want to believe that."

He could hear the hitch in her voice. In all these months, she hadn't really said much, but now she was crying. He felt relieved that she was finally coming to terms with it. So, he held her as she cried. She cried for a long time, and after her crying tapered off to sobs, she suggested they just get rolling.

As he drove out of his old town, he passed the Coconut Room on the way out, and gave Bobby Kennedy a wave as he drove off into the empty road. He wasn't sure if he felt the sadness that Demi did. He supposed that there was only one way that he could let go of Sloan, and that was to leave the town. There was nothing else to tie him there, but bad memories of something that never quite made it to marriage.

His cell phone sounded as they entered the interstate. It was a simple ring, no song tune, or clever chime. Demi was asleep, so he didn't want to wake her. He reached into his coat, and pulled it out.

Allan wasn't ecstatic, but there was relief in his voice. "We've got a lead?"

Damien was hardly able to keep the excitement out of his voice; "We've got a match, actually. The guy's name was Kevin Davis. The arresting officer thought he was acting pretty funny about being stopped. Kept trying to evade questioning, and talked his way into getting searched. At the last moment, he tried to make a run for it."

"I don't know. That sounds awfully easy to me. I didn't think our guy would let himself get caught so easily."

"Well, there's more. When the officer asked to see his license in such, the guy didn't even show them. He offered some excuse about going to some family affair, and claimed that he couldn't be late. The officer suggested that he call his family by cell and tell them about the delay. This guy brushes it off by saying it's in the trunk. The officer offers the use of his own phone, and he says he can't remember the number offhand. This guy is asked to open his trunk, and they find a small crowbar, brand new. They also find a torn skirt, a girl's jacket, and a soiled pair of panties."

"Would our guy really make a stupid mistake like that, though?"

"Well, they called us up when they heard he had put a search out on the license plate. It matches the one reported by the guy from the garage. I've run a check on the vehicle, and get this; it belongs to Lieutenant Harold Quartz in Saffire Falls. I went ahead and made a call because he never reported it stolen. When I asked him about it, he said he had sold it, and that the paper work might not have fallen through properly. When I asked who he sold it to, he got crabby and said he couldn't remember."

"So, we've got a dead-end there."

"Not quite. I don't think the Lieutenant is being completely honest with us. I think he might know who this Kevin Davis is."

"Relative, possibly?"

"We'll have to ask him."

"Where is be being held?"

"He's in a jail just outside of Saffire Falls."

"Why'd it have to be that town? Well, at least he's been pinned before he could start something there."

"Let's hope we can keep him in. I talked to the trooper that stopped him, and made sure he went through proper procedure when arresting him."

"Otherwise, he walks, I know. That's the last thing we need. What'd the trooper say?"

"He said he did everything by the book. He said that he was actually going to shoot the suspect, but something made him chase the guy down, and pin him."

"Thank goodness for that."

"If this is the guy?"

"We start making calls around. See if anyone else has missing girls. We've already put out an all-points search, so hopefully someone fesses up."

"If he's not?"

"We can still see what this guy has done. The stuff in his car is a little too suspicious. I don't think I'd want that guy wandering either."

"I can't imagine anyone letting him. How long before you get here?"

"Give me five hours. That's with pits stops, and food breaks."

"Understood. What'll I tell anyone from the press?"

"Tell them that we might've found a rapist. That's all."

"What about any questions about our ad, and anything relating to this guy?"

"Don't say anything yet. The moment the press gets their hands on any information, they're on the next hour, giving away important parts of the case."

"Alright. Have a good trip, Allan."

"Thanks. You take care, Damien."

"You too. Send my regards to your little sis."

"Will do."

Harry Quartz went to the impound yard, just outside the city. He gave his license plate number, and ID. He was able to claim the car as stolen property. He drove it to a junkyard, and had the car compacted, and left aside.

◕◑

Becca and Ryan watched the moving truck roll into his neighbor hood as she walked with him. It came to park two houses before Ryan's as the two were coming up to his place.

"Wow. You're happy."

"Of course I am. I'm with you."

"You squeezed my hand just now. So I figured something got you excited."

"Well, yeah. It feels a little weird being the only new one in town."

"Want to go talk to them?"

"I don't know. They might be busy."

"Well, it never hurts to say hi or something."

"Really?"

"Sure."

They came to a stop in from of the porch as the new neighbors tested the keys. It turned out to be what seemed like a father and daughter.

"Hi, there. Hope everything's cool, and we just wanted to welcome you to the neighborhood. I'm Becca and this is my boyfriend, Ryan."

Allan and Demi turned to smile at the couple.

"Thanks!" Demi was all smiles. She put down the box she was holding and went to hug Becca. Allan was getting a call on his cell phone, and opened the door so he could have some privacy. He never talked about police work in front of Demi. He felt it would only jade her later in life. He went inside for a moment a moment, talking into the earpiece as he carried a box in.

Demi watched him go in, and turned back to face them. She gushed, "Maybe you can show me all the cool places around here."

"Sure, when you're done with unpacking."

"That'll take a while." Allan said, joining them. "I just got called into work, too."

Demi looked to Becca and shrugged.

"That means the unpacking will have to wait."

Ryan offered, "If you like, I could come and help with the unloading later."

Allan nodded, "I'll take you up on that. Not now, though. I will ask that you look after my little sister and show her a good time."

Demi looked back to Allan, "You mean it?"

He gave her some money, "Go on, and have fun. We'll unpack later, when you get home. We'll also have Ryan's help, right?"

"Yes, sir."

"Just Allan is fine."

Becca offered her hand to Allan, "We'd be glad to help. Allan."

"Great. For now, just hang out with her, k?"

"Sure. It'd be our pleasure."

"Great. Take care, sis."

"Yup."

Allan locked the truck and the house, handing Demi the keys to their place. "Be home before dark."

"Will do."

He got into his car, which had been parked and waiting in the drive way. He'd had to maneuver the truck into the small double drive way, and cursing the whole time. That had been earlier, and that helped Demi to laugh a bit, which let her come to her current light mood. He seemingly grimaced as he started the car, waved at her, and drove off.

Ꙩ

The officer at the car impound was told, only later, that the car was to be kept intact for evidence. Damien didn't take it very well.

Allan went into the Saffire Falls Police Station, and asked if Damien had arrived yet.

Just outside the interrogation room, Damien waved him over, and he was fuming. "I can't fucking believe this."

"Detective Greene?"

"That's right, I'm Damien Greene, and you're Allan, right?"

"Yes, I'm Allan Hollister, and glad to finally meet you. Having talked to you on the phone a few times, I sort of felt like I got to know you. So, what happened?"

"They took the fucking car. Someone took it, and trashed it. When I asked them if anyone had come to claim it, they said they couldn't tell me."

"What about the suspect?"

"He's still in custody."

"What are they holding him for?"

"For the moment, they're holding him for drunk and disorderly."

"Will that work?"

"We should go in and talk to him now."

"Has anyone from here tried to shake him down?"

"That's just it. They haven't really questioned him. They said they could not be a party to a man being wrongly accused. I think they know him."

"What makes you say that?"

"He's been asking for shit .all day. Whatever he wants, they just get it for him. It's sickening."

"Let's talk to him before they try to move him."

"Where's your sis?"

"She's staying with a friend from here."

"Wow. Made friends already?"

"It's one of the new neighbors, Becca something or other."

Damien nodded, "That works."

"You know her?"

"Let's just say, she's an old friend."

Allen moved his head to one side, slightly puzzled, "Meaning?"

"Don't worry, Allan. Your little sis is in good hands."

"I sure hope so. Let's talk to this Kevin Davis."

Damien looked into the room where Lester was sitting, his face was determined, and his voice had a subtle tone of anger. "How do you want to do this? This department set it up so we can't record an interview. So, I guess we'll have to take notes."

Allan was taken aback. "What? That's ridiculous."

"We'll have to make do with what we have."

"How about surveillance footage, so we can use it later?"

Damien swore, "Shit. This guy must have a lot of pull here because the cameras to the interrogation room have been shut off. They did that when they learned we'd be interviewing this guy. I can't figure it out."

"Maybe someone's trying to cover for him."

"Do you think so? That'll make things a lot harder for us."

Allan didn't care. He wanted to see what this guy might know about Sloane. If he found out that this guy had killed her, he'd find a way to pin the rest of the missing girls on him. Only then would he have some peace of mind.

"Any suggestions?"

"A few. First of all, don't go in there with a face that says you're judging him."

"I'll be plenty steamed if I find out that he's killed those girls."

"We don't know that yet. We have to go in there with an open mind. If he says he's innocent, then we'll let him talk about it. He might remember something, and let that slip."

"Like if we mention one of the girl's names."

Damien shook his head, "The names mean nothing to him. It's their face, or their body. Whatever it was that a lot of the girls had in common, we have to use that as a point of reference. We could mention locations that we've been to. That might jog his memory, if he's the one."

"What if he's not?"

"We'll ask where he got the stuff that was in his trunk . . . That might be enough to keep him in confinement."

"Good enough."

"Also, if he does happen to mention something that might implicate him, keep cool. Do not change your tone or refer to him in a condescending manner. He won't talk if you do that. Got it?"

By the time he returned to the police station, two out of state police officers were questioning his son.

He went to the station chief and demanded that he be left to handle his son, and for the other two officers not to harass his son.

"Those little bitches are trying to pin shit on my kid?"

"They're looking for someone that might've been killing all those girls in the papers."

"Now, we don't know that. It's not my kid. These fucking FBI wannabes are trying to make it seem like they're big shots, and making my kid admit to shit he didn't do."

"They seem pretty sure. They also showed me a lot of the reports, and even some of the surveillance photos from some of the security systems they've been looking at. I don't know, but the character on there looks an awful lot like your son, Harry."

"Come on. You know Lester. He's a sweet kid. He wouldn't hurt a fly. Just let me get him home before they talk to him."

"You'll have to let them finish."

"What do you mean?"

"They're already setting up the interrogation room as we speak."

When they entered the interrogation room, Lester was sitting on the chair backwards, resting his arms on the backing. He was also given a smoke, and there was a bag of garbage from some fast food joint. When he looked up at them, Allan could've sworn he saw two black holes swimming about in his eyes. They seemed to swirl this way and that, making Allan turn away. He looked up at the light fixture instead, so he could see what made the bright reflections.

"-Lan, turn on the recorder."

Allan looked back and announced, "I didn't think we were supposed to."

Damien nodded, "Good. It's great to see that you're paying attention to the here and now."

Lester took a drag, and smiled up at them, his teeth having yellowed a bit. "Hi, there."

"Hello, Kevin. Do you know why you're here?"

"Well, someone over reacted and dragged me in here for no apparent reason."

"Of Course, there's a reason. Kevin, what were those clothes doing in your trunk?"

"What? My girlfriend's sweater?"

"What's your girlfriend's name, Kevin?"

"Marie."

"How about Karen Chastener? Ever heard of her, Kevin?" That earned Damien a puzzled look from Allan.

"I have no idea what you're talking about. Also, I don't like the tone of your voice, officer. You seem to be accusing me."

Damien turned to Allan and nodded, He knew that the Lester would try to dissuade the use of any names. "That's the girl who owned the jacket in your car."

"Oh. Well. I saw it in the garbage, in some alley, and thought I'd pick it up."

"She was reported missing over a week ago. Also, she was last seen wearing that jacket in your car."

He had forgotten that he had gotten her early in the morning, just as she was going in from morning cheering practice. He had looked like one of the students, so he had asked her where the restrooms were. As soon as the got there, after seeing that no one was around, he had knocked her out. Then he took her to the janitor storage room, and went on sodomize her while he shoved a kerchief down her throat. He had worn rubber gloves, and protection. After he had finished with her, he had gone to the bathroom, and flushed his condom down the toilet. He came back for her, and found her undisturbed. He had taken her to his car, drove out to the deep desert, and buried her there. He hadn't bothered to put her clothes in a bag, though. He had been done playing with her around sunrise. Burying her took longer than he'd thought. So he had been in a hurry to get dressed and go. He thought he could deal with the police if they were like that elderly officer. So, he had just left her clothes in the trunk.

Now, here he was. He was paying for his mistake of not having gotten rid of the evidence before hand. Leaving them in the hole would have raised far too many questions, but leaving them in his car had placed the target squarely on himself.

"I didn't know. Was she?"

"Which alley did you find this in?"

"Are you calling me a liar?"

"Well, no. If you say you found it, we believe you. We just need to know where you found it. Maybe we can catch the real killer if we knew where he left the body."

"Oh, well. I don't know the streets, too well."

"Are you sure?"

"Sure."

"Had you seen the body, or just the jacket?"

"I didn't see any body around there."

"Just so we get this straight. You're not a vagabond. Correct?"

"Do I look like some bum off the street?"

"Then why would you need to go around digging in the garbage, Kevin?"

"I recycle. So I collect bottles and cans. When I saw the jacket, I thought it'd be a waste to throw it away."

"Do you often like collecting girls' clothes, Kevin?"

"What are you trying to say?"

"A pair of panties, and a torn skirt were found in your trunk. Do you have a sort of fetish, Kevin?"

"No look, I'm not like that."

Allan leaned forward in his chair and asked, "Why did you lie about the clothes, Kevin?"

"I just didn't want people to know I dug around in the garbage."

Damien looked over at Allan for a bit, and then went on, "Would it bother you if people knew that you dug in the garbage?"

"Well, yeah. Look, some girl must've thrown away those panties. I just got whatever came with the jacket. I didn't know all that shit was under it."

"Oh, you didn't?"

"No, I just grabbed the whole thing up, and hugged it to myself."

"So, you carried it to your car, just like that?"

"Yeah, I did. That's right."

"Was the crowbar yours, Kevin?"

"What?"

"There was a brand-new crowbar with the other things. Was that yours?"

"No. I mean, yeah. I put the stuff over the crowbar without realizing it."

"What were you doing with that crowbar in your car?"

"No, wait. I think it did come with the stuff."

"So, someone threw away a perfectly brand-new crowbar. Is that what you're trying to tell us, Kevin?"

"No, wait. That's mine. I thought your were talking about the jacket."

"To which, you thought was a waste, correct?"

"Yeah, I did. I mean. It looked all new and shit."

Allan was getting frustrated, and asked, "Did you do anything to her?"

Damien looked over at him with a scowl, and tried to pull it back to a safe and comfortable level for Lester, "The jacket, Kevin. Did you play with it?"

The door slammed open, and Harry looked at the two cops. "Alright! That's enough! You're harassing the suspect."

Allan stood up, "We're not done yet."

Harry grabbed him by the lapels, and put his face to Allan's, "Yes, you are."

Damien pulled Allan back, and added, "He's right. We have a lot of questions to ask this fellow, and you're breaching protocol as we speak."

"Bullshit. I'm not breaching a damn thing. You guys come in from the big city, all talking big shit. Enough of that."

Allan sat down next to Lester, and placed his hands on Lester's own, the one he had on the table. He looked at Lester directly in the eyes, and it was the stuff of nightmares. Yet, he continued on. "When you had her, did you have to fight her? Or was she easy going?"

Lester's eyes glazed over for a moment, and he slurred, "She was so easy."

That was when Allan felt a bolt of stars as he was hit hard. Damien was trying to offer a hand to help him up, and fending off Harry at the same time. Allan waved him off, and pointed at Lester, "Get him! He's leaving! He's leaving!"

Damien turned to see Lester go out the door of the interrogation room, as Harry hurried out to follow him.

"Runaway!" Allan yelled, moving after Lester. That was when the other police officers turned and grabbed Lester.

Harry turned back to face them. "Alright, boys, we've got this covered. You can go home now."

"I don't think so!"

"This case is no longer yours. He's in our place. It's our jurisdiction."

Damien had to restrain Allan from hitting the bigger guy.

Harry grabbed Allan by the lapels again, and snarled, "It's our problem."

"He's the one, you bastard! You've been protecting him, haven't you? You knew he was dangerous and you let him go!"

"Hey, shut up."

To the rest of the officers, he declared, "This sick guy has been using the lieutenant's car to go cross country, and kill a whole bunch of girls!"

Harry was about to hit him again, when the chief came out. He looked at the two out of state officers.

"He's been killing girls all over the country. My wife! My pregnant Wife, you killed her, you bastard!"

Lester muttered, "She was a whore, you should be thanking me."

The chief turned to his own officers, and told them to take Lester to a holding cell for the moment. Then he turned to the newcomers, "Lt. Quartz is right. This isn't your problem. We'll deal with it."

Damien looked at him for a moment, and bit out, "If he gets out, it's your fault."

"Just get out of my station!"

Harry offered to help Damien drag Allan out, to which both refused. He helped to push them out, anyway. Once outside, he looked at them both menacingly, and told them what he did know.

"I know he's fucking crazy. You don't think I know that?! I'll keep him behind bars if that'll make you feel better!"

Damien was puzzled, "What are you trying to say?"

Harry took in long breath, and let it whistle out, sounding like a rusted kettle that was due for being thrown out. "He's my son. His real name is Lester. I guess saying I'm sorry won't help you much, at this point."

"It won't." Allan bit out, "Your bastard son killed my wife."

Damien released him for a moment, and struck Allan across the face, telling him to get a hold of himself. Then he turned to Harry, Allan behind him, and both with grim expressions.

"You better pray that for everyone's sake you can keep that promise. If he crosses our paths again, we'll take him in, and charge him to the full extent of the law."

Harry was shaking, his head slowly going from side to side, as he looked at the two of them. Then he told them something that chilled the both of them.

"I can't bring myself to do it. If he comes before you again, you have my permission to kill him. I'll cover you and say you did it in self defense."

With that, he walked back into the station. Watching as Harry trembled and closed the glass doors behind him.

They couldn't figure out what just happened. They couldn't fathom that a father could ask two complete strangers to finish his son. Allan wiped at his face, rubbing his eyes as they both left the station, and went to one of the local cafes in the area.

9

Why Aren't You Fighting?

Why just sit there? Aren't you one of us? Are you a patriot, waving your flag in my face?

Think of this, though. Take the word, patriot. Take out a letter, say the first one,
What's left forms the word, Traitor.

So don't be so eager to claim yourself one, For when you call yourself a patriot,
You are a traitor to your soul, For you've given up your right to disagree.

I know it seems like another rant, Think of what you stand to lose, though.
Can you think of the graves you'll plant? It's so easy to lose everyone with one blow.

Is your pride in the cause enough, What is that worth to you? Is pride in nation worth
more than your living treasures, Worth more than their smiles and tears?

If you want to give that up, and then call it loyalty, and then you have lost them already,
You've signed their death warrant.

Hate me if you like, For what, though, telling you the truth,
For saying what's totally possible, If the truth hurts, reality is that much more painful.

I won't lose, though; you can call me traitor, if you like,
Remember what I told you, though, It still means Patriot, just to my own flock.

So, you can wave the flags, then send your children to fight.
When they come back, though, if at All, Will they be the same you knew?

I will go myself, In place of my brothers,
Since I don't care if I die, Even if there's no reason to fight.

Still I ask though, didn't this happen before, in Viet Nam?
Another war, same purpose, waged by one who has not learned from History?

The higher-ups have, Can't fight a war without a reason, So our leaders cry wolf, sending
us to hunt in the wilderness.

Think now, though, our leader cries loudest, How'd the wolf get past the gate?
Who let it in? Or has the wolf been there always? Our leader's shadow.

If you have no mind, Rise then to the call of the horns, Like the expendable heroes, or is all
your anger just a front from fear.

Be very afraid then, For the Wolf is inside,
Smiling widely as it begs to fight, And snapping at the black sheep.

> \-   Songs of Lester,
>   <u>Coffee, No Sugar</u> Album.

Allan looked up at Damien and muttered, "I'm sorry for fucking things up, back there. Now we can't go after him."

"I think we can. We just have to get the feds to transfer that guy out of here. You see, this might be his sanctuary."

"Do you think that Quartz meant what he said?"

"I think he did. However, I don't think we should take him up on it. Who knows what he might be thinking."

"It's him, Greene."

"Damien . . . just call me Damien."

"Alright, Damien . . . It's him, though. You could tell that when you looked in those eyes of his. It was like drowning."

"What made you ask that?"

"I wanted to see how he would respond. If he freaked out, and said he didn't do anything. That would be a more natural reaction. Didn't you see how he stopped to think about it?"

"It was as if he were reliving it."

"Exactly, and that's why we have to get him now."

"Are you talking about actually going in, and using an FBI shield to put him some place more secure?"

"I guess."

"Alright, I know that this might be the guy that killed your wife."

"He might've also killed that waitress, and those other girls. No, wait. I think he might've done them all. Think about it. His car was seen at those places at those particular times."

"We're presuming that based on obscure surveillance photos, and fleeting reports from people who might have seen him."

"Wait. Where are those two witnesses you have?"

"Oh my god, you're right. They're in this very town."

"Think you can get Harry to pull a mug shot for us to show around?"

"I doubt it, Allan."

"Give it a try. If she can ID him, then we've got our case."

"What if he asks what I want it for?"

"Tell him that you're going to send it out to other areas, so you can get a confirmation of where he wasn't. That way, he'll think we're trying to eliminate his son as a suspect."

"I guess that way he'll think we're getting out of his way."

"Or, it might be a way to test his stance on this. If he's willing to help, we'll know about it through this."

"I'd hate to put this to the test when we might have a contact, or a connection."

"I don't want to lose the connection either. However, if we depend on him, and he drops out on us without warning? It might be better for us to test this ground now."

"Still, we should keep what we have to ourselves. There's something about that guy that I don't like."

"What about the girls in the witness protection program?"

Damien shook his head. "Well, I don't think we should reveal them yet. I'm just afraid of what might happen to them if this Lester found them."

"Had they dealt with him before?"

"One of them was right under the knife, so to speak."

"My god, it was a miracle for her to get out of that. She must've been terrified for a while after."

"She was, the poor girl. It was all she could do to keep from breaking down during the debriefing."

"So, she got a good look at him."

"That she did. When we make sure that Lester Quartz is in a secure location, then we'll go ahead and get our prosecution team ready."

"Let's not count our eggs."

"You're right. I guess it's just that it feels like we're so close."

"Think we might be able to link him with the other girls?"

"I hope so. I don't know what we might be able to do without his car, though, since it was destroyed."

"The devil seems to be on his side, huh?"

Damien raised his hand in the air, signaling for more coffee. When Damien turned his attention to Allan, his face was somber. "More like, he's the devil incarnate."

"Exactly. So, how do we fight him?"

"We'll have to look through the evidence we have."

"Well, we should try to get a DNA sample as well. See if you can get them to get a cotton swab to pull Lester's saliva sample."

"As well as hair and fiber, I know. I'm sure they must've gotten him to submit to taking blood and tissue samples."

"Not with his father calling the shots."

"Good point. I'll go ahead and see if I can talk to their forensic specialist."

"Are you sure? What if he loses the sample?"

"Loses the sample?"

"Think about it. We're in his town."

"Well . . . Let me see if we can call one of our people over here."

"That's a lot better. Then we'll know for sure."

"If we find proof and link him to a lot of the cases, he's going to fry."

"I certainly hope so. I can't bear to think of how many girls our still out there, buried in the middle of nowhere."

"I know. I'm going to make the call now."

"Go ahead. I'll start listing what we need to follow this guy, build a history so we know what we're dealing with."

"Hopefully his father doesn't interfere with that."

"My feelings exactly."

Damien got up, and went outside to make the phone call.

Another waitress came to refill their cups. She almost over-filled Allan's cup, as she watched him read over reports. Allan lifted them off the table and got up before the coffee could spill onto his lap.

Pam reached out to clean the coffee. "Oh my god, I'm so sorry."

"It's fine. It's fine. Just be more careful."

"It's just that while you were sitting there, reading over that case file stuff, it reminded me of my boyfriend."

"I see."

"Well, not boyfriend now. We broke up, and so we're not talking."

"I'm sorry. Pam?"

"Yes?"

"I have a lot of work to do. Would you please clean that up so I can sit down?"

"Sure. Did you already order your food?"

"We just came in for coffee." Allan pointed out the window, motioning to Damien.

Pam's face seemingly dropped, "Oh, you're gay. I understand."

"No, we're not." Allan placed money on the table, and gave her a scowl, "Just annoyed. Thanks for the coffee."

Just then the manager had approached Pam, and asked her to go to the back of the house.

They were standing in the kitchen, just outside his office, and he let her have it then and there. "What the hell were you thinking, talking to customers like that? You're fired! Got that? Don't come back here."

After getting changed and leaving her uniform in the office, she went out to see if those young men were still there. She had seen that the other one was still on the phone, and Allan was actually just sitting in the car and waiting to leave. She walked by the car, and bent over to poke her head into the car.

"Look. I'm sorry. That was totally out of line."

Allan rolled his eyes, "Don't worry about it. Is that all you wanted to say?"

"Well, yeah. That, and . . . Are you free tonight?"

"I've got a lot of work to do. So, no."

She wrote her number on a scrap of paper with her lipstick, "Here. Call me in case you change your mind, ok?"

"Um, sure."

"Do you have like a uniform? If you're wearing one of those, you'd look totally hot."

"Thanks."

"Have you seen that movie?"

"Which?"

"Cops on the Beat. It's like actual arrests and incidents on the road."

"No. I guess I haven't."

"You should. It's pretty good. I thought the guys on there were pretty hot too, you know? Not as hot as you, but pretty damn close."

"Great."

"Omigod. I'm talking too much aren't I?"

"Yes, you are."

Pam's eyes were casts downward, "I'm sorry to bother you, then."

Allan noticed that she reminded him of Sloane somewhat. The last thing he wanted was to be with someone else that was a lot like her. It was enough to be handling the case. He didn't need his personal life to become a problem too. With that in mind, he leaned towards her, and said, "Listen, Pam. I'm sure you're a very nice person."

"No, I'm not. I'm a total bitch. So, you don't have to lie to me."

"You seem really nice, but I really don't have time for a personal life at the moment. I've too much to deal with."

"No, it's ok, really. I mean, you've got shit to do, and you don't want to waste time with someone like me, right?"

"I didn't say that. I only said that I have a lot to do."

"No, you can say it. You think I'm a whore, right?"

Allan shook his head, and began to fidget uncomfortably. "This really is not the time to discuss something like that. I've got a lot to do."

"Fine, do what you want!" Pam snapped. That was when she felt a tap on her shoulder. When she looked back, Damien was standing there, looking impatient. She tossed her head up, and walked past him.

When they got into the car, he asked, "Now, what the hell was that all about?"

"Don't ask. I don't think that even I know."

"What'd she want?"

"She wanted me to ask her out."

"So, why didn't you?"

"Maybe it's because she's nuts."

"She's a little old for you, too."

"That doesn't bother me. It was the fact that she reminds me of my wife."

"Is that a good thing?"

"Not really. Times with her were pretty tough."

"It was that bad, huh? Too much like history repeating itself?"

"Exactly. Let's just get back to work."

"You got it." Damien said, as he drove off to gather more resources.

When Ryan and Becca got to her house, her father was ordering a pizza. It was combo deal with chicken and fries. Ryan took a seat next to Becca, and Demi sat on her other side. She felt glad to have someone to hang out with, especially since Allan would be busy a lot of the time. She supposed he still had to get over her sister. She didn't think it would be that hard, though. Sloane wasn't quite the memorable person that Allan made her out to be. She remembered that when she was a kid, Sloane would be watching the midnight horror flick on TV, and when Demi complained about oncoming nightmares, she was kicked out of the room. Sloane didn't care if her father yelled. She'd dog him until he couldn't argue with her anymore.

Now, here she was. Allan had made a great home for the two of them, so far. He had also tried his best to be her big brother. Demi had to wonder, though, just how did he put up with her all those years? When she got up the courage to ask him that on the road trip, he told her that he was trying to hang in there for Demi's sake. Also, he wanted to come to an understanding with Sloane, even if she was a bitch. As she sat around the table, she found out what it was that she and Allan were missing.

"-The taters."

Demi awoke from her daze, and found that Ryan was talking to her. He asked her again, "Would you pass the taters?"

"Oh, ooh yeah. Here."

Becca looked over at her, a little worried, "You ok? If you like, we can take you home."

"I'm ok. No, don't worry about that. I'm cool. I was just looking around."

Ryan nodded, "It is a pretty nice place."

Becca's father looked over at him, and asked, "So, what do you see yourself doing in five years?"

"Maybe begin a career in social services, and help kids out of abusive homes. I hope to do a lot of good."

"Sounds like a noble dream. Have you thought about how you will go about it?"

"I'm planning to take some classes at the University for Psychology, and child psychology. I don't quite yet know enough, but I will do the research."

"That's excellent. Isn't it, Matthew?"

Becca's brother had been broken out of his reverie. He had been staring at Demi for a while now. There was something about her that made his face warm, and his hands go numb. He wasn't even sure he could talk in front of her, without having his words come out in slow spurts. He decided he would try some other time. In the meantime, he would enjoy the pizza, and chicken. Ryan had been noticing him, and felt for the kid. He knew exactly what that longing was like. He had felt it, himself, with Becca. He had tried to approach here a few times after Eric had introduced them. He couldn't bring himself to do it, though. His lucky break had been that day when he had been rushing to school on a holiday. That only made Ryan feel more embarrassed. He supposed it couldn't be helped at the time. He also supposed that Matthew would have to go through his own dilemmas, and setbacks. It was painful to watch, though. Inwardly, Ryan wished the kid luck, and hoped that his own luck would continue going well. He looked over at Becca, and found that she had been looking at him. She squeezed his hand under the table, and it made him feel warm all over.

"More Pizza."

Everyone got a chuckle out of it. Demi snickered, but she gave Matt a wink that would carry him through the whole night as well as a whole bunch of different dreams with Demi. He would see himself with Demi at the beach, at the shopping center, or even at a movie with her, alone. The possibilities were endless.

"Ryan, do you think you might want to do police work?" Matt asked suddenly.

Ryan was slightly puzzled, and could only incline his head. "The thought had crossed my mind a few times. I just don't think I would make a good cop. I'm a little too shy for that."

"Well, I'm guessing they teach you how to toughen up there."

Demi interjected, "Well, it won't completely change you, if that's what you're worried about. I mean. My older bro is a cop, and he's the nicest guy in the world. You met him too."

Ryan nodded.

"They pretty much teach you how to defend yourself, and stuff like that. I'm guessing you might be good at that."

He hadn't meant to tense up, but his voice was controlled. "What do you mean by that?"

"Well, you look like you do some body building, so it wouldn't be that much of a stretch, you know?"

Becca had her hand on his arm, trying to soothe him. Her father hadn't noticed either, so she was relieved. She was also proud of Ryan for being able to keep his voice level. She supposed that the conversation might've turned toward the subject of his father, and she was worried about Ryan having to deal with that. However, his father would not be brought up all night, much to her relief.

When Ryan got up to leave, Becca turned her eyes up to him. "Want me to walk you back home?"

"No, it's cool. I have a lot of homework to do. Oh yeah, Demi. Let your brother know that I'd be totally all for helping you guys unpack. Just let me know when."

"Totally. Are you going to bring some extra help too?"

"Do you have some heavy furniture to move around?"

"We might. It's arriving over the weekend."

"That's fine. Let me know, k?"

"Yeah."

"Oh wait. You want me to wait until you're done? I forgot about you being two houses down now that I think about it."

Becca stood up for a moment, and pulled him back to the table to sit down. She was actually pretty relieved that he wasn't leaving just yet. She squeezed his hand, and felt a rush as he squeezed back.

"I just wish this could last longer." Demi sighed.

Matthew look puzzled, "Dinner?"

Demi gave him a smirk, "No, silly, this moment. Everyone's so cool."

Becca's father folded his arms on the table, and inclined his head, "Well, you know that you're always welcome here, Demi."

"Really?"

Matthew readily agreed, nodding furiously as his father smiled, and told her, "Oh, yeah. Next time though, Dinner's got to be your treat." He winked as he said this, making Demi chuckle a little.

After dinner, Demi offered to help Matthew pick up the table. In the meantime, Becca took what little time she had so she could be with Ryan.

They were sitting outside on the swinging porch bench, Becca pulling Ryan's arm over her shoulder. She was now leaning on his chest, as he caressed her back.

"Do you think your dad liked me much?"

"Sure, he does. He didn't give you the full-fledged boyfriend test."

"Does he do that to everyone?"

"Just people he doesn't like. Anyways, I kind of told him how we met, so he thought I'd be good for you."

"Wow, that's cool."

"Oh?"

"I mean, it's cool that your dad would look out for me like that."

"Your dad doesn't?"

"My dad wishes I were dead."

"Don't say that."

"That much is true. No lie, seriously."

She sat up so she could look at him, feeling him shiver as he told her that, "It can't be all bad."

"It is."

"Oh, Ryan. I'm here for you, too, you know?"

"I know you are. I'm used to the whole deal with my father. He's pretty much lost his worth in my eyes."

"Will he mess with you if you go home now?"

"No, I got the feeling that he won't be messing with me for a long time. My brother's got him on the run, too."

"Well, there you go. You've got your brother to look out for you too."

"For how long, I wonder."

"What do you mean?"

"He told me not too long ago that he wouldn't always be there for me. I'm wondering what he meant."

"He means that you'll outgrow him one day."

"I thought about that, too. We always promised each other, though, that we would stick by each other until one, or both, of us find our path."

"That's deep."

"Well, I guess he always thought that he had to look after me after our mom got killed. I guess I've always felt like I was a burden too him, though. I mean, it's something that I felt."

"You're not a burden. Not to him, and definitely not to me."

"I know that. I'm just hoping everything goes cool for my brother. He deserves it, you know?"

"You deserve to be happy too."

"Well, yeah. That's why I'm sticking to you."

"Meaning?"

"In the past few weeks, you've made me really happy. Do you know that, Becca?"

"Yeah, I do." She leaned in to kiss him, and they stayed like that for a long time, holding each other closely.

Demi cleared her throat, "I'm wondering if this is to walk me home, or it's a field trip for you two lovebirds."

Becca gave her a playful mean look, and smiled, "Ready to go home?"

"Sure."

Ryan smiled over at Becca, and then looked to Demi. "Well, let's get moving before it gets any darker."

"Are you kidding? Looking up is like being in space."

"Night sky is usually pretty clear."

"I can tell." Demi nodded. "The one on the left is Orion, I think, and the other one farther up is Sagittarius."

Ryan shrugged, "I wouldn't know."

Becca playfully hit his shoulder, "Don't be so serious all the time."

"Ok, ok."

He started walking, and Demi smiled back at Becca as she joined him.

As they walked, Demi asked, "So, how long have you two known each other?"

"A month now."

"Wow, you two are pretty close."

"I'd like to think so."

"Well, my big brother was in love with my older sis. He's actually not related to me, but he was cooler to me than my sis was."

"Were they close?"

"No way. She was a total bitch to him. She always made him feel like crap a lot of the time. It was like she knew how to hurt him, so she did it over and over again."

"That's pretty bad." Ryan nodded.

"Not just bad, but oh well. I think now that I can appreciate a nice guy."

"Well, I'm sure you'll find Mr. Right some day. Takes people a while to find the One."

"I know. I wonder if my bro will find the One, soon."

"Well, he'll decide that when the time comes. For now, it's just a matter of healing. When my mom died, my dad never really got over it. He's been blaming me for it, ever since. Sometimes I feel bad for him. There are other times when I don't care."

"You might not think so, but your dad needs you. I know that sounds like I'm getting too much into your business, but that's what I think. Your mom was his world, and now she's gone."

"Well, what are me and my brother? He totally thinks my brother's the best thing since the internet."

"Well, there's that. Your dad, though, knows you'll both leave one day. That part of him that was with your mom is gone. He doesn't have that to lean on. When your mom was still around, was your dad the same way?"

"Actually . . . No, I guess he wasn't."

"See? He probably doesn't know how to talk to you."

"He says plenty if I give him the time of day."

"Then just listen. Eventually, he'll run out of crap to say. I guess at this point, he just needs to get all the crap out of his head."

"Here's your house."

"Ok, thanks. Think about what I said, though. My sis was the same way. I could tell she didn't want to be saved, though."

"What did your older bro type do?"

"He hung in there. He still feels bad, but at least he knows it wasn't his fault."

"Thanks. I'll think on it."

"You better."

He stood there until she was able to get the door open, get in, and lock it. Some part of him told him that it was completely necessary to make sure she got in. If he had been facing the street, he would've seen Dave Thompson, stopping for a moment and leering at her. She had seen him too, but tried not to make Ryan feel bad. So, she smiled, and whispered a good night to him.

The next day, Ryan brought Eric with him as they helped Allan and Demi unpack all of their furniture. Allan even bought a large bottle of water for the two of them, and gave them both lunches. He was looking at the two of them, and wondered aloud. "Wow. How do you guys have energy for all this?"

Eric pointed at Ryan; "Dude keeps me on my toes, always getting in trouble."

Ryan scowled, and muttered, "No, I don't. I'm totally cool."

Eric patted him on the head, and said, "If you say so, little one."

"Shut up, dude."

"Becca was right. You can not take a joke."

Allan smiled, and looked over at the clock, which read two in the afternoon. He looked over at the boys, and said, "I'm hoping we can finish today. Think we can do it?"

Eric gave Allan thumbs up, "You better believe we can."

Ryan nodded reluctantly, "Yeah. What he said."

They all laughed a good long moment, and then finished up their meal. Demi was upstairs vacuuming, and yelled down at them, "No fair sharing a joke when I'm not there."

That made them laugh even harder.

As the evening wore on, Eric told Ryan to go on home, while he helped Allan with a few last things. Ryan wasn't sure he even wanted to leave, feeling so good at that moment. He resigned himself to having to explain their evening to their father, though. It wasn't like their father would be in any mood for explanations, anyway.

◌◌

Then, there was silence. He was surrounded with just his thoughts. About his father, his older brother, he felt a distance that he hadn't felt before. It made him sad, but he shook his head inwardly, and went on to his house. When he got home, he had seen his father on the floor of the living room, knocked out. Only, his body wasn't heaving and contracting. Ryan knelt by the body quickly, and listened for a heartbeat. It was very weak, and when he looked over his father's shoulder, he saw a puddle of vomit. His first reaction would've been to turn the old man over to lie on his back. That would've killed Mr. Sandler. Instead, he began to slap his back, making him cough up, and regurgitate even more. At least now, though, he was coughing and moaning. He helped the old man sit up, and looked around.

"You're home, boy?"

"Yes, father. What did you drink?"

"I don't remember."

"Father, this is important."

"I don't know, I said. I was just having a pull on my scotch, and it just got stuck. I don't know."

"That's your body telling you it doesn't want anymore. Do you know that?"

For a moment, the old man's eyes seemed to glaze, and then come back into focus on Ryan's face. He finally recognized him, and didn't try to push away, or try to hit his son at all. He only held on to his son's arm.

"I've been so crappy to you, no?"

"It's alright."

"No, not ok. Your mom would be mad as hell if she knew."

"She's gone, father. She has been for years, now."

He looked up at his son, "She's not coming back, is she?"

"No, seems she won't."

His father's face seemed to crinkle and scrunch as his eyes watered, "It's not your fault, boy. Your mom, she was always like that. She used to make me put out milk for stray kittens, and all that. She was so nice like that."

"I know, father."

He looked up at his son, "I really miss her, boy. Is it ok to miss her?"

"Yes, father. We all miss her."

"I know you did, boy. You kept them dogs she gave you."

Ryan fought to keep the tenseness out of his hands. He only held his father, sitting on the floor with him. He couldn't help asking, though. "What about them?"

"I left them there because I know you missed her, too. Then I came out here, and thought it'd be better for you if I weren't around anymore."

"No, father. That's not true."

"Yeah, it is. I've been bad to you. I know that."

"What woke you up?"

"When you hit me, that's when I woke up."

"Father . . ."

"Don't you say sorry for that, neither. You did right. I was being an asshole, and I said some lot of bad things to you."

"It's ok."

"You're just saying' that. Oh gah." Mr. Sandler began to vomit again. This time, it didn't seem like he could stop. Ryan pulled over a metallic bucket with ice, and emptied it out, throwing the ice onto the area rug. He figured there wasn't much point to keeping neat if his father was puking all over the place.

Eric ran in, dropping his equipment at the doorway. "What's wrong?"

Ryan looked up, shaking his head, at a loss, "I don't know. I think he just had a bad drink."

Eric pulled the keys off its rack, and motioned his head to the car. "C'mon then, dude. We'll have to drive him over to the MC."

"Can you drive?"

"Of course, now come on!"

They helped their father into the car, keeping the bucket a little below his chin, and Ryan sat in the back with him to keep him from moving too much. Before they took off, Ryan ran into the house, grabbed one of his mother's quilts, and ran back to drape it over his father's shoulders.

Between coughs, the old man managed to croak, "No. was your mom's. She'd get mad if she knew I got it all dirty."

Ryan tried to smile, "She'd get mad if she knew we let you get cold."

His father smiled up at him gratefully, and turned back to puke more. Although Ryan was usually squeamish, and hated any bad smell to the point of gagging, he was able to hang in there, and hold on to his father as they all went to the medical center.

☙❧

A few hours later, the doctor was explaining to him that their father's liver was almost gone, and he only had a short time before he died.

Ryan thought he would be ready for that, but when he looked up at the doctor and asked about how long, he felt his voice cracking.

The doctor inclined his head, and muttered, "Four or five months, possibly. If he stops completely, it could buy him a year at the most."

Eric held his brother's shoulder, and squeezed it. When he turned to the doctor, he was already in parent mode, as he had been since their father had started drinking. "Well, then. It seems we have a long time to think about this, then."

Ryan nodded, and looked up at his brother's face, solemn and stony. He almost winced when his brother had said, "I'll have to quit football, and get a job."

Noticing his brother's alarm, he added, "It'll be alright. Mom left us enough to last for years."

"I'll be leaving you something too." Their father added. He was fully sober, and he needed to lean on the wall to keep up straight. They went over to him, and helped him back to his bed. "Father, you shouldn't be up and walking."

"I know. I heard." He allowed himself to be escorted back to bed, and as soon as he was done easing in, he looked at the two of them. He took in a deep breath, and when he opened his eyes again, he said, "I know I haven't been easy to deal with all this time. I know I've been an asshole, even."

Eric was about to reply when their father held his hand up. "Let me finish. I've been actually working while you've both been out. Except, my work hasn't been easy, and it hasn't been at all any help when I see that your mom is not here."

"It's because of me, isn't it, father?"

"At first I thought it was, but when I looked at the facts of your mom's case, I realized it was easier to just blame you. The one that hit your mom was a plain clothes officer named Harry Quartz. They covered for him pretty well, though. Even if I tried to bring this case up, no one would ever listen. That's why I drank so much, I guess. Trying to get anything mentioned seemed so useless, that I drank more than usual."

"Dad," Ryan found himself whispering.

The old man smiled at that, "I know I haven't been very worthy of that name lately, but thanks anyway for the thought."

Ryan seemed as if he were about to retreat into formality again, but his father patted his head gently, "I'm sorry for all I've done to you. I'm sorry for all I couldn't do for you. I wish that I could've done more for you."

"You still can, dad. I mean. We've got some time."

"I know. It won't be enough, though. Never. I want you to find this guy, Quartz, when you're older. That is, when you're old enough to do something about it, go ahead and raise hell. I know your mom would want to do the right thing, and let this go. I can't though. It's not fair that your mom is gone, and that piece of trash is still walking around, and having a good life."

"What should we do when we find him?" Eric wanted to know.

"Do what you need to do. I know it's not fair, putting this on you two. There's a lot of things that haven't been fair for you two, but you've pulled through. I guess that's why I don't mind dying so much. You're both actually men, and I had nothing to do with that."

"Dad, you have."

"Yeah, I know. I've become the example of what you don't want to be."

Ryan shook the urge to incline his head.

"It's my turn now. It's ok, boy. I haven't been very good to you. Now, here I am, and leaving you my grudge. I also got some money from my retirement fund."

"You've been drinking a lot, though."

He smiled at Ryan, and for once he was being the dad he always could've been but had missed his chance. "Thanks a bunch professor. The liquor was stuff I made on my own. I had to pour it into brand bottles, which is why I never let you take the bottles for recycling. I guess that experimental stuff is bad for you.'

"Even the processed stuff is bad for you, dad." Eric chimed in.

"Well, I'm paying for it now body and soul. I didn't want to leave you both empty handed, though. You'll find my safe in the basement. It's got all you'll ever need, as well as a savings bond that will start giving out cash as soon as I'm gone. Also, you'll see all the files for your mom's case. That's the guy that killed your mom, Ryan. You didn't get her killed. I know you think you have. I've made it worse. It wasn't you, though."

Ryan inclined his head.

Mr. Sandler lay back, and waved them off, "Now, let me get some sleep. I'll see you at the next visiting hour."

Eric nodded, as did Ryan when he felt his brother's hand on his shoulder. They sat there watching their father sleep, and did so for a long time.

When Becca met Ryan on his way to school, he smiled at her weakly. She wrapped her arms around him, and looked up into his eyes.

"What's bothering you?"

"My dad . . . He's dying."

"Oh, my god. Ryan, I am so sorry."

"So am I. We took him to the hospital last night, and that's when he found out."

"I hate to ask this, but . . . Is he sober now?"

"Dry as this sidewalk. It was weird too. He was different from what he's usually like. It's almost like he was a different person."

"Is he going to stay sober."

"I hope so. The doctor told him that if he does, it'll give him a year. If he doesn't keep to that, he won't have much time left."

"I guess it's hard to talk all at once, huh?"

"Well . . ."

"You know I'm here for you."

"Yeah, I do. I just hope I don't-"

She held her fingers to his lips, "Lose me? No. Just don't say it, either. I don't want to have something happen because of some jinx. I know I want to be with you, so you won't lose me."

"Well you could lose that bad sense of humor."

"Aren't you so bold? Any more suggestions?"

"I've got a few."

"Ouch. Is there that much room for improvement?"

"No, don't worry about it. I like you just the way you are."

"You better." She playfully punched his shoulder.

"I know, I know." He rubbed his shoulder, feigning pain. Then he wrapped his arm around her. She leaned on his shoulder as they walked. They passed Demi's house, and she smiled as she ran to join them both.

"Morning, you too. Are you always this lovey-dovey this early in the morning?"

"No, just this morning."

"Did you talk to your dad?"

"Yeah I did. Thanks for that."

"For what?"

"If I hadn't talked to him when I did, I get the feeling I probably wouldn't talk to him again."

"Oh my god, what happened?"

"He's in the hospital. He had poisoned himself with some homemade alcohol. I guess he had been hiding a few things from us, too."

"Ryan, I am so sorry."

He smiled over at Demi, a sort of relieved smile. "It's alright. I mean it. It's too bad it had to happen like this, but at least I got to talk to my dad."

"Well, at least you got to talk to him, right?"

"Yeah, more than the usual grunts and yelling."

"Don't do that."

"What?"

"Just be glad for what you have. You know you won't have it for much longer."

'True. How's Allan doing?"

"He came home yesterday a little bothered. He eventually told me it was because of someone he met while putting some files together."

"Who was it?"

"It was just some lady that reminded him of my sis."

"Is that bad?"

"You didn't know my sister. She wasn't a nice person. That's all I can really say."

"Gotcha."

"Yeah."

Becca kissed his cheek, and whispered, "You think too much."

"Do I?"

"Yeah. It's almost like you have to think out every word."

"Oh, come on. I'm not that bad."

"Yeah, you are, silly."

"Still love me?"

"Always."

Demi cleared her throat again, and smiled when Becca told her to shut up. She felt like she was finally with friends. These were real friends, who looked out for her. Then she looked up the street, and Dave Thompson was walking towards them. He had a single rose in his hand, and had a cocky smirk on his face as he approached Demi.

Instinctively, both girls got behind Ryan.

"Outta my way, squirt."

"Um, no. What do you want?"

"I just want to talk to your hot friend, there."

"She's a little young for you, so no."

He reached up to grab Ryan's shirt, but got both of his wrists trapped in Ryan's grip. Ryan squeezed both wrists until Dave knelt to the ground in pain.

"Let me go, you bastard."

Ryan raised an eyebrow. "That's my line. What do you want?"

"I just want to talk."

"So talk."

"In private. Just me and her."

"Then, no. Get lost."

"I won't hurt her."

"I never mentioned that. If you're saying it, it's been on your mind. So again, back off."

He tried to raise himself on one knee, and use the leverage to throw Ryan to the ground. Ryan held his ground, and pushed down on David's back. "Very bad idea."

Dave felt his face hit the concrete, hard enough to chip his two front teeth and scrape his nose.

He tried to grab Ryan's ankle, and felt a hand on his neck. It was his current nemesis, and he was pressing Dave's face to the ground.

"If you stay in that position with the blood clotting your air passage, you'll black out. I assure you. I can make it worse than that. Don't make me."

"I'll back off."

"Really?" He was pressing Dave's head to the ground with the one finger, which had extended up to the back of David's head.

"Yeah, yeah. Let me go."

"Alright." Ryan stepped back two paces, and held his ground as Dave got up.

"You are so fucking dead, boy."

Ryan rushed him, and drove his fist just below the ribs, making the other crumple to the ground, coughing and groaning.

"Alright, that's enough. Let's leave it at that. Come after either girl again, you'll be dealing with me. Do you understand?" Ryan added the bitterness to the last word, making it clear that he was very serious about protecting Demi and Becca.

"Fine, I'll go away."

"You'd better. Cross your fingers with that promise and I'll break them. Do you understand that?"

"I got you. Dude, you kick ass. Want a ride to school? My car's right over there."

He didn't need to look to the girls. He knew what they would say.

"That's alright. Let's just say we've come to an understanding, and leave it at that."

"Well, if you ever need my help, I got your back."

"Um, thanks."

"Sure. That's like my guarantee of protection."

"I'm guessing you might need me more than I would need you."

"Whatever. Later, dude. See you at school."

"Sure. If you say so." Ryan watched Dave drive off, but knew better. As it turned out, Dave tried to be Ryan's friend after that, but there was always an eerie sense that the girls were being watched by him.

--10--

<u>That Road</u>

I decided long ago, I'd be on my own. I decided I'd be able to go on without anyone.
I told myself, it's always easier when one is looking at a book, or just keeping close to their
favorite things.

So why can't I feel like I did before? Why do I feel so distant, even from me?
I can't even write as much as I used to. I can't even think.

The road I take is the road for self-reliance. However, it's also self-damning for me,
Because self-reliance means leaning on No One. Why can't I just be on my own and not
need anyone?

I wish I could just be on my own again. I'm glad I met all the people I have.
But I haven't done enough for anyone. I've done plenty for myself.
I've bought myself several things, gorging in everything that was delicious.
But I still don't feel filled. Why is that?

Why can't all the old things that used to make me happy
fill me anymore? I don't know. I really don't.

There used to be a boy, Who was used to just reading?
Never looking up from that book, And wanting to just stay in the book.

It was safer in those times, Safe from all the turmoil and pain
Which seems too all consuming now.

I supposed there must be some reason for all this. I supposed one must go through all this
for the sake of growing up. If this is what growing up means, I don't want it.
I want to stay as the bookish child I was.

It's always been safer there. Now I know why some people don't want to grow up,
Because being an adult means being in pain. Being an adult means worrying about what's
going to happen the next day, and the day after.

I've done that all my Life, Now, though,
When it's a must, I don't want to do it.

For that I'm called spoiled, For that I'm called selfish.
For that I'm made to feel like a child, But not a safe child,
I'm seen as a stupid child.

"Grow up" I'm told, several times, I keep wanting to say, "I have grown up, and now I
want to stop growing." Because the older I get, the more their words hurt.
The older I get; everyone's words seem to have a sting to them.

I'm not giving in though. I'm going to keep trudging.
I still have a brother to think about. I have a girl to think about as well. At least I hope I
do.

She sees through my words, and when I'm in pain,
She knows enough to ask me "what's wrong?"
She knows me well enough to see when I'm moody,
She knows me well enough, Because I trust her, With my very life.

She's told me that she trusts me just as much, Yet I still feel like I can't give her as much,
Not as much as she has. But I realize, now, We'll always try to be there for each other,

And when the other is sad, We'll say to each other, "Aren't I helping?"

But I guess that's how love is, Giving, trying to give the best of yourself
To another person, And hoping it's enough.

She told me already, though, Many times, She loves me just the way I am, As I do her.
I suppose, that's why I feel so overwhelmed, When I asked myself what I've done to deserve
her. Though I know I won't ask.

If I did, she'd just smile, Then squeeze my hand,
And say, "Just being here was enough."

She tells me to be myself, but I no longer feel that's enough,
Because the old me was untrusting, Protective and very selfish.

She saw past all that, and I'm glad for it,
That's why I love her, She's filled me in a way that books,
And other little things couldn't fill me.

That's enough for her, and she tells me that she'd love me,
No matter how snobbish I was, Just as long as she knows that I love her back.
I've promised her that, Already, and she smiled. That's enough for me.

I fear sometimes, I will not be enough,
But she clears all doubts, With her gentle words,
And soothing voice. I feel complete, for once, I feel totally filled.

> — Songs of Ryan
> <u>Light of Hope</u> Album

By the time Ian got a block from the university, he saw a girl just run past his car. He had to brake hard so as not to hit her. He made a quick right turn, stood out of his car, and slammed his car door shut as he gave chase to the girl in the long black coat. He was able to follow her for at least three blocks, and then she seemed to disappear. He looked around further, and went down an alleyway. He saw her standing by the door of an Italian eatery, and hid as he watched the owner open the door, and hand her a bag of food. When she began looking through the contents, Ian spoke up.

"Well, I'm glad you're not in too much of a shock. At least you recovered enough to get yourself some food."

"Do I know you?"

"No, you don't. I actually came to see if I might've hurt you with my car."

"I'm fine. You really should get back to your family."

"I have none."

"Well, that's sad. I'm afraid I don't have family myself to speak of."

"There must be someone."

"Parents are dead. My brother, too."

"Tell you what; Let me buy myself a pasta dish and we can eat dinner in my car."

"Is that what all you men think about?"

"Getting food? Yes, it is."

"That's not what I meant."

"I know what you meant. I'm not one that would try to hurt you, Miss."

"Thorne. Scarlette Thorne."

"Scarlette, huh? Cool name."

"Thanks. I thought of it myself."

"Come on."

Ian was able to get himself a take out lasagna with a sausage He ate calmly as he watched Scarlette pick at her food.

"What's the matter?"

"I'm not hungry at the moment. What a waste."

"Do you have some place to stay?"

"For the moment, no."

"I have a spare room. You can have that one."

"Whatever for?"

"So you have a roof over your head?"

"No. I mean, why would you get a new place and have an-other room if you just said that you were alone."

"I guess I got used to renting out for two. The room would've been my step-daughter's."

"Where is she now?"

"She's gone."

"Ah. Ran away?"

"No. She was killed. Her mother was no prize, either. So, I left."

"Did you kill them?"

He shot her a glance, and snapped, "No!"

"I'm sorry. That was quite rude of me. No, you don't seem like a person that would hurt anyone."

"I think my wife did enough hurting for all us combined."

"Well, in that case. I accept your offer. On one condition . . ."

"What's that?"

"My body is off limits. I don't care if you are doing this out of the kindness of your heart."

"Of course, it is. I wouldn't, either."

"Oh?"

"I took care of my daughter, after all."

"Was she yours?"

"It felt like that."

"What did her mother do when she died?"

"Looked for another of her boyfriends to comfort her."

"Sounds awful. You are not considering returning to her, are you?"

"No."

"I'm sorry. I seem to be asking too many questions. That's my nature. Living with a man like my father had required me to be quite careful."

"That's understandable."

"Is it? You're not a woman. How would you know?"

"I think we as human beings do not like others hurting us. So, we put up defenses that we hope will keep us at a level where we are somewhat comfortable."

"That was quite pretty, um."

"Ian Fanning."

"Well, Ian Fanning. Would it be all right if I left this in your icebox? I'd like to eat it later at least."

"Of course. Do you have another place where you keep your belongings?"

"There was an older house not too far from here."

"The Frankfurt place?"

"Yes. Do you know of it?"

"Everyone in town does. A schoolteacher went home one day after having been the victim of a vicious prank. She didn't have the nervous breakdown at that moment, though. Instead, she went home and picked mushrooms from her garden. They were white nightshades, which she used as the ingredients for a chicken stew she had made. Her husband had to come home later, so he's still alive. However, her children were not so fortunate. She'd had her eldest son when she was very young, at fourteen. So he was at least sixteen. The other two had been twin boys, both twelve. The last had been a daughter, nine, and her favorite. Oddly enough, her daughter had the largest portion. The other three died within the hour, all were excruciating deaths, I hear. Her daughter died within only a few minutes of having the stew. She began to bleed horrendously, and well let's just say she died badly. The mother hadn't eaten her own stew. She instead took her husband's hunting rifle, and proceeded to blow her brains out."

"That's horrible. Is that why the house was empty?"

"Indeed. That was when I was still a kid, even. All the kids used to run past the front gates of the house as a dare. 'Be swift lest Crazy Annie take ye.' Or something like that."

"Did you believe it?"

"I looked it up when I was old enough to understand."

"Ah, ever curious and eager. Did you do that so they wouldn't scare you with it?"

"I did it because I would have nightmares about that house. Mine was only five houses down. So, I had to walk past it every-day. So, one day I read on her. That's when I found out what had happened."

"Did it help?"

"Made it worse, actually. I still had nightmares. They got so bad I had to take Valium for me to sleep."

"Why did you look into it, then?"

"I thought if I could look at the incident logically, I might be able to dispel any of the hokey BS that surrounded that house."

"Did you move out?"

"Sure, I did. Also, wherever I live, I just make sure it's nowhere near that house."

"Childhood fears are the worse."

"You said it. Hey, you're still pretty young."

"Well, yes. I feel older than my years, though."

"I suppose you would. Was it bad for you, when you were younger?"

"Bad enough. I suppose everyone has a rough time of growing up, though."

"That's true. Here we are."

They got out of his car, and he helped her bring her belongings to the car. She had looked over at him before he got out of the car.

"Are you sure you want to go in there? It might start your nightmares up all over again?"

"I've dealt with worse since then."

She nodded, and went into the house, grabbing the bag of money and whatever clothes she had. He helped her with the rolling suitcase. They got back into his car, and she watched him the whole time.

He allowed her into his apartment. The walls were bare. Usually, he would have pictures and pictures of Dara. She was gone now, though, and he had to accept that. It was a harsh truth that still made his breath hitch, and his throat tighten. Scarlette also noticed how lonely the place was. She supposed she understood, having lost her own brother. It would not be an easy pain to deal with, for either of them. For once, she was glad to meet someone else she could share that grief with. She watched him as he sat down, leaving his lasagna to sit on the coffee table before him. He leaned forward, and rested his elbows on his knees. She had seen her brother do that when he was thinking deeply. She thought she might know what thoughts might be running through his head, since his eyes began to leak.

"What's wrong?"

"Dara used to love Lasagna."

She leaned over, and held his shoulder gently. It was the most she could do. She hadn't even told him about Lenny, but she figured she would tell him later. For now, it was her turn to be the one to comfort him.

Dave watched as Ryan walked Demi home, and cursed as he stayed until the door was locked. How he wanted her, and it drove him to the point of getting the nerve to bang on the door, claiming to be the police.

To this, there was a resounding answer. An unmarked police car pulled up to the curb. Two plainclothes officers had gotten out, ready to draw their weapons.

Dave's hands went to the air, as the two looked him over.

Allan spat, "Who the hell are you?"

"I was just messing. I didn't know this was your place! I swear to god."

Damien dipped his head to the side, his eyes burning into the young man, "Get lost."

"Come back here, and I'll have you in on trespassing charges. Got it?"

Dave ran off the scene.

Both went into the house, and Demi made them coffee.

Damien closed his eyes, and sighed as he swallowed a sip, "Hmm . . . This is great coffee. It's a lot better than that diner crap we've had to drink not too long ago."

"Thanks."

"No problem."

"Would you like some cupcakes? Allan just got some yesterday."

Damien smiled, "Sure."

After she got them the cupcakes, she went to her room to watch her TV that sat on the floor, and prepared her sleeping bag for bed. The wooden floor was cool, but she still slept well enough.

Allan went up to check on her, and returned to the living room.

"She's a trooper, Allan."

"Yeah, she is."

Damien sighed, "So, what do you think we should do about Lester?"

Allan rapped his fingers on the table. "One of your girls in protective custody could ID him, and we could get him on the attempted kidnapping, and aggravated assault."

Damien shook his head. "That won't fly in this town, not with Lester's father calling the shots."

Allan rubbed his chin, and let his words draw out slowly. "What about the stuff that was found in the trunk?"

Again, Damien shook his head. "The department's seemed to have 'misplaced' it."

"It gets worse and worse, doesn't it?"

Damien patted his friend's shoulder. "Don't let it get to you. We'll nail the bastard. I've got people to protect, and so do you."

Allan fought the temptation to swipe away the hand. He couldn't help cursing under his breath. "Shit . . . I know. The question is if they will let us."

Damien looked him in the eye. "If they insist on protecting him, we could bring in the big guns."

Allan was still wary. Again, his words came out in a cautious tone. "Well, I hope that will be enough. I mean, we've got the evidence from the other sites. I'm afraid we might not have much, even if we do find Karen Chastener."

"What makes you say that?" Damien asked, eyebrow raised.

"When you mentioned her, he didn't seem to budge."

"I told you he wouldn't react to names."

"No. It's more than that. We will not find her alive, I think. Even worse, I think despite the fact that he left large clues in the car, he might've been much more careful with the body."

"Meaning?"

"The evidence might've been her full wardrobe, at the time. He might've actually gotten to her when she was changing, or was barely clad. He stripped her down, and probably buried her."

Damien whistled. "Well, that's a long guess."

Allan raised one finger to count out his points. "Think about it. He wasn't worried about whether or not we would find her. He hadn't left enough traces of himself on her to be nervous about it."

Playing Devil's Advocate, Damien blurted, "Or, he could be a total psychopath, left plenty of clues, and not have cared."

Allan was shaking his head, "He's too careful about that sort of thing. The girls that we have managed to find were just bones. In fact, none of the girls we've found have had even tatters of clothes, ripped, worn ragged or otherwise."

"So, we know he's stripping them down from the previous finds."

"We also know he's been knocking them out, somehow. Remember that on the skulls we have found there was a fracture on the area just above the neck. Some of them were even broken inward."

Damien shook his head, and whispered, "Bastard."

"Worse than that. I think we should call the Bureau in on this."

"Well don't go around waving that term. It might make them nervous enough to let him go."

"Quartz didn't seem to want him out."

"Who can tell with that guy?"

"You're right. Damn, I wish we could put him away right now with everything we have."

"They were right. We're out of our jurisdiction here."

"I just moved here. That makes it my business. I have a sister to protect."

"Careful. They might use that against you."

"How so?"

"A young man about your age, tooling around the country with a girl that young?"

Allan stood up, "You know it's not like that!"

Damien made a dismissive gesture, "Easy. I know that. However, Quartz has this area under his thumb. Who knows what they might be able to do, or say? They will find a way to screw you over, if you let them."

"I can call a press conference announcing our findings, and my willingness to protect my sister."

"Careful with the press. It could backfire, and the one thing you do not want to do is to use the press to play mind games."

"This is no game, Damien."

"To them, it is. They're trying to cover for one of their good ol' boys, remember?"

"I really hate them." Allan whispered under his breath.

Damien nodded, and drank his the last of his coffee. It had gotten cold and bitter, but he swallowed it anyway. It was Demi's coffee, and he liked her very much, just as he had liked Becca. The two were alike in some ways.

The two looked out the window, into the darkness. They could only sit there, and stare into the darkness. Still the solution to their problem would not present itself to them until some time. It would be a long and bloody malaise of pain until then.

Claudia bumped into Becca in the high school hallways, and noticed how bright her friend was these days. She even said so.

"Oh my god. It's like you're a different person."

"Wasn't that the whole point to coming here?"

"I guess so. I just didn't think that you'd take to it so much."

"What's that supposed to mean?"

"Nothing. I guess I'm just being weird."

"You're always weird, silly."

"And you're in love."

"Yeah . . . I am."

"Is he anything like Derek?"

"No way. Ryan's been pretty cool."

"Awesome. I met this guy, myself. He's got his own place, and a cool truck."

"I didn't think you were into boys that sported their toys."

"Oh, shut up."

"So, what's his name?"

"David. David Thompson."

When he spoke from behind her, it was all Becca could do to keep from cringing at the sound of his voice. It made Becca whirl around to face him, and slowly step back on the heels of that. There was Dave, sporting his football jersey since he was on the team.

"Hey, babe."

"Becca. This is my guy, Dave."

"Pleased to meet you." Becca's voice was strained.

He winked at her, "Same here."

"Well, I won't keep you two. I've got to go to class."

Dave chimed in, his voice almost melodious, "Hope we meet again sometime."

Becca kept walking, not wanting to look back. She wanted to warn her friend, but she supposed she would have to do that later. She knew there was something wrong with that guy the moment he had tried to brush past Ryan. It was even more disturbing that he wanted to get at Demi, who was definitely too young for him. Then she saw Eric coming down the hall as well, wearing his own jersey.

"Hey, bro."

His voice was playful, "Hey, sis?"

"Oh, funny. I need to ask you something."

"Shoot."

"Do you know this guy named Dave?"

Eric's face grew dark, "Sure. He's pretty creepy actually. He seems to have an eye out for the younger girls. I mean the ones that are like way too young for him. He'd chase skirts from the second grade if he could. Why?"

"He was trying to mess with a friend of mine the other day."

"Oh, yeah. Ryan told me about that. Don't worry about him. If he messes with you again, I'll deal with him, myself."

"Don't like him much, do you?"

"There's been a rumor floating around that he's been molesting his younger sister lately. Knowing him, I totally believe it."

"Why is it just a rumor?"

"She goes to here, too. We all try to keep it on the low so we don't make her feel bad. She's a cool kid, despite having an asshole for an older brother."

"Wow. Ryan's right. You really do act like a dad a lot of the time."

"Someone's gotta watch out for Ryan. He doesn't seem to care what happens to him, sometimes."

"I care."

"I know you do. Take care of him, Becca. He's only going to have you and me when my dad dies."

"I know. I wish there was more I could do."

"Just be there for him."

"I am. Where's that sister of Dave's? Maybe I can back her up, with Ryan and Demi."

"Wow. My brother has his own circle of friends. I never thought I'd see the day."

"Meaning?"

"He's always been pushing everyone away. I've known him a long time, and he's been feeling so bad since my mom died."

"I know. It's like a bad dream that he hasn't waken up from."

"Exactly. Look, I have practice in a few, so I have to let you go. I'll keep an eye on Dave, though. I've had my eye on him for a while."

"Alright. And Eric?"

"Yeah?"

"Thanks."

"For what?"

"For being Ryan's big brother . . . Mine too."

"I just want you all to be happy. I think if I can help you with that, I'll be a content man." With that, he was gone, and Becca had to smile at his back. After he was out of sight, though, Becca's face became grim again. She had to tell her friend about Dave, or at least warn her somehow. She became more determined to look for Melissa Thompson.

The man who sat in Harry Quartz's office at the moment had several DUI charges on his record. He was also being held for a hit and run from the next state. The other police department asked Quartz's people to hold him, since he was suspect for a hit and run that had killed two kids. The kids were ten and seven, and they had been crossing on the green light. The suspect had been barreling down the street in a large SUV, and hadn't even noticed hitting them. When Quartz got the fax on it, he called the fellow into his office. The suspect had been nervous, but Harry showed him the fax from the other department, and went on the place it in the shredder. The stranger looked up.

"What's your name?"

"It was on the fax, man. They saw it was me."

"I never saw any fax."

"What?"

"I'm letting you go, Lucifer. Your dad always said you would get into trouble, and he was right. I've had to cover your ass several times. Now, I need you to do something for me."

"What would you want me to do?"

"You got a band, don't you? Always on the road, right?"

"Yeah, so?"

"Well, maybe you might need an extra hand, to help you with the equipment, and all that shit."

"You want me to take your son with me."

"Right?"

"What's he done?"

"Never mind that. I just need you to help Lester lay low for the while."

"How long?"

"As long as it takes."

"So, you'll let me go? What about the other police types look-ing for me?"

"I'll just tell them I never saw any fax, or even you for that matter. You just need to do me that one favor. Can you dig that?"

"Yeah, I can dig it."

"Now, I know you were always into that satanic shit, so I'll tell you something that might make you feel more at home. You want to be the devil? You take my son under wing, and cover him. Then, you can call yourself Lucifer, himself. Got it?"

"Is he that bad?"

"How would you know? We never met as far as everyone else is concerned."

He handed the thug a keycard, and whispered, "Get out quick. No one can see you when you leave. Swipe that through the maintenance only door, and that'll get you to the parking garage. Leave the card behind the wheel of an old car with my personalized plates on it. They will have just my name on them, Quartz. I'll get it later. Got it?"

"Yes, sir."

"Who are you again?"

"Some guy that got lucky, right?"

"No. You are fucking Lucifer, himself. You are the first and greatest devil there ever was. This is your time to shine."

Lucifer's eyes glazed over dreamily and his mouth curled into a sick smile. Harry inclined his head, gesturing that he was dismissed.

Quartz watched him leave, and hoped that the travel would get his son to quit what he was doing. The truth was that he wanted to go with them, but he figured this was Lester's journey. It would have to be enough.

Lester sat in a cell, trying to lie in his cot. He was wondering how he would get out of this mess and he didn't know if his father would even help this time. If he could've only found that first girl that would identify him, if he could've killed her in the first place, he wouldn't be here, rotting slowly. He was letting out short frustrated breaths when he heard someone laughing from the shadows. The laughter in the shadows came from Harry Quartz's friend.

He sat up, and Lester's temper flared immediately.

"What the fuck are you laughing at?"

"You."

"You want to die, don't you?"

"Oh, c'mon, little man. In here you sound like a little dog trying to bark like a big dog. No one buys it."

"Then what do you suggest?"

"Keep barking, but bark loud enough so the whole fucking world hears you."

"How am I supposed to do that?"

"You'll figure it out. In the meantime, let me introduce myself."

The figure stepped out of the shadows, and he was tall, this stranger. Lester didn't know what he was looking at until he looked up. That was when he realized that the top of his head only came up to the stranger's chest.

"Who are you, anyway?"

"Hope you guess my name."

Lester looked at him eerily, making the gentleman laugh. He felt the man's booming laughter pound into his ears again.

"Shut up! You'll make the guards come down again."

"Don't worry about them. They were told by your dad to pretend I wasn't here. I am Lucifer, and I've got the black magic touch."

"You know my dad?"

"Yes. You could say we're old friends. He did a few favors for me a while back, so he called me in for a favor."

"What's that?"

"To get your ass out of here. I cannot hide you forever, though."

"What the hell am I supposed to do, then?"

"I told you, already. You have to bark loud enough for the whole world to hear you. Only then will you be untouchable. That will be later. I'll let you know when the time comes."

"I don't know what the fuck you're talking about."

"I've got a rock band waiting for me, just beyond these doors. We just signed a big contract, We might need another lead singer down the line."

"I can't fucking sing."

"You don't have to. All you have to do is to scream the words we give you. For the while, you'll just be a roadie."

"How will that solve my problems?"

"I can hide you for now. When the time comes, though, I can make you one famous motherfucker. So much that no one could touch you even if they wanted to."

"The cops got my balls in a vice, dude."

"'Dude?' Did you pick that up on your trip across the country?"

"More like I was born in Dude country. Get to your point."

The stranger pulled a card out from his coat, and swiped it through the card reader. Then unlocked the door while the lock was still green. Lester stepped out of his cell, and looked around with a vicious grin.

The stranger reached down to grab his face, and forced Lester to look at him in the eye. "Not yet, Lester."

"How do you know my name?"

"Your father, remember?"

Lester followed him through the parking garage and got to Lucifer's car, which was sitting on the next level down. Lucifer grinned because he knew Harry had pulled his car out of the impound yard, and pulled out his cell phone.

"Yeah, I'll meet you guys at the end of town. I've got a new guy with me. He's cool. Just starting moving out through the south road out of town. Keep driving, and I'll catch up."

He looked to Lester, and opened the door for him. Lester got in, and his own face had caught Lucifer's infectious smile.

They were gone before anyone noticed.

❦

Ryan and Becca held hands as they walked down the hall. She was looking at him as he looked straight ahead, and seemed so distant at that moment. She didn't mind, though. She figured that he was thinking about his father, and everything else that had been going on around them. That was when she saw a younger girl approach them, or was it that she seemed younger than them? She wore her long red hair loose, with great curled locks.

"I've seen you two around, but I've never had a chance to say hello much."

Ryan inclined his head; "It's alright. I'm Ryan and this is my girlfriend."

She offered her hand as she, said, "Becca."

Scarlette regarded the hand for a moment, and offered her own. She was actually gazing at Ryan. For some reason, she felt that he reminded her of Lenny. It was a scary moment for her because she felt as if the whole world had backtracked, and she would have to watch her brother die yet again. This, time, though, it would be Ryan that would die. She shook her head as if the shake of a nightmare.

Ryan's voice was full of concern, "Are you alright?"

Scarlette smiled, and nodded. As she walked off, she looked at the both of them over her shoulder, and said, "I do hope we meet again. Perhaps we can catch a movie or something."

After making sure that Scarlette was some distance away, Becca finally announced, "I don't like her."

"Becca . . . We just met."

"Doesn't change the fact that she bugs me . . . in a big way. There's something about her."

"I'm sure it's just the fact that we just met her. I'm sure she'll grow on us after a while."

"I hope not."

Now it was Ryan that was looking at his girlfriend. She seemed deeply disturbed by the whole talk. He was wondering what was on her mind as they walked down the hall. Yet, when he tried to loosen his grip her own had tightened around his own. He leaned in close to kiss her forehead, and that made her feel better. She looked up at him, and smiled. She was feeling better already.

☯

Melissa Thompson was in the bathroom. She was in a stall and lifted her skirt to see if the bruises had gone away. They had

faded somewhat, and yet she still felt that they would be seen.
It bothered her because Dave insisted on her hiding their secret
meetings. How could she do it, though, when he would leave
bruises whenever he would get so rough with her? She did all she
could to keep their activities from being discovered, and how she
hated him. She had just walked out of the stall when Demi came
in, and then the skirt caught on the one of the loose screws that
held the latch on. It pulled her skirt up, and the bruise caught
Demi's eye.

"What is that?"

"It's nothing, I swear."

"Girl, that is the tell-tale sign that someone's been messing
with you."

"Leave it alone."

"Who did this to you?"

"You don't even know me."

"Then tell me your name, girl."

"If I do, will you leave me alone?"

"No way. What's your name?"

"I can't tell you."

"You tell me right now, or I'll call my brother. He's a cop, and
he'll start looking around."

Demi could see the tears in her eyes, and the desperation in
her voice as Melissa cried out, "No, Dave will kill me!"

Melissa's hands moved to cover her mouth, and she realized
the name had come out. She began to cry, deeply. Demi pulled her
into an embrace, and held her close as the tears came.

"I j-just d-didn't w-want anyone to know."

"Why not, girl? This is bad, and it sucks that you're trying to
handle it all by yourself."

"Melissa."

"Demi. I'm Demi. Look if you like, I could walk you home after school."

Melissa was already shaking her head, and the tears seemed to stain her cheeks with the mascara that Dave demanded she put on. Demi pulled a handkerchief from her jeans, and wiped Melissa's face.

"You're not alone, anymore. I'll walk you home. I'll even ask my big bro if I can stay over your place, and make sure you get some sleep."

"He'll try to hurt you, too."

"Who will?"

The voice echoed in the bathroom, as he announced himself. "Me, bitch."

"Oh, so you're the asshole."

"Bitch, you watch your tone with me."

"I can't believe there are brothers out there like you. You're scum."

"What did you tell her about us, sis?"

"No. Leave her alone."

"You brought her into this."

"No! I was trying to cover the bruises you gave me."

Dave tried to rush in to grab her. He felt his foot catch on to something, and went down. He put his arms out in from of him so they could break his fall. Demi spun to face away from him, and dropped her weight on the small of his back. His arms weren't enough to keep him up. His elbows gave, and he was kissing the floor.

"Melissa, kick him! You've got to take a stand."

Melissa kicked his face, and she felt free for once. So much that she kicked him a good five times. He reached back to grab Demi, but she was no longer sitting on his back, and she was standing beside Melissa. He used his other hand to lift himself back so he could support himself on his knees. Demi and Melissa allowed him to get up, when he reached out for Demi, she took his hand and held it. She looked over to her new friend, and winked. Both girls pulled one foot back, and they connected with Dave's crotch section. He dropped to the floor again, this time on his side. Also, he was grabbing his groin, and cringed when both girls knelt by him.

Demi was so angry at the moment that she reached for his head, and pulled at a tuft of hair to keep him facing her. He could barely manage a groan. She looked him in the eye; his own were red, like his flushed face. He was trying to keep himself awake. He would have reached out for her if he weren't protecting his balls.

"You listen to me, asshole. You touch her again; you'll have to deal with both of us. I won't be going away any time soon, so you better get used to that. She's off limits, got it?"

He tried to nod furiously, but he was running out of breath, and to do so would make him choke on his own spit. Melissa pulled her foot back, and kicked him in the stomach. It was all he could do to keep lunch from coming up; it was his way of showing strength, despite his bad situation. After kicking him a third time, she knelt by him, her eyes locking with his. His eyes widened when he saw that she breathed in deeply. When she opened her mouth, she yelled out, "Help! Oh god, help me, please!"

Her eyes were still locked on his when they heard steps coming. She leaned in and whispered. "Demi's right. You won't touch me again. If you do, I'll do worse than kick you in the balls."

The security officer entered, and she regarded the girls proudly, "Wow. Still need my help?"

Demi smirked, and added, "Just don't tell my bro about this, k?"

"I will need you two to fill out a report, you know?"

The security guard kneeled by Dave, and shoved him back to the floor. She pulled his arms behind his back, and cuffed him. He didn't resist, but he did glare at Melissa as he was being pulled to his feet. Demi looked to her new friend, and found her glaring right back at him. Demi was proud of her.

He was trembling as he seethed, "This is not over, you little bitches."

The guard was slightly taller than he was, so she was able to push his head forward, making him cough. "You know, you may not be under arrest, but anything you do or say can and will be used against you. Now, move along."

As soon as Dave was hauled out of the girls' bathroom, Demi looked to Melissa, and put her arm around Melissa's frail shoulders.

"We so kick ass, Melissa."

"We do."

"Let's book it to class, though."

"Cool, I'll grab my bag, then."

"Need me to walk you to class?"

"Want me to walk you to yours?"

"Good point. Let's go."

11

<u>Hopeless Memories</u>

I sit sighing as I cry for just a little bit thinking what if I'd been good child

If life had not been so sheltered. Would've I been very different

I sit and think some more then give up and find I'm nothing when I look in the mirror

that's before me.

Best if I disappeared best

if I stopped being someone I'm not

best if I just became the wind and let go releasing everything else

because the pain is too great to handle on my own

to handle alone I dry off my tears staring out the window.

Watching the snow, which falls. I hear a silent voice.

The voice which calls to me through time and space.

Telling me that I don't belong

Though I'd rather be here, thinking of how I would like to be loved by those that I love..

that is my wish it is just that a wish . . .

an empty request that means nothing to the stars . . .

just useless words that have no value in the eyes of others just mine

Saw you there standing against the light post looking back at me, with those cold eyes

That seemed to hate only me, though I saw your smile, that smile you held for everyone else.

Was I just another face you wanted to block out, and ignore . . . because I wasn't ideal?

I'll never be Ideal. I'll never be the ideal.the star, or the treasure.

I am one of the strangers without faces, the strangers without care

If I were that special guy, if I were anything . . . Would you look for me? Or would you

rather I fade out? Would all rather I just fade away?

Would it be better if I were a memory, or not even that an image . . . maybe an ideal?

I guess that's why I'm not with you or with anyone

-        *Songs of Demi*
         <u>*Light of Hope*</u> *Album.*

Derek wandered the halls of the high school; his eyes darting back and forth as he tried to look for the girl he knew as Kendra. He knew she had to be somewhere here, and felt he had to yell at her for just picking up and leaving. In his mind, she was a stupid bitch that was being overly sensitive and left for some stupid reason. Never mind that he had left her at a street corner in the worst part of town, or that he had admitted to sleeping with another girl while with her. He felt he had been wronged, and that was enough reason to look for her. He saw several girls that looked like her, but he knew better, and when he saw her walking with another boy, that just about tore it for him. He grabbed her arm, and pulled her back.

"Let me go! What do you want?"

"All this time, and you can't even say hi to me?"

"You're the one that called it quits, remember?"

"I did no such thing. I told you I had gone to the club already and didn't feel the need to go again."

Ryan stepped beside her, and held out one hand protectively.

Derek seethed, "Get the fuck out of my face, homeboy!"

Becca placed a hand on his shoulder, and Ryan subsided. Derek smirked and bit out, "That's right. Listen to the bitch, since she's got you on a leash."

"I assure you. There is no leash, and I'd be glad to deal with you."

"What the fuck you mean you'll deal with me, asshole?"

Becca stepped in his face, and yelled, "Hey, you leave him alone. I'm the one you want to yell at. Now that you've done that, you can take off."

He pulled his arm back, and Ryan was behind him before he realized what had happened. Ryan pulled his arm farther back, making it hard for Derek to breathe.

"Alright. Now that you've closed your mouth a moment, you'll have to listen to me."

Derek tried to curse, and choked a little as Ryan pulled on his arm.

"You were being very rude to my girlfriend, and to me. Now I don't care one way or the other what you say to me. What you try to do to her, though, is my business, and I do not take threats to her, lightly. Give me a thumbs up if you understand me."

Derek frantically waved his thumb in the air.

"Good. Now, you will leave us alone. You got that?"

Again, Derek waved his thumb frantically, and Ryan let him go. After leaning on his knees for the moment, Derek got his breath back. He was about to say something, and Ryan was seemingly bouncing on one heel.

"Keep her, then. I don't care. She wasn't that great anyway." Derek walked away, nursing his neck.

Ryan looked back to Becca and saw that she was crying. He took her into his arms and held her. She looked up at him, and whispered, "I need for us to go someplace where we can be alone."

"Let's go to my usual spot by the tree, ok?"

When they got there, the grass had grown well enough so that they could sit there and feel the cushion of earth beneath them.

"Did you know him?"

"I knew him when I wasn't very proud of myself."

"It shouldn't matter. He's your past."

"You're my future?"

"If you want me to be."

"I do. I just wish I didn't have to face that person I used to be."

"You know? When we first met, I wasn't all that great myself. I think it was you that helped me to become a better person."

"You were always a great guy, Ryan. Even your brother sees that, and now your dad."

"Then you're a great girl, no matter what anyone says, alright?"

"But I used to be such a bitch, and I used to treat my brother like shit. I used to be such a bitch to Amy, too."

"That's what you used to be. I think it's safe to say that you've grown out of it."

"Well, that's because you were there."

He shook his head, "I think we helped each other. Don't you?"

She nodded, and though tears streamed from her eyes, she still tried to smile.

"That's my girl." He whispered as he held her, and she felt like she could stay there for a long time.

Ryan's cell phone went off. He hated carrying the thing around, but Becca had insisted that he get one.

He looked down as he talked into it, feeling that he might not want to hear what might be said. "This is Ryan."

Eric was on the other end, and he could barely keep his voice from cracking as he spoke. "I think it's close. Dad's been coughing all day. They managed to sedate him, and it calmed down for a bit. When he woke up, though, he was at it again. Ryan, when I held a towel to his chin, the towel was red. He is really sick, you know?"

"Is he?"

"Dying? I'm no doctor, but I'm willing to bet he's pretty close to it."

"How long?"

"I don't know. They said at this rate, he won't last the hour, let alone the night."

"Alright. I'll be there as soon as I can."

When he closed his phone, he looked up and he seemed so helpless at that moment that Becca nodded. She knew that he had to go to face his fears, but she stood up with him, and walked by his side. It was the most she could do for him at that moment, and she felt good that there was something she could do for him.

⟜⟝

When they arrived in Mr. Sandler's room, Eric was sitting by him, his face somber. When he looked up, Becca swore that Eric seemed to be dying, himself. His face was drawn taut, and he was so pale. It may have been that he hadn't enough rest for the past few days. Ryan's own face lost color as well. She knew what to expect, so she led Ryan slowly towards the bed. He seemed to walk slower, and she understood his hesitation, so she held his hand, squeezing it. He seemed to draw strength from that, and was able to join Eric, also standing vigil. They all regarded each other, and Eric audibly swallowed before he spoke.

"Hey, dude."

"Yo. Well, I'm here. Didn't think I'd make it, you know?"

"I know. You didn't have to come you know? This is hard, and I would've understood if you'd blown me off."

"No. I couldn't let you forgive me for that. Is he going to be sleeping a while longer?"

"I-"

"Ryan, my boy."

Ryan looked to Eric; his face was suddenly stricken with shock. Eric could only incline his head, and Ryan found himself stepping past Eric. He took his father's hand, and couldn't believe his throat had dried so quickly.

His voice was hoarse, but Ryan managed, "Yeah, dad. I'm right here."

"I wish I could've done more for you, boy. I keep thinking that I wasn't there for you like I should've been."

"It's alright."

"It's not, and it'll never be enough, that measly amount I left for you. I left it with it a lawyer friend of mine. He'd been wronged by Quartz too, you know?"

"Dad, don't talk."

"No, you listen to me. This is important. His name is Ian Fanning. Some awful guy killed his daughter a few months ago. So, he left her mom because she was always playing around, and leaving him to do all the parent work. I felt for him, you know? He was finishing his law career, though. So, I asked him when he would finish up since I had a job for him. He did finish-" the rattling cough began, and Eric moved to hold the handkerchief to his mouth. The old man trembled violently against Ryan as he tried to settle down.

"Dad, it's ok. I'll figure it out."

"No, I got to finish. This guy, Ian, finished school. He's a full-fledged lawyer now, and I asked him if he could settle my last will and testament. He wrote out the sweetest deal for you boys that I almost cried, I was so happy. I'm pretty sure if we could've gotten a settlement from your mom's accident; you two would be well off enough. This will have to be enough though. Between the two of you, you've got Fifty million. That's from all the stuff I've sold a few years back, and put the profit in a bank. You can get another fifteen million if you sell the house. So, I hope that'll do you boys up for-" he began to spasm again. The nurse almost came in, her face grim. She seemed like she was about the yell the three of them to let the man rest. Mr. Sandler looked up at her, meeting her gaze, and waved her away. She shook her head and went on her way.

"There, dad. You see? She thinks you should rest up, too."

"You look for Ian after I die. Got it?"

"Yeah, dad. I got it."

"Eric?"

"I'm here, dad."

"You play football, boy. You're set for life, and you don't ever need to quit. You got it? If that's what you dream about, and that's what you want, you do it."

"Dad . . ."

"Don't fucking quit on my account. I'm about to meet your mom, again, if she'll have me."

"Of course, she will."

"Well, when I get up there, I want to be able to see the two of you do what you want, and be happy, you got it?"

The boys nodded, and Mr. Sandler smiled at them feebly. "Eric, you know why I didn't ask you to take care of your brother? It's because you do that anyway, boy. You're more like his dad, than I am."

"Aww, dad."

"Becca?"

"Yes, sir?"

"No, you call me dad, because you know you gonna be with my boy."

Becca had to smile at that, and the old man beamed back at her, "You're so pretty, too. I want you to take care of my boy, Ryan."

"I will, dad."

"He doesn't know he's a great kid, and maybe that's my fault. So I want you to make him the happiest man alive, to make up for what I couldn't give him."

She nodded, and now she felt tears streaming down her cheeks. She couldn't help it. She couldn't believe this was the same man that Ryan had been so angry at the whole time they had been going out. He reached up, and squeezed her hand. Then he called the boys to stand by him again.

"I love you, boys. You make yourselves, happy. I made sure of that. I want your mom to know that you'll be happy."

Ryan and Eric had their heads down, trying not to show their eyes. Becca reached up, and wrapped her arms around both their shoulders. They all watched as Mr. Sandler gave his last breath. At least, he was able to close his eyes, and smile. Ryan tried to speak, but Becca shushed him, gently squeezing his shoulder. They all watched Mr. Sandler for a moment longer, and went to the front desk. The nurse had been there, the one that had told them to leave. Only now did she understand that the old man had been trying to tell them his goodbye. She motioned her head to the door with a gentle, sympathetic smile, gesturing for them to go home.

The next day, Eric and Ryan couldn't bring themselves to look for Ian Fanning, since that would make their father's death seem too final. Instead, they went to school, despite their moody state. They had gone to sit by Ryan's favorite tree. Demi had approached them, in tow with another girl. She started talking really fast and left herself tongue-tied. She tried starting over.

"Hi, guys. Sorry I couldn't walk with you to school since I was walking with Melissa here. She's my new best friend." She placed her hand on Melissa's shoulder, and nudged her, "Say something, silly."

"I'm Melissa Thompson."

Eric looked up, "Dave Thompson's sister?"

She looked down quickly, and was about to walk away. Demi held on to her, and Eric got her to calm her down. He placed his hand on her shoulder gently, and said, "I've heard a few things about you."

Her voice was trembling, poor girl. "Are you one of my brother's friends?"

"No, I'm not. I'd heard he'd been hurting you."

"He did more than that."

Demi perked up, "Until we kicked his ass."

Ryan looked up from his spot, "Demi, you went after that guy alone? You know how dangerous that was?"

"He came after her, and I just happened to be there. We totally sent him packing his nuts."

Eric's face was somber; "He's not the type of guy to let it go at this."

Melissa found it hard to look up.

Ryan stood up, and Becca stood by him. "So, we'll have to fend the bastard off."

Her eyes meet theirs as she slowly lifted her head to look at them. They were being completely serious. She ran over, and hugged them both. She couldn't help it.

Eric almost fell back, but held his ground.

"I guess this means we're friends?"

Melissa nodded furiously, and pulled back to look at the two of them. Becca smiled at her too.

"Hey, I'm Becca. I'm the shorter guy's girlfriend."

Ryan made a face, muttering, "I am not short."

Demi nodded, "See? I knew you guys would stick up for her."

The boys smiled at her, and Ryan reached out to muss her hair. "Yeah, you know everything, don't you?"

Demi playfully slapped his hand away, and then she looked to Becca. "Say, have you guys eaten yet?"

Ryan answered, "Not sure about her, but to tell you the truth, I haven't had an appetite all day."

She looked to Eric, as he nodded. At that point she knew it was about their dad, and gave them both a hug, whispering, "You guys won't be alone. You have Becca and me, and Melissa now."

"We know. Thanks, Demi."

Eric cleared his throat, "Well, she's right. We should get something to eat."

"What do you suggest?"

Demi put her hand to her chin in a thinking pose, "Well, I heard that our cafeteria serves some really good gourmet stuff."

Ryan cleared his throat, "Sometimes. At other times, it's like the kitchen that should've never been."

Melissa shyly put in her two cents. "Let's all go to the NY Pizza place, then. I heard they have really good pizza."

Eric wrapped an arm around her shoulders, and smiled. She looked up at him as he boomed; "The new girl hath spoken. Let us go eat some pizza."

Ryan rolled his eyes, "Wow. Are you supplying helium to the group now?"

"Shut up, dude."

"Yessiree."

As they left the courtyard, Scarlette could only watch them from afar. How she wanted to join them at that moment. Something inside her, though, told her that she did not belong there. So, she stood in the shadows and looked as the walked over to the pizza parlor, laughing and talking all the while. As she watched Eric hold Melissa, it reminded her of how her brother used to hold her. In order to resist the urge to go to them, she reached down, beneath her coat. She found the item she had asked her lawyer to procure for her. It was a full-fledged katana designed and made by Hikaru Masaki, himself. He was said to be an excellent sword master. She had come to know him from the exquisite dagger he had made for Harold, the orderly. Something told her that Harold hadn't been completely honest with Masaki. She could only imagine the flights of fantasy Harold must've gone through to get the sword master to make him such an exquisite dagger. She had found it after emptying out his locker, and taking his clothes. It was so fitting that the blade should land in her hands. Shortly after arriving in Saffire Falls, she had set up an address at the old house, and set it up as a place to receive any of the goods that would come from abroad. She had written to Masaki and had told him her situation about her father, and what had happened to her brother. He had written to her in return, and his English was extremely eloquent. The letter read:

Dear Ms. Scarlette Thorne,

It seems that your situation would require dire action. However, I would suggest calling the authorities before taking action into your own hands. If you feel the need to avenge your brother, I can very well understand that. I will caution you, though. Once you take a life, there is no way to gain that innocence back. It will affect you for years to come. So, when you raise this sword, I do hope you raise it to defend yourself. I would be very dishonored if you were to simply use my work in order to satisfy some warped sense of justice. I realize I am speaking quite candidly. It is because this is such a delicate matter. I do hope you use good judgement. Also, I hope you enjoy my piece as more of a symbol of such. If I hear that you have used it otherwise, I will not hesitate to come after you, myself. This is not a threat. I do not make threats. I make promises.

Respectfully Yours,
Hikaru Masaki

She had to admit that the sword master had sounded quite serious with his threat, despite the fact that he denied it as such. She would try to help girls like Melissa, even if it meant staining her hands. She felt that Dave Thompson deserved to die, though. He was scum, much like her father had been. So, she caressed the handle as she thought of what she would wreak upon David Thompson, and all those like him. She took rather fondly to Masaki's last words. So, she would say the same. She would not make threats, only promises.

Becca looked back suddenly, shivering violently as she looked around. Ryan asked her if she was all right, and she honestly could not answer him. She felt like someone had walked over her grave. She hated to think like that, in light of trying to comfort the brothers in their moment of need. She couldn't help it, though. She had a sort of feeling, and it felt like a premonition. She wrapped an arm around Eric, as well and asked if they could just stay there a moment while she gathered her senses. Melissa made her way to Ryan, and placed her arm around his shoulder as well. Demi turned to watch them, and slowly walked over. She joined the embrace, coming in between Ryan and Melissa. For a moment, they all stood there, holding each other as the noon soon glazed through the overcast clouds, and they were sprinkled with tears of heaven.

Harry Quartz had his own connections with people in high places. It was through them that he found out that Lester hadn't finished two girls. He cursed his son for getting that sloppy. He had really thought that going cross-country had taught the boy a few things, but it seemed that Lester took girls at random. The problem was that he didn't finish with these two girls, and from what his contact had told him, the two outside officers were trying to build a case against Lester. It was even worse because the evidence against Lester was out of his reach. If only he had kept Lester in town, then it wouldn't have come to this. He blamed himself; too, because he had told Lester he wouldn't cover for him anymore. So, the boy felt that he should go elsewhere, and they were places that Harry could not reach. He sat behind his desk, wondering what to be done about the evidence that was spread throughout the country. If Lester had crossed any borders, he wouldn't have tried to come back to town. Then he realized why. He held the pictures of Becca and Claudia in his hands. In their old lives they had been Kendra, and Amy. They stared back at him, smiling. How he hated that, because they seemed to mock him for not being able to control his son well enough to even kill them right. He was interrupted when another of his loyal boys poked his head in.

"We just got another psycho at school. He was trying to go after his little sister."

"Really?"

"Yeah. He's in the tank for the moment, but I'm guessing you want to talk to him."

"What makes you say that?"

"I'm sure he could help you tie up a few loose ends."

Harry gestured for him to come in, and close the door. The younger officer did so, just in time to feel Quartz' fist just below his ribs.

"Don't think out loud anymore."

"I won't do it again." The officer croaked, trying to pull himself back up.

"See that you don't. I'll go talk to him. If he goes along with my thinking, you fix it so he escapes, got it?"

"I didn't lock the cell properly. The card reader on the cell door was red, so I thought he would be in there all night."

"Now, you're thinking right. Get down there, and only set it up when I give you the signal, got it?"

"Yes, sir."

Harry went down to the holding area and saw Dave pacing around in his cell like a lion in a cage. Strike that; this guy didn't even rate that. He was big, though. He only needed to learn a few tricks, and he'd be the perfect killer, and the perfect patsy. When Harry stepped up to the cell, Dave rolled his eyes at him.

"What the fuck do you want?"

"Typical kid. You are lucky to be alive. If everyone knew why you were here, you'd be wearing your guts for garters."

"So fucking what?"

"Ah, ok. You wanna play rough? Hey boys, this guy is one sick motherfucker. He-"

Dave's eyes widened, and he looked at Harry, "What do you want?"

"Ah, good boy."

One of the older prisoners, a big bruiser named Harley, was eager for a fight. "So, what'd he do, Quartz?"

Harry smiled at Dave, knowing he had full control. "He blew off some store clerk's head, and licked the blood of the walls."

The rest of the cellmates stood up, and put some distance between them and Dave.

Dave's eyes raced back and forth in their sockets, "What the fuck you do that for?"

"I got a little proposition for you. You ready to listen now? Or are you going to be a tough little shit, and try to play big dog. You can. I helped you on that end, but you won't last long without my help."

"What do you want?"

"Good boy. I have a job for you."

"If I do it, I go free?"

"We'll talk about it in my office."

The youngish guard pulled Dave from the tank, and locked the door properly. As Harry walked with Dave, he leaned in close, and whispered, "You try to run, and I will shoot you like a dog. Got it?"

"You need me, though."

"Right now, yeah."

"I got it."

So they went to Harry's office, and Dave took a seat. Harry threw Kendra and Amy's picture onto his lap.

"I've seen these girls around."

"I know you have. You're about their age. You go to the local high school with them."

"So, what do you want me to do? I can't talk to them, they'll freak out."

"I don't want you to talk to them, idiot. I want you to rape them, and kill them."

"So, you can come in and play hero? Shoot me like a dog?"

"No one will ever know it was you."

"How do you know?"

"I'll cover your ass. You have to do it quick, though."

"Well, I can get the second one. She's like my girlfriend right now."

"Then you can do what you like with her."

"Make it look like an accident?"

"Leave that to us. As for the other girl, you have to totally kill her Jack the Ripper style."

"I'm not like that, dude."

"You raped your little sister a few times, and now you're getting all moral and shit? I don't buy it. You do this, and I might leave you alone."

"Why them?"

"Is there a problem?"

"The other girl is always with her boyfriend."

"He can't be around all the time."

"She's always got people around her. I think she's even friends with that new cop's sister."

"I'll deal with him, and his friend. Just get rid of her."

"Do you want me to like do it berzerker style with her?"

"Do it however you like. Never mind the little details. I'll worry about that with my boys."

"Ok. Whatever you want. After this, though-"

"After this. I'll be calling in favors when I want. I own you."

"You said you might leave me alone."

"I said that I might. Might and Will are two different creatures. Understand?"

"How do I get out of here, though?"

"One of my boys has that all arranged. You do what you need to do, though."

"I might just smother my girlfriend. She's been cool with me, you know?"

"Whatever gets your rocks off, kid. Let's get you back to your cell."

So, Harry walked Dave back to the holding area. Only this time, he placed Dave in his own private cell in the corner. When the other inmates asked Harry why, he answered them with a sick smiled, "You don't want him to eat you while you're sleeping, do you?"

They all chewed on that for a bit, and Harry turned to wink at Dave. As horrible as Dave was, even Harry Quartz gave him the shivers. The Deputy Jo-Bob told him to settle down until midnight, and he would be pulled out, and left on the street. Dave sat in his cell, and couldn't help laughing at how the others kept trying to avoid looking at him in the eye. He wondered what they had done, but that didn't keep him from being amused at how they seemed to think of him as a monster.

Midnight came, and Dave walked the streets of Saffire Falls, a free man with a mission. He even managed to seem like he was Royalty.

Scarlette watched him, walking into the night. She caressed the handle of her sword, yet left it in its sheath. She didn't feel the need to do away with him at that moment. She saw him walking calmly, and yet he dug into his pants every so often that he almost limped along. She knew where he was going, though. She walked through the bushes, and watched as he made his way towards the house where Ryan and Becca's new friend lived. She had her curtains drawn so she couldn't see him as he stood by the bushes, and began to masturbate then and there. He was beginning to breathe hard, and Scarlette made her way towards him. She stood among the tall bushes that surrounded him. No wonder he chose this spot. Even if anyone had heard him, he was covered enough so one could simply dismiss him, and go his or her way. Once he climaxed, he zipped up his pants, and made his way to the trellis, and began to climb. Unknown to Dave, the two brothers had just moved into the new Thompson home. It was at that moment when Eric and Ryan came out the front door, and he cursed loud enough to be noticed.

Ryan turned to the sound, and grabbed him by the waistband of his jeans, and pulled him down. Dave had fallen hard, but he was able to recover pretty quickly. It sickened Scarlette that he was so energized because he had seen his sister's silhouette changing. He was about to fight them both, and they were ready. He changed his mind at the last moment, and decided to make a run for it. He was down the street, and he had enough energy to sprint down the street. Scarlette followed him, At the end of the block was a black sports car, and Derek was driving.

"Hop in."

"Huh?"

"Get in, moron."

Dave hopped into the car, and could've sworn he saw something blur past him on his left when he was getting in. Derek turned to him.

"What's wrong?"

"Nothing."

"Dude, those brothers are fucking pissing me off."

"Oh, yeah. I've had a few scuffles with the younger one."

"And you let him beat you?"

"Dude, he's tougher than he looks."

"Yeah, I know. Did you need to mess around with him?"

"He's fucking my ex."

"Holy shit, that girl?"

"She looks like a whore, don't she? Now she's trying to play all nice and shit. She was a total bitch when I knew her, though."

"I'm sorry to interrupt your bitching, but who the fuck are you?"

"I'm Derek."

"Dave, just Dave is fine."

"I got to teach her a lesson for cheating on me like that."

"What a cunt."

"I know. I'll show her."

"How do we do that?"

"That younger brother. We have to get rid of him, somehow."

"Like kill him?"

"That'll work."

"Then fuck yeah, I'm in."

Scarlette had heard enough, She dropped out from under the car but the long coat took a lot of the damage. She waited until they were a good distance away. She figured she could deal with them before they could do anything to Ryan. She got up from the road, and made her way back to Ian's. She supposed he would be worried.

When she got there, Ian was still up, and watching TV. He was also finishing some paper work for the Sandler case, and getting the paper's finalized. When she knocked, he opened the door quickly enough for her face to feel the wind getting sucked in.

"Where have you been, Scarlette?"

"I was with some friends."

"Well, the next time, please call me ok? I've had a rough night like this before."

"With your daughter? Did she come home late one night?"

"She didn't come home. It's a bad memory I'd rather not have to relive, you know?"

"I got it. I'll try not to be late again."

"Well, alright. I'm going on and on. Get some sleep."

"Goodnight, Ian."

"Goodnight, Scarlette. Sleep well."

Ian was about to get to sleep when he heard the phone ring. There was a young voice on the other end, "Mr. Fanning?"

Ian would've actually hung up, if not for remembering Mr. Sandler's two surviving sons. Ian cleared his throat, and spoke up, "Speaking. Who's this?"

"This is Ryan Sandler. I believe my father might've spoken to you some time ago about our family estate matters."

"I'm looking at the case right now. I really am too tired to discuss it right now, though. If you like, we can set up a meeting tomorrow afternoon, and talk about it then."

"That would be good. Also, my girlfriend wants to talk about something that happened to her not too long ago."

"Really?"

"Yes. She'd been attacked, but got away. They never caught the guy, but she wondered if you might be able to help her if they ever did manage to catch him."

"That is a rather large request, Ryan. However, I am your family's lawyer from now on. So, we can discuss that, if you like. She has talked to the authorities about it, though, right?"

"Of course. I will give you all the details tomorrow."

☯

Ian sat on the patio of the Italian restaurant where he met Scarlette. He had ordered a lasagna dish, remembering how much Dara had liked it. Ryan approached, a tall brooding boy, who was too young to wear the grim expression that was a seemingly long-term fixture. Next to him was his girlfriend. He hadn't said her name on the phone, so he hoped that Ryan would introduce her now.

"Hello, Mr. Fanning."

"It's cool. Call me Ian. And you are Miss?"

"Stratsford. Rebecca Stratsford."

"Now, Ryan tells me that you had an incident a while back."

"It was this young guy that tried to kill me. I just wanted to know if I had a case since I had gone with him."

"Well, if he tried to rape you, even kill you, then you have a case."

"I just wanted to make sure that I didn't mess up the case because I had gone with him in the first place."

"Unlikely. You didn't know what kind of person he was until he thought he'd have you all to himself."

"How did you know?"

"That's how a lot of these rapists and murderer types pull in their victim. They act like they're just some dork that doesn't know any better. Then they take you to their location of choice, and a lot of the times they have their way with the girls. It's the sad truth, but types like that don't look like tattooed psychotics that you can spot in a crowd right away. A lot of the times, they look like everyone else."

"What can I do for now?"

"For the case? Well, as long as you gave the report to the authorities, they'll have it on record. Hopefully you talk to the right cops, though."

"What do you mean by that?"

"Well. In my case, it was handled badly. They said my daughter was some runaway, and she was trying to get away from me. I know something was wrong, because when they kept pushing me on it. I said I would be quite willing to go to a Federal office, have them review my case, and even take the polygraph."

"Which cops were those?"

"Some of the cops in this town. I'm sure not all of them are like that, but I had the bad luck of running into them. Do you know the officer's name, the one that questioned you about the incident, took your report?"

"He actually gave me his cell number. Would you like to talk to him?"

"Definitely. With him, I could definitely help you build your case against the one that attacked you. However, this all depends on whether or not he is apprehended. Until then, it's up to the authorities to conduct the manhunt. I can only take care of the court room aspect of it."

"Sure. Here's the number."

"Thanks very much. Here's my card for each of you. Would you two like something to eat? My treat?"

Ryan had to smile at that. He rather liked Ian since the guy didn't talk down to them, and he was being very specific about what was going on. He and Becca had to go meet Demi and Melissa, though.

"Rain check?"

"Definitely. You two take care now. Also, watch out for the cops in this town. I get the feeling that they're not what they seem."

"Meaning?"

"Think about the officers that took care of your mother's case. I don't know, but I think there's definitely something wrong with them."

While Becca and Ryan were going to her house, Harry Quartz had called a press conference. It was perhaps his first aggressive move against the two officers that were trying to prosecute his son.

Becca called Damien the first chance she got; Ryan had gone to the market with Eric and Matt to get some chips for their pizza dinner with Melissa and Demi. Her father was ordering the pizza, and was glad that Becca had gotten so many friends. She now waited for Damien to pick up the phone.

"This is Damien."

"Damien. It's Becca."

"Hey, little one. What's up?" Even his voice sounded like he was smiling.

"We talked to Ryan and Eric's Lawyer. He's totally cool. He said he'd help with my case if you ever catch them guy."

Damien seemed to hesitate, and then, "That's Great. Now, we'll have something to nail him with."

"What's wrong?"

"Nothing. Look. There are a few problems here and there, but those cop problems, you know? Trying to get the paperwork right and all that."

"Well, ok. He said he'd need to talk to you about me, and what you got on the reports and such. That way, he can help us build a case."

"Sounds like he knows his stuff."

"I think so. He said he would call you. If you like though, I can give you his number."

"Would he mind?"

"I don't think so."

"Well, alright. You take care k, Becca?"

"I will. Good luck hunting the bad guys."

"Good luck avoiding them. Take care. Bye."

Damien had been on his way to meet Allan at the local diner. Shortly after Becca left him, he got a call from Ian.

"This is Damien."

"Hello. This is Ian Fanning. Becca has told me so much about you. I would like to discuss her case with you, if that's alright."

"I'll be at a friend's house later this afternoon. His name's Allan. He's also after the guy that tried to kidnap Becca."

"So, this fellow's been at it a while?"

"We've got a lot of cases far. I can't tell you much more on the phone. I'll give you Allan's address, though. We can talk there about everything. I will fill you in on all that we have. Is that alright?"

"That would be fine."

Damien gave Ian the address, wished him god speed in this forsaken town, and hung up.

Allan looked Damien in the eye for the moment. His voice was intense when he announced; "I want that bastard. We should go ahead and use the attempted kidnapping charge he had in your jurisdiction. We should be able to control the situation better once he's in your court."

"That would be lovely . . . if he were still here."

"What do you mean?"

"Quartz had called me last night, and said someone had ordered he be transferred."

"Knowing him, that would translate to letting him go. Son of a Bitch!"

"Keep your voice down. This pisses me off, too. I just about fell off my chair when I heard it."

"It's all too sordid. I don't like it at all."

"You shouldn't. I came to the same conclusion you did. We sent faxes all over. If anyone had any charges against him, they would've called us first."

"Unless Quartz got to them first."

"A lot of the others didn't strike me as the type of person that would get taken in by someone like Quartz."

"How do you know that?"

"Because they ran several check-ups on me before they would even talk to me."

"That was probably to make sure that you weren't the actual killer that might be taunting them."

"Exactly. I respect them for that. Also, it doesn't seem like Quartz may have a very clean record. When they said they would try to look for his information, they got back to me a week later, and said that their superiors told them to lay off."

"He may have a stooge within the higher ranks."

"That's what I gathered, too. So, I stopped asking around about him altogether."

"You still feel like he's covering for Lester, don't you?"

"I think he's doing more than that. He's doing his best to make sure we never find Lester. After I got word from him that Lester was transferred, I called all the local districts. I'd asked if they had requested that Lester serve a summons or a subpoena in their area. They all said the only info they had gotten on him was the fax I sent just after the interview."

"Did any girls disappear in their area?"

"Not yet."

"I don't like the sound of that."

"I think he's long gone, and I think that Harry Quartz helped. He's not done yet, either. He's still trying to find a way to kill without having to worry whether or not they can be traced back to him."

"So, he's out there right now, trolling, waiting." Allan felt a shiver roll down his back. As he said the last words, he couldn't help feeling a sense of foreboding.

"Let's watch some TV. "

"Sure."

When they turned on the television, the last thing the expected to see was Quartz holding a press conference. It was worse than that. He was feigning a cry of outrage, and saying that he was being harassed for something his son wasn't doing.

"I refuse to be held under scrutiny for these wild allegations against my son. He has done no one any harm, and does not need these upstart officers coming to my town and telling me that my son is a common criminal. The real criminal, here, is Allan Hollister. He's been traveling all over the country with his ex-wife's younger sister. Now, a year and a half ago, his wife had disappeared, and he had decided to come here."

Allan slammed his fist on the café counter as he stood up, "That low-life son of a bitch!"

Damien placed a hand on his shoulder and pulled him back down. "Let's see what else he's trying to spin."

"There's also the fact that he's got an unusually close relationship with his fourteen year old sister-in-law."

Allan looked to Damien and shook his head. "Sloane didn't even want to marry me. I took Demi in because she was a good kid."

"I know that. I did tell you, though. He was going to try to use that against you."

Quartz went on, "Such a man shouldn't be questioning my character. He is the last person to do so in light of the fact that he has had sexual relations with his younger sister. I suppose his wife wasn't enough. I'll go further. I propose that he might've killed his wife, himself, and covered the whole thing up. Well, I have this to say to him; Saffire Falls does not tolerate child molesters. There will be justice, and I refuse to allow him to come after my son in order to distract everyone from the fact that he is sleeping with his younger sister. That is all the time I have. No questions."

"Bastard!"

"Allan."

"You corrupt son-"

"Allan!"

Allan's eyes darted to Damien. "What?"

"Is any of that true?"

"What? How dare you."

"Sit down."

Allan sucked in his breath and took his seat along the counter. "What is it?"

"Have you ever had close relationships with Demi?"

"No, of course not. How could you even ask that?"

"Good. Then, we have that clear. Allan, you're acting exactly the way he wants you to. Let's get going back to your house."

They asked for the bill as they pulled their coats on. As soon as they were in the car, they were on their way to Allan's home.

"This is exactly what he wants, Allan. He wants you to get mad and have a shit attack."

"Wouldn't you?"

"I know. However, we have to get there and show him that we are not afraid of him if he tries to confront us."

"How do we do that?"

"Becca's boyfriend. He has a lawyer working for his family now. Becca put me in contact with the lawyer."

"How will that help?"

"The boyfriend's father had a beef with Quartz. Maybe we can pull a counter card against this corrupt bastard and he'll leave us alone."

"I hope you're right."

"Me, too."

Allan didn't find Demi when he got home. He called her cell phone, and she seemed cheerful enough, but she could sense that Allan was slightly bothered.

"What's wrong?"

"Where are you right now?"

"I'm at Becca's. Want me to come home?"

"No. Stay there. Something just came up at home. When you're ready to come home, call Damien, ok? He'll be the one to pick you up. I have to handle some things here."

"Ok, Allan. Hope it turns out good then."

"Me, too." He hung up.

"You know they're going to bring someone from child services don't you?"

"Not if Quartz is in charge. For all we know, it might be one of his boys pretending to be child services."

"Now, you're getting paranoid."

"If I were being investigated for that sort of thing, my people would've called me by now, and told me that I was under disciplinary action."

"Yeah. That's true."

As if on cue, the pounding on the door began. When Damien looked through the viewing glass, he saw Quartz standing there, with five other men in tow.

Allan opened the door, and barked, "What do you want?"

"We have reason to believe you might be tapping your little sister."

"I've never done such a thing."

"All the same, I brought someone from child services. Ike?"

Ike Sellers was of slight build, at five foot three inches. He had horn-rimmed glasses that did nothing to hide the sick gleaning in his eyes, which shone like a rat's.

Allan looked at him briefly as he spoke.
"I really do need to talk to your sister. I must do so, alone." When he said that, the corner of his mouth seemed to tremble as he attempted to keep from drooling. Allan knew what he was thinking about.

"What are you going to talk to my little sister about?"

"Confidential matters. It is a breach of protocol to talk with the abusing parent any terms of the case against them."

Allan reached for his hip, forgetting his that his gun was no longer there. Damien was relieved at that, and moved to calm Allan down.

Then another voice spoke, despite the cold bitterness within; the newcomer was able to drive back Quartz's team with his professional approach.

Ian announced, "Quartz! You will cease and desist all these groundless accusations, or be placed before a Federal Board of Inquiry over the Gross Negligence in handling my daughter's case. Now, I know there is more behind it, but I will prosecute you for that this very moment if you insist on pursuing the case against Officer Hollister."

Quartz tried to stare Ian down, but Ian glared at him. "This is trespassing. Do you have a warrant?"

"We heard complaints from the neighbors."

"Which ones?"

"Never mind that. We have a right to search."

"Not without a warrant you don't."

"We have just cause. A little girl's life is at stake."

Ian stepped up to Ike Sellers, "Hello, Mr. Sellers. Has the school, you were teaching at, allowed you to reenter the campus? Or are you still considered a sex-offender?"

Sellers began to sweat profusely, and looked to Quartz. Ian spoke again; "There's nothing wrong, here. You heard a false report of abuse filed by someone trying to pull a prank. Or would you like to be brought back before the parole board for that incident in the next town?"

Sellers shrugged at Ian. "There's nothing wrong. Must've been a prank."

Ian looked to Quartz; "Do you concur?"

Quartz grudgingly nodded, and muttered, "Those damn kids don't know when to quit. We'll be on our way. Sorry for the trouble."

When Quartz's people left, Allan couldn't help but shaking Ian's hand, and bowing his head.

"Thank you so much for helping."

Ian scratched his head and looked at Damien. "Um. It's all right, really. You can stop shaking my hand now."

Allan still had his head down; "I don't know how to thank you."

"You can start by calling me a friend. I'm Ian Fanning."

Allan could hardly believe how he turned things around on Quartz, "H-how did you know to come here?"

"Well, we could go through the quick version. Or we could sit down and talk. I can tell you everything then."

"The guy who tried to rape and kill Becca was in this town." Damien began.

"How do you know it was him?"

"Well, we have two living witnesses, and they both were able to identify him from what little pictures we had."

"Do you know what else he's done?"

Allan bit out; "He killed my girlfriend. I'm the only family her little sister has."

"Ah, so you're acting guardian. Damn Quartz try to pin a molestation charge on you?"

"That he did. That's why he was here. I could tell, though, that other guy he had with him was definitely not from child services."

"You're right. Sellers is an ex-convict. My mentor put him away when he was still doing DA work. He might be able to help us. So, this fellow who tried to kill your two star witnesses, what's his name?"

"Lester Quartz. We think he was connected with at least fifteen other cases around Dalian alone. He might've done more, but even after we put out the all points alert, we haven't been able to get anything on him."

"He doesn't leave traces of himself?"

"Not a one. We think that he might be removing the heads, though."

"Why do you say that?"

"The heads we have found don't seem to match the bones we do find. Our person in forensic paleontology says that the skulls are one week fresher than the bones we've managed to find."

"What can you tell from that?"

"That the bastard is probably taking them home with him so he can fantasize over them. There have been times when all we've found is just that, the head."

Ian coughed out his drink, having felt like he'd just been punched. His eyes widened as he face grew into a snarl. "It's him, then. He's the one that killed my step-daughter."

"Ian?"

"A few years back or so, I was married to this one flake, and took care of her daughter. She was a great kid, but she went missing. When they found her, they said they could only find her head. I was devastated. Since, then, I've stayed around town to see what had happened to my daughter. I had thought about leaving, but then I would never know, so I stayed."

"He killed my girlfriend, as well. When I asked him about it, he said he had done me a favor."

"Have you brought the federal agencies into this?"

Damien spoke up, "We tried that, but one of his stooges within the Bureau has been able to slow down or stunt any case against Quartz or Lester. So far, we've been able to keep the evidence in their perspective districts, and before they can actually remove it, they need a release form with both of our signed consent."

"Just in case it gets lost."

"We know how evidence tends to disappear when it comes to Lester and Quartz. I am so sorry about your daughter."

"It's a terrible thing to lose a child."

Damien turned away, "It certainly is."

Allan chimed in, "Is there something you're not telling us?"

Damien cleared his throat; "I just got word from my brother that my niece was found last night. She disappeared a while ago."

Allan looked down at his hands.

Ian spoke up, "Alright. This guy has hurt all of us. Now it's time for us to take a stand. We find, and bring him to justice."

"I think he's slipped through our fingers, yet again."

Ian looked puzzled, and then scowled when he heard Allan say, "We think Quartz helped him escape. We're not sure, yet but we haven't heard anything from Lester because last we saw him, he was grinning like the cat that swallowed the canary."

"Or bit its head off."

". . . And still prowling."

"So, what now?"

"Well, we'll have to see if we can play Harry's game. I know he expects us to just take it. However, I know that he's under scrutiny for a hit and run that involved my client."

"Well, if you got to know the kid, you'd like him."

"I know, Damien. He's a great kid. I can't argue with that."

"You don't know if you can really present his case after all this time."

"There may be something to it. After all, the damages caused have cost Ryan his parents."

"His negligence also got your daughter killed."

"If it's as you say, he's indirectly responsible for my daughter's death. He is aiding and abetting a felon."

"Not quite. We don't have the conviction, yet."

"We will, soon enough."

"Did you talk to our lab people, Ian?"

"Indeed. We found one fresh burial site. The girl still has her clothes on, so there may be a chance of pulling something out of her."

"Depends on how old the site is. If it's been a while, we've lost any chance of getting any sample of his bodily secretion."

"It's fresh enough. We also found Karen Chastener with search and rescue teams."

"Who's we?"

"My mentor has some links to some federal resources. He was able to get his specialist to use spectral analysis to track Lester's car that day, right to the burial site."

"We thought Quartz disposed of it."

"Ah, yes. Not before his boys got into the impound yard to take a few pictures of the car. We've got hair and fiber, We even grabbed the clothes in the trunk."

"That son of a bitch was going to burn it all."

"When he went to the impound yard to grab the car, it was an empty shell. There was nothing in there. We took everything we needed."

"Well, if you didn't get a warrant, it can all be thrown out."

"I thought of that. The bureau thought that Quartz might be covering his son. He will have a warrant out for his arrest too."

"What about his stooge?"

"Ah . . . That's the best part. He's actually in league with my mentor. They planted a set of merchandise so that the stooge could traffic the decoy through Quartz. Of course, Quartz covered him, but not without a price. Information was to come in and out."

"A decoy. Was all the information encoded?"

"They gave him old information on certain departments. Now they know what kind of person he is."

"What about the warrant?" Allan wanted to know.

"It's a federal decree to search said property, and pull evidence as necessary."

"If you don't have the car, you can't pin him."

"We can. Their specialists built a facsimile, and left that in place of the actual car. We have it, in federal impound. We can nail his son, and tie him to a lot of the crimes that get called in."

"Well, we still have the missing persons' cases. In each case, no one really saw him."

"Except for Becca. Claudia was lucky enough to survive, but she wasn't conscious when he attacked her."

Damien nodded, "If we can get her to state for the record that it was Lester who attacked her . . ."

Allan finished, "We can nab him on attempted kidnapping and aggravated assault."

Ian shook his head, "Not so fast. We have to find him first. As far as everyone else is concerned, he's a regular Joe."

"Until he kills again. Ian we have to get to him before then."

"Well, you guys can worry about the all points alert. I will go ahead and handle the case against him."

Damien muttered, "When we find him, I wonder if we'll really feel like arresting him."

Allan looked him in the eye, "If he tries to run, we'll have no choice but to act."

Ian looked over at Allan; "I want this scumbag, too. When you find him, arrest him. If he runs, you chase him down, and cuff him. We have to make people see what kind of monster he is. Then we go after Quartz."

Damien muttered, "And bring them all tumbling down."

Ian nodded, "That's the plan."

Allan couldn't help beaming at Ian, "If you had all of this set up, why didn't you tell us?"

Ian breathed in deeply, and braced himself. "We didn't know if you were with Quartz, or if he would try to force you out of the equation. When he came up with those allegations against you, then we knew he definitely wanted to discredit you."

"So, you were able to argue him down."

"Allan. That guy is unpredictable. We don't know what he's been doing. For all we know, he might be just like his son. I went to my mentor after my daughter died, because I knew it had been handled badly."

"You wanted peace of mind."

"And got more than I bargained for. We are in the Dragon's Lair, gentlemen. So, we armor up, or get out. I'd rather pull everything together, and take these bastards all down to hell. I'm doing this for Dara, and your girlfriend, Allan. As well as your niece, Damien."

"What will we do while everything's in the works?"

"Same thing you've been doing. Act frustrated over everything."

Allan looked up at him with a scowl. "That wasn't an act."

"It is now. Ham it up, folks. He has to believe he has control."

"So we can catch him at his worst."

"By the way, who's the stooge in Quartz' department?"

"We'll call him by his regular name, for now. His name's Bobby Kennedy."

"You're kidding."

"You know him."

"I'm glad I do, now."

"Try not to show Quartz any sign of relaxation on our part. He may be able to detect that we have an advantage."

Two days later, the boys were getting the rest of their things moved in.

"Just a little to the right," Melissa told the boys as they helped Ryan with his dresser. He had hoped there wouldn't be much trouble in bringing it to Melissa's house, and there hadn't been. The trouble had begun when they tried taking it up to the second floor. When Ryan suggested that the Thompson duo should get an elevator, Eric almost laughed his head off. Now, he could see what Ryan meant. Even with the drawers removed, and the clothes all packed into their sports bags, the mahogany dresser was a pain to move. At this moment, they were finally setting it down on the far wall by the window. They had already moved all of Eric's things into his own room the day before.

"Wow. Thanks, dude."

"You have way too much shit."

"Oh, shut up."

Melissa was beaming at both of them, and finally giggled at them in spite of herself. They both turned to her, and started tickling her. By the time Mrs. Thompson was home, she was squealing with laughter.

"Stop rough housing, you kids."

Ryan settled down, and Eric followed suit. Lorna Thompson could've sworn that Melissa was a tad disappointed.

"I'm sorry, Mrs. Thompson."

"Now, now. What did I tell you? You live in my home, and that means you can call me mom, if you like."

Eric smiled, and nodded when Ryan looked to him.

"Yes, mom."

"He's shy. He'll get used to you, like a terrier."

He had to nudge Eric for that, and that got Melissa giggling all over again.

Once they settled down, the four of them sat on the table. Eric and Ryan looked at each other, and nodded.

"Well, we've decided that we can contribute at least fifteen hundred to the house, and hopefully, that should cover the both of us."

Lorna was shaking her head, "You boys should know that you shouldn't have to do that. Also, Ian said that I would already be getting that much as current executor of the estate. That was the agreement. Once you both find your own place, Melissa and I will be on our own, but we've gotten through it."

Ryan inclined his head, solemnly. He didn't want to mention David at that moment. Also, Melissa seemed so happy that he could hardly bare to bring that name up, and see the sadness and pain in her eyes. For that, he hated Dave for that unforgivable act of violating the sibling relationship. So, he had decided that he would be the big brother that he knew Dave had never been. Also, there was something that bothered him every time he thought about it. That was the fact that Dave had been at it for a while, and he wondered how long the fantasies existed before he decided to act on them. Had he been thirteen or fourteen? Ryan figured that he had gotten fixated on Melissa as soon as she was old enough to menstruate. However, he figured it had to have been before then. He had already known how she was developing, which meant that he had to have been watching her closely before then. That meant that Melissa could've been around nine, and Dave was starting to fantasize about her. He had to shiver, but he fought it, and it made him cough harshly instead. That's what he got for trying to stave off an impulse, and he was sorry for it when the cough lingered for a good two minutes. When he got it under control, he had asked Lorna if she had known when Ian would be coming around to serve some documents and get things finalized.

Lorna nodded, "Oh, yeah. He should be coming around. He's also bringing a young girl he's recently adopted."

"Really? Wow."

"Why do you say that?"

Ryan became pensive, and muttered, "I don't know. He seems like he might be a tad busy for that."

"Well, he's got a lot to do, no doubt about that. Some people try to make time not matter their schedule, you know?"

"I guess you're right. Well, hope he gets here soon."

"Well, he said he'd be stopping by Southern Fried Pop's Chicken before coming here. So, he'll be bringing lunch."

Ryan could hear Eric talking it up with Melissa and thought how wistful Mrs. Thompson looked as she looked over at them. She looked back at him, and whispered, "I know it's such an awful thing to say, but sometimes I wish that Melissa were an only child. I've tried to understand . . . .her brother. He was so odd a lot of the time, though. I really didn't know what to do with him."

They all turned when they heard the knock at the door. Melissa frowned playfully as Eric got up; "I'll get that."

Ian was standing at the door carrying a briefcase in one hand, and carrying a bag, which held a bucket of chicken. Scarlette was coming up the walkway, herself, with yet another bucket, and a tub of mashed potatoes. "Hi, Eric."

Eric went ahead and took the bag from Ian, "Come on in, Mr. Fanning."

"You guys can just call me Ian, you know?"

Ryan went over to help Scarlette with the rest of the food, "Well, have a seat, Ian, and I'll get you a drink in a moment."

"You don't have to. There's like seven bottles of soda in the car."

Melissa got up; "I'll get those. You guys just settle down."

Scarlette left the food to Ryan, and went to join Melissa; "I'll help. You guys can set up the table."

Melissa smiled at Scarlette as she helped with the sodas. She hadn't even noticed that Dave was standing across the street, watching her. When Melissa grabbed four, and turned to go back into the house, Scarlette glared at him, making him nervous enough to leave.

When Scarlette got back into the house with the rest of the soda, she was pleased to see Melissa bantering with the boys. She helped Mrs. Thompson set the table as she watched them. Lorna, herself, found that somewhat disturbing. She felt like Scarlette was projecting something that wasn't there as far as watching the boys with her daughter. It was as if they boys reminded Scarlette of people that she deeply distrusted. She turned away when Scarlette turned back to ask her about where the plates were.

Through her teeth, she managed a cheerful reply; "They're on the cupboard by the refrigerator."

Ian was looking through his briefcase, and making sure he had all the files he needed so he could go over them with the boys. He was pretty sharp, and at times, he seemed too young for all his years. In some ways, Lorna also saw Ian as one of the boys, like she had with Ryan and Eric.

Then two more girls appeared at her door, and at that moment she was so happy for her daughter that she almost cried.

Becca had her hands on her hips, Demi following suit, "Oh, wow. I can see we're not needed here."

Ryan walked over, and reached out for both their hands, "Yeah, you are. Come on over."

Demi went over to hug Melissa, "Hey, sis."

They plopped onto the couch and began to talk just about anything when Ian pulled out an ancient rustic bell, and began to clang on it as he announced, "Lunch is ready."

Ryan started handing out the silverware when they all heard a knock at the door, and saw two figures that made Becca smile. "Could you get two more sets, baby?"

Ryan nodded, and went into the kitchen as Becca opened the door. In the doorway, stood Allan and Damien both holding up their own bag of food. Only it was Chinese and they had several boxes.

"Wow. I guess we came over prepared."

Lorna went over to take the bag from them, and chuckled, "There's no such thing as too much food with this group."

Eric and Ryan looked slightly embarrassed since they had managed to keep the Thompson fridge filled to the max.

The two detectives sat on either side of Ian, and Scarlette took a place by Melissa while Demi chatted it up on her other side. Lorna sat by Allan, and looked on as the kids all talked amongst each other. The brothers sat together, though Becca seemed to cling to Ryan's side. Scarlette found that bothersome, but said nothing. They all began to dig in, and for a moment, it actually felt like family.

When lunch was over, Ian cleared his throat, and looked to Demi and Melissa for a moment. "Would you girls mind excusing yourselves? There's some things we need to discuss with the boys and Becca."

Melissa shook her head, and Lorna was about to give her a scolding look, but she stood her ground, "If it's something serious, then I have a few things to say on that, myself. Besides, Demi told me about what happened with her sister. I can take it. I've heard worse."

Ian looked to the two detectives, and they nodded.

Ian pulled a manila folder from his briefcase, and handed it to Becca, "Alright, Becca, it seems they had someone in custody just recently. I want you to take a look at the photo in this folder and just nod if you know him."

Becca received it, and almost whimpered when she saw the picture. Ryan wrapped his arm around her shoulder. Realizing the photo had her transfixed, he tried to reach up and close it. Demi held his hand firmly, and gave him a tense look when he turned to her. It was as if she were saying, *This is something she has to do. Leave her be.*

Becca finally closed the folder, and handed it back to Ian. He looked at the others, and made sure he had their attention. "I'm going to have the rest of you pass this around, and tell me if you've seen him."

The two detectives knew he was going to do this. They hadn't planned on the other girls being there, though. They sat, and decided to ride it out when Melissa looked up, her voice trembling. They could all tell, though, she was eager to get this out of her system.

"I've seen this guy before!"

Ian regarded her a moment, and looked to the detectives.

Allan asked her, "Where have you seen him before Melissa?"

"I was walking home, and saw Dara in his car. Once when I was going to the market, and the second time, as I was coming out. He was circling the area. He actually looked at me as I crossed the street in front of him. He looked at me for a moment, and it was the way some jock would look at a brand new sports car. It was creepy."

Ian's voice caught in his throat, but he managed, "Was he with Dara?"

"She was there, but I think she was sleeping that second time. I asked my mom about it the next day, you know, to report it. So we did."

Allan watched as Melissa seemed to relive that moment, "They wouldn't listen to me, though. I kept telling them that something bad was going to happen, or already had, but they said I was just some kid trying to send them on some red herring. For a moment, I thought that maybe they didn't want to listen."

Allan seethed, "No, they wouldn't."

Damien shook him by the shoulder, and looked to all of them, "This guy has been taking girls all over the country. We have reason to believe that his father, a cop, has been covering for him. We also believe that he may be at large again. Now, Melissa, since you saw him with Dara, that confirms the first crime we can connect him with."

Ian uttered, "A cover up. The whole time, they were covering it up. That little creep killed my daughter, and they covered him."

Ryan looked to him, and told him, "The older one had killed my mom. It had been a hit and run, and for a while my father thought it had been my fault. He had later told me it was Quartz, but could do nothing about it because his boys kept covering him up."

Damien whistled through his teeth, "I don't know which is worse."

Melissa finally announced her own troubles, "My brother. He's the worst of them all. He's been . . . you know . . ." Demi held her friend, and that gave the girl courage to finally say, "He's been messing with me . . . a lot. I don't even know if I want to go into detail, but I do know I want him out of my life." She began to sob, "S-so, he c-c-can't touch me, anymore!"

Ryan placed a hand on her shoulder; "We dealt with him. He's rotting in jail as we speak."

Scarlette shook her head. "Not quite. I saw that little fag not too long ago. It was just a few hours ago, in fact."

Damien and Allan looked at each other, "Quartz."

Eric cleared his throat; "I just want to know one thing. Why is this bastard covering for all these psychos? I don't get that. What could he possibly gain from something like that?"

Damien looked at Eric, "Well, supposed that there was some-one Quartz didn't like. He could go ahead and talk to an inmate, and tell them what he wants them to do for him. Once the job is done, Quartz comes in, plays the hero, and kills the inmate."

"So, he sends them out like hit-men?"

Allan nodded.

"Well, that's horrible. What an asshole!"

"Harry Quartz is a horrible person." Ian shrugged. Then his voice grew intense as he told the rest of them, "I remember when I first called in to report my daughter missing, and it was Quartz that answered. His first step was to accuse me directly of molest-ing my daughter."

"What did you tell him?"

"Well, he had threatened to call child services on me for an interview. I told him that he could do it by all means. Now, I'm glad I didn't. He would've gotten one of his own people to do the interview. I've got a few contacts, though. I think we can bring him down. I can take all of this information, and put a case to-gether against him."

Damien shook his head, and muttered, "This round goes to him."

The others looked to him, horrified.

When he looked to each of them, he told them, "Don't you see? While we've been talking about putting Quartz away, he's already helped his son get up and go."

"We'll have a case when we find him." Ian reassured them.

"If we find him, you mean."

Ryan was thoughtful, and looked out the window, where he could see the sky had suddenly become overcast, and the drizzle had begun. Finally, when he spoke, he agreed with Damien, "He's past tense now, until we read about more missing girls. We'll just have to pray, I suppose."

The mood around the table was quiet, and the only thing to punctuate the silence was pounding of the fat drops of rain that beat against the windows. For a moment, Becca saw a vision of herself, not having been able to escape Lester, and the drops were her blood splattering onto the window of his car, as he beat her skull inward.

Claudia knocked on David's door at least five times before he answered, and even then he wasn't completely coherent. His hair was a mess and he looked liked he hadn't shaved a few days. He reluctantly invited her in and said he couldn't offer her more than a beer or and old can of vegetable juice. Although she declined, she agreed to wait for him in his room.

She plopped onto his bed her feet swinging backward knocking his stack of photos loose. Two of them peeked out from under the bed. It gravely disturbed her because the girl in the pictures seemed to be only fourteen or fifteen. She bent over quickly to snatched them up and take a closer look. The girl in the pictures was crying. She was also wearing lingerie that was too big for her and yet the ropes tied around her pressed the clothing to her skin just below her breast. She was also wearing a spiked collar with a leash attached. Another picture had her standing on her knees, while yet another had her positioned on all fours like a dog.

Claudia quickly slid off the bed and got on to the floor so she could look under his bed. The three photos she had on her hand were from a set of fifty, maybe sixty others. In some of them Dave was behind his sister and fondling her with a predatory grin on his face. Claudia quickly stood from the floor pocketing the pictures she had on her hand. She had done it just in time because David had just come out of the shower, soaking wet and fully ready to pounce on his girlfriend. When he started reaching out for her, Claudia slapped his hands away. She quickly bent down and grabbed a few photos from under his bed, positioning herself for a tackle if he tried to hit her while she was bent over.

She shoved the photos into his face and demanded, "What the hell is this?"

"It's nothing. Don't worry about it."

"It is something, something very big, very sick. Who is this?"

"Alright. I didn't think I would have to tell you this. The thing is, my sister took pictures of herself and planted them under my bed. The little bitch has been trying to blackmail me with all those."

He plopped down on the bed, on the spot where she had been sitting not too long ago. She almost shuddered, and she kept wondering why she was still there.

"You understand, don't you? And now she's got these two guys, who are probably doing her, acting as her bodyguards. Makes me sick."

"You make me sick. I'm leaving now."

She turned to head for the door, and she felt his hand grab her arm. His hand slid down to her wrist, and he began to squeeze hard. She grabbed a bottle of beer he had on his night table, and brought it down on his arm, breaking it. He let go and started cursing at her. She hit him again, this time squarely on the jaw with her bare fist. He seemed like he was trying to recover. She leaned close, holding the broken bottle with the other hand at a distance.

She breathed in deeply, and when she spoke, her voice was quiet. "Now, you listen to me, creep. Come near me again, you'll have a lot more to worry about than these cuts. Got it? Don't come near me again."

If she had been screaming, he would've dismissed it, and took advantage of her hysteria. She knew that much, and for that reason, she had told him everything in a low voice so that he would understand that she was serious.

He held his cut arm, squeezing it so he wouldn't lose too much blood. With whatever wits he had left, he seethed, "If I see you again, I'm going to fucking kill you, bitch."

"I would say that you're barking like a big dog, but what kind Of faggot would rape his own sister?! It's good you get the message, though. Now you know how far I'm willing to go."

His eyes widened as she left. He had only thought that she was talking about calling the cops or something like that. However, she was talking about dealing with him, herself. It was a startling revelation for him to realize that he could possibly be the target, being such a predator, himself.

As the door closed, he called out her name. She no longer heard him. She was down the street, having dropped the broken bottle in the nearby bushes. It was all she could do to keep from running frantically. She looked back at Dave's house, and shuddered in relief as she realized that she had been able to get away from him.

Becca was about to go to sleep when she heard a banging on her front door. She looked to the door from one of the windows, and was relieved to find Claudia there. If she had taken a closer look, however, she would've noticed that Claudia was shivering violently, and was staving off her tears so she could tell her friend what had happened at her ex-boyfriend's house. Becca unlocked the door to let Claudia in, and methodically fastened all the locks as soon as she was in.

"Oh, god. I hope he didn't follow me. If he did, I'm so sorry, I shouldn't have come here, Becca."

Becca reached up, and held her by the shoulders, "I need you to calm down, alright? Let me get you some water."

"I'll go to the kitchen with you."

"Ok. Come on, then."

They went into Becca's kitchen, and she took the bottle of water that was offered to her. She was still fidgeting, and looking out all the windows.

"Listen, Claudia. I need you to tell me what just happened."

She got no response; Claudia was still frantically looking around at all the windows of the kitchen. She felt a moan in her throat, and whined, "Why did we have to come in here?"

Becca took her hand, and squeezed it. Then she led her friend to her room on the second floor of the house. Once there, it was all she could do to keep her friend from bursting into tears. She remained firm with her, yet guided her through the simplest of motions such as sitting down, and taking deep breathes.

"Now, Claudia. I need to know what happened?"

"Something's really wrong with Dave. He's got this weird fixation on his little sister."

"I know."

"You knew?"

"Well, I just met Melissa a few days ago. She only told Ryan and me tonight. We were having lunch at her house."

"You knew and you didn't tell me?"

"He seemed creepy to me to begin with. I wasn't sure you would listen to me if I had told you that up front."

"Well, that's not fair."

"Well. Would you have listened to me if I had told you?"

"Well, I guess I don't know."

"The important thing is that you know about him, now. It's also good that you got away from him when you did. I was really bothered by him when you first introduced me to him. I swear I felt like screaming when I saw how he was leering at me."

"You might have been paranoid."

"No. I've seen that look before. The guy who attacked us, Lester, his eyes were like that too."

"That's his name? The guy who made it so we had to come here?"

"Yes. Now, I know you may not want to hear this, but he's still on the loose."

"How can you be so calm?"

"Because I know my friends will protect me. You know Detective Greene? He's been cool with me since this whole thing started. He'll protect you, too if you let him."

"Well, from now on, I'm sticking by you. I told that jerk not to come near me."

"Good. Melissa hates him too."

"Oh, my god. How could I have been with him?"

"Come on. You didn't know. Hey, I was the dummy that went with that Lester when he first approached me. I'm lucky to be alive."

Claudia laughed nervously, "Well, so am I, apparently."

"Yeah, you are." Becca agreed, sticking her tongue out.

Claudia leaned in to hug her friend, "Well, I guess we're stuck in this town."

Becca accepted her friend's hug; "At least we're stuck to-gether."

Claudia cried deeply, and Becca held her for that moment. They stayed like that for a long time. When Claudia calmed down enough, she pulled back from her friend, and smiled.

"When did you get so tough?"

"I guess it helps to have a guy that's been standing by me."

"Yeah, it does. He's been really good for you. Hopefully, you'll never have to see that Derek asshole again."

"Too late. I saw him a few days ago. He tried to pick a fight with Ryan."

"Did he start talking shit?"

"Ryan didn't really give him a chance. Sent him packing."

"Awesome. I like him already."

"Hmmm. Get your own Ryan."

"I will. I will." After a moment they both settled down, and Becca got a sleeping bag for Claudia. Ever the gentleman, Matt offered his own bed, and volunteered to sleep on the couch. "I've been meaning to test doze on it for a while."

Claudia woke up sometime in the middle of the night, star-tled, confused, and unsure where she was. She looked around and saw Matthew's model airplanes. She relaxed herself, and fell back asleep. It was the first quiet sleep she had in a while.

Ryan told Becca he would meet her at school. He had wanted to go to his old house before it was sold off. Nonetheless, Becca had asked Matt, since he went to school later, if he would be cool, and hang with Ryan. Eric would've gone with him, but he had to go to morning practice. Matt came up behind Ryan, and tapped his shoulder.

"What's up, dude?"

"I'm alright. Just looking at the old place. I guess it's hard to believe I used to live there."

"Well, I guess at one point or another, you have to say good-bye."

They both heard Derek seething, "Yeah . . . like now."

Matt turned around, just in time to see Dave's fist flying towards him. He was able to dodge it, losing his footing in the process. As soon as Matt hit the ground, he stuck his leg up, and hit Dave in the stomach. Dave's own leg went forward, and Matt held it at the ankle, again, kicking upward into the stomach. Derek hadn't fared any better, since Ryan had whirled inward, and leaned forward so he could drive a fist into Derek's torso, just below his ribcage. The two stepped back from them, and each pulled out a weapon of sorts. As Matthew got up, he picked up one of the large rocks and threw it. Ryan followed suit, and threw some, as well. Dave dodged two of the rocks coming at him, and charged forward, holding the knife high. It was at that moment when he brought his knife up towards Matthew's face. Matt turned away just in time to save his eyes, but received a deep cut on his cheek.

"Ain't so tough now, are you, you little shits?"

That was when Dave saw a long blade come into view, which moved slowly and came to rest just an inch from his neck. His eyes darted left, and there was Scarlette, holding the sword out at shoulder height.

She hadn't taken her eyes off the two thugs, but she motioned with her head for Ryan and Matthew to leave as soon as they could.

Ryan stood there a moment, and said, "Now, don't actually hurt them, Scarlette."

She smiled at him innocently, "Who me? Don't worry about them. Get your friend to the school's clinic, or at least some place close by that offers first aid. Just don't wait for what I'm going to do."

"Promise me you won't do something rash."

"I'll honor that promise, if you can disregard me and look after your friend."

"Deal."

As soon as Ryan had gotten far away enough, Scarlette regarded the two with a smug look, "Now, listen. You two are going to regret trying to hurt that boy. I don't care about the other, but Ryan is my prey. Do you understand?"

Derek nodded furiously, and waited until she removed the katana from Dave's throat. The two slowly walked away, and Scarlette watched them as they took their time leaving. Perhaps they thought she would turn her back on them. Very unlikely since she knew one of them had a knife. She had bluffed when she had told them that Ryan was her prey, if only to frighten them. Perhaps they thought she was quite mad, and she would readily prove them right, if they gave her the chance. She was actually hoping that they would turn on their heels and try to charge her. They didn't, however, and that made for a boring day to her. She finally did walk away when she was sure they had gotten into Derek's car, and had driven away. She couldn't help feeling that Ryan had begun to think of her unkindly in light of this. Had he really thought that she would kill the two, then and there, right in front of him? She brushed off the remark, and went on her way. It was all she could do to keep from relishing the look of fear on the face of the two thugs. She had been very willing to take their lives. Such a thing would not be much of a loss, but when it came to trying to stay in Ryan's circle of friends, she measured her own temper, and figured she would have to settle for putting fear into people that deserved it. She would punish them, later, and the punishment would be swift, and violent.

Ian looked to Allan and Damien as he sat with them, at a table just outside the Italian Restaurant. They weren't very hungry so they had only ordered a plate of garlic bread, and the garlic butter that it came with.

"I need to know what it was that prompted Quartz to move against you two. He must've been really desperate when he pulled that press conference bullshit."

Damien shrugged, and nodded at Allan, who took a deep breath, and said, "We went to the station to claim the last of Karen Chastener's belongings."

"No wonder it was such a bitch getting it out of there. I had really been dreading that they were in a rush to get rid of it. One of the operatives told me that they had put everything in the car. I was afraid they would burn it."

"You knew about that?"

"There's one federal agent in the division posing as one of Quartz's people. We had to do a lot of work for him to get inducted into the fray."

"Like what?"

"Can't tell you that. Listen, from here on in, you guys have to tell me everything you're going to do."

"Why is that?" Allan demanded.

"To prepare himself for any rash movements Quartz might make. You're lucky he was there when he heard the rest of you talking."

"He heard that you were trying to gather all you could from the Chastener site. It was an admirable effort, but quite a spectacle."

Allan creased his eyes, and asked, "What would you have done?"

"Just what I've been doing. That is to hang back and watch his movements. He is covering up a lot. If you keep going in with your hair on fire, though, he's going to start taking more precautions. He's afraid of you guys, otherwise he wouldn't have pulled that press stunt."

"Should we feel honored?"

"You should be satisfied that you got him that scared, however foolhardy your actions. At least it's more than what the courts can do at this point."

Damien folded his hands under his chin, "Meaning?"

"Karen Chastener's family is suing for psychological damages, and for gross negligence on the police's part."

"Let me guess. You told them about your operation."

"Our operation. However, that was before the press conference. I didn't know what he was thinking, or if I had managed to rattle his cage."

Allan looked aside, "I think we all did. Now, he's scrambling to pull his pants up, and tighten his belt so we don't catch him like that again."

"Well, with that being said, we have to sit back and watch him. We can't upset him anymore, or he'll start making other plans, and he might learn how to cover his, and Lester's tracks better."

Ian perked up, and smiled at Allan, "By the way, we cleared up everything on your molestation charges. They won't fly in court because you've been able to give us a good record on the finances you've covered for her. Also, one of the people from child services did talk to her at school and got an excellent report about you. If Quartz tries to press that, he's going to run into a brick wall, and have himself pulled in for his unusual interest in your daughter."

"Damned if he does, and all that, right?"

Ian and Damien could hear Allan's voice losing the tension that had been there all afternoon. He had been deeply worried what would happen if Quartz's people ever got their hands on Demi, but at least now, he knew that they both had some sort of protection.

Damien stood up, "Come on, you guys. Ryan and Eric invited us for dinner. So, we've got to get moving."

Allan looked to Ian, "Is Scarlette coming?"

The young lawyer shook his head, "I honestly do not know. She's been very distant lately. Also, she goes out, and comes back at odd hours. What do you make of that?"

Damien squeezed his shoulder, "That's called, being a normal teenager."

Allan pulled his coat on, "By the way, what about Mr. Sandler's funeral preparations?"

"I talked with the boys about it. They're going to have the full mass, and the procession will be just the family and friends, mostly other students."

"Poor kids."

"Yeah. I'm guessing Becca can help Ryan pull through. I'm wondering who'll be there for Eric, though."

"I don't know. I think in a way, we'll have to be their support system, and hope that's enough."

"Are they taken care of financially?"

"Oh, yes. They'll be well off for the rest of their lives. In fact, they might have to take up unusual sports, and such to even start moving any of their inheritance."

"What about a suit against Quartz for the boys' mother?"

"Ryan said to let sleeping dogs lie. Besides, he wants us to expose Quartz first, and then we can start dogging him about that."

"Well, if that works. Did they sell the house?"

"Yes, they did. It's a foregone conclusion that they would be moving out, but Eric told me that it would be too hard to stay there any longer."

Allan scratched his head, trying to bring up a point, "How much do I owe you, Ian? I mean, for all you've done, there's got to be something I can do."

"Help me bring this bastard down. You're already doing that, though. So, don't worry about it."

The sun colored the town red, and they were bathed in the rays of sunset. For once, they all felt serene as they walk towards their car as the red sun glazed gently on their backs, and went on to the Sandler's and the Thompson's home.

Lorna Thompson asked Ryan to get the door as their three guests arrived, and she finished the trimmings on the home made chicken dinner. As she brought the bird to the table, she smiled at the three men as they entered.

"I figured you boys might like some home cooking." She gushed as they smiled back gratefully.

Ryan was setting the table and Eric was bringing over the extra chairs for them to sit on. Becca, Demi, Melissa and Becca's old friend were helping with the salads, and bringing out the bottles of soda for them to drink. Claudia, having joined the group for Becca, had asked them what they would like to drink. When she came back, she had given each a huge glass mug with ice and their drink of choice.

Ryan sat down in his place on one side of the table, Becca and Eric sitting on either side of him. Demi and Melissa sat next to Eric, while Claudia sat next to Becca. On the other side, Lorna stood by her chair as she cut the chicken. Allan sat across from his little sister, while Damien and Allan sat on either side of Lorna. Even Matthew had come, sporting a bandage on his cheek. Melissa looked over at him, feeling bad.

"Oh my god. My brother did that?"

"Ah, don't worry about it."

"Still, that looks bad."

"Looks pretty roguish, if you ask me. Can't say I look all that tough, but I do have that tough guy air about me now."

Ian looked over at him; "You're lucky to be alive. Next time you're confronted like that, don't try to take them on by yourself."

Ryan looked up at Ian; "We had no choice in the matter. We had to fight back whether they had a weapon or not."

Ian grudgingly acknowledged this. How he hated this town sometimes, and its abilities to crush dreams, like those of his daughter. He wished Dara could be there with Ryan, and Becca and the others. How she would've loved them all. Again, he wished there were more he could've done for her. He felt a hand squeeze his shoulder, and saw Damien looking back at him. Ian could only nod, and smile.

Becca spoke up, "Alright, I think you all know the two of us. I haven't told you about the first time we met, though."

Ryan did a mockingly horrified face, "No, don't tell them about that."

Becca shushed him by putting her hand to his mouth, and blowing a kiss his way, while winking. Everyone laughed, and Ian felt a whole lot better.

Ryan smiled as he looked over at Becca. She indeed did start talking about the first time they met, and she was laughing here and there because she had remembered how shy he had been around her at first. Eric laughed himself.

"Hey, it was not a bed of roses the first time around."

Ryan threw his brother an angry look, "Dude, don't tell them about that."

"Why not? Everyone has *got* to know how obnoxious you were the first time, since I was the one you were giving lip to."

Becca put a finger to her chin, "Oh, yeah. You were a bit of a smart ass that first time we talked."

"Oh, come on, now. You can forgive and forget."

"I'll forgive . . . Not so sure I'll forget now, though. Hmmm."

Everyone laughed again, and Ian stood up. Raising his mug of soda high in the air, smiling as his eyes watered slightly. "I'd like to make a toast. All of you have come to mean a lot to me. So much that I would like to call the rest of you family."

The rest raised their glasses in unison, and clanged their mugs together as they stood as well. Ryan and Eric looked around, and never felt so much at home themselves, hoping that they indeed had all become a family.

Ian looked at everyone, and said, "I think all of us have gone through some pretty hard times over that past few months. I know it's been rough for me. We've all been able to push though it, though. Now, it seems as if all of that was meant to bring us all together in some way. I think I had told my two partners, here, exactly how I felt about our plight. We are all knights, I think. We have come into the dragon's lair, and have born the armor that will help us get through all of this. We've lost much, yeah. At least, we have all found each other. Therefore, I dub this group the Knight family. I think we've sufficiently earned that right."

The boys in the group nodded, as did Allan and Damien. When Ian sat down, they asked if he was really going to get something put together that would actually make them all a legal family.

"I think we can bend the rules, in our own way. Shows how much strength we have."

Matthew spoke up, "That shows that we've got balls." At this, everyone laughed, but Matt knew it was more out of surprise.

Ryan looked over at him, "We certainly do."

❧

The town seemed to stand still as Ryan looked out the back panel of Lorna's car as the procession followed them to the Grant Hill Cemetery. Becca held his hand as they rode over. The mass had been a small service with just those proclaimed among the Knight family. Allan, Damien, Ian and Eric had agreed to be the pallbearers. They were riding in another car. Demi was in this car, too. She was sitting next to Becca, as Melissa sat up front with her mother.

The minister was a friend of Ian's, reciting something Ryan couldn't quite hear himself as he watched his father being lowered into the ground. He hadn't been sure what he could say. There was so much he hadn't been able to say, and so much he wanted to tell his father. If only Mrs. Sandler were still alive, she would've made sure these last dark years never existed. Becca looked at him as he buried himself in that thought. He couldn't help it, though. The last years hadn't allowed him and Eric to be close to his father. He wanted to blame Quartz, but that would be too easy. He felt he should've tried to understand his father a lot sooner. Demi reached over and placed her own hand on Ryan's shoulder. The thing that made Ryan feel even worse was that he couldn't cry, nor did he feel the overwhelming grief at that moment. Eric, though, was allowing his own tears to fall; though his face was still. Had there been more to this death that just burying his father? Ryan felt like perhaps he was burying part of himself, here. This would be the end to all his childhood grudges, and his constant effort to prove himself to his father.

All that was left as his father was finally in the ground was Ryan and Eric, the Sandler men. The boys had died with their father, along with their dreams of one day making him proud as he watched them accomplish their dreams.

Not far from the procession, Scarlette stood there and watched. She hadn't been able to give her own brother a funeral. She had only been able to bury him, in a dirty grave by a girl that wanted to die with him. She wished there could've been more of a legacy for her brother. She was his legacy, she supposed. She had promised him that she would strike down people like her father. At that moment, she just stood, and let her tears fall. She saw that Ryan could not cry. So, she cried for him, as she cried for her brother, and for Jamey, that waitress of long ago that had given her a bowl of soup, and played big sister for that one moment that they knew each other. Most of all, Scarlette grieved for Mina Thorne, who had died with her brother. As Ryan had, she also buried her childhood with this. All that was left was Scarlette, and she felt that was a poor substitute for the girl that Lenny had struggled so hard to protect. They all grieved.

12

Loving From Behind a Wall

In my secret little world,

I never thought or imagined that someone would find me the way that you had on that day.

I gave up on everything, and everyone but the little characters in my stories.

Never stopping to think that you saw beyond that, being close, you opened me up . . .

Now all I can think, Why did I stay there, all this time?

Though I think I know why, Part of me always was waiting for your touch.

I have always been afraid, but with you I am not.

I'm thinking right now, all I want is you, love, because there's no one else for me.

Whenever we are close,

Together, All I want to do is hold and love you, protecting you from any pain.

I'll do it all for you, love, take the pain for you if I could. Cry your tears for you; take your pain and sadness. Even then, hoping it's enough

I'll hold you close to me, wishing I had met you before, Wishing I knew you then and wanting you now and forever not letting go.

You're the only one that I have opened myself to, The only one who has seen

The true me that was afraid now I run to you trusting you fully.

Let me get closer, I'll dry your tears looking in your eyes,

I'll be smiling at you, hoping you'll smile too. Or I'll share your tears with you.

Because all that I want is to understand your heart, Which beats along with mine.

Our two hearts are as one. Together, in pain, happiness, and love.

- *Songs of Demi*
  Light of Hope Album

Melissa knocked on Ryan's door around midnight. He was barely asleep so he didn't mind. He poked his head out of the door, and asked, "What's wrong?"

"I can't sleep. I think Dave might be out there, tonight."

"How do you know?"

"I don't know. I just have that weird feeling again."

He opened his door, and walked her to her room. He went in, checking the frame of the window, and making sure the two latches he'd added were secure. He was trying to figure out if there was some way to open them from the outside. He had actually been on the roof that afternoon, testing the latches with any tools he could think of. When he had mangled three crowbars trying to open the window, he had looked in at Melissa and gave her a thumbs-up. He wasn't sure why she was so worried now. He told her so at that moment.

"I totally burglar-proofed this window. What are you worried about?"

"The thing is, I heard from Scarlette that Dave was hanging out with this other friend of his. She told me he might be just as crazy."

"He is. Why would she tell you that, though?"

"Well, the thing that bothered me was for me not to worry about them because she would deal with them, herself."

He slowly turned his head to look at her, in the dark, and he hoped that she could not see how he strained to keep the worry out of his face.

"What's wrong?"

"Nothing. She told me something like that, too."

"What do you think?"

"I don't know what to think of her, sometimes. At times, she acts like a friend, at other times she acts like someone I don't even know."

"Did you get to know her in the first place?"

"I guess I hadn't. She was the one that introduced herself to Becca and me."

"I guess she was feeling lonely."

"I hope that's it. When I look into her eyes, there's something about her that makes me feel like she sees someone else when she looks at me."

"I can't sleep. I keep having bad dreams of Dave coming back."

Ryan nodded, and held up one finger for her to wait a moment. He went back to his room, closed the door and turned on the lights. When he came back out, the lights were off again. Also, he was holding a large bundle in his arms.

"I'll put my futon by the window, and sleep on the floor ok?"

"You sure?"

"If you have a bad dream, all you have to do is call for me, and I'll be around, ok?"

"Do you think Becca would mind?"

"Why would she? I mean, you're my little sister now, right?"

"I guess. Thanks for doing this."

He winked at her, like Eric would so many times when he had felt unsure, but tried to keep appearances that everything was fine. He even smiled for her. Eric came out of his room, and playfully hit Ryan on the back of the head.

"You make way too much noise. What's up?"

Melissa looked down, and muttered, "Bad dreams."

Eric did just as Ryan did, bringing his own futon and a sleeping bag. He smiled at Melissa, and muttered, "Well, we'll protect you from the bad dreams. Let's get our stuff set up before mom wakes up, though."

They had their sleeping bags set up in moments, just under the window where Dave used to come through. Even if he found his way in, he would have to deal with them. As they fell asleep, Melissa watched them both. Just that afternoon, they had buried their father, but here they were, trying to make her feel better.

As she fell asleep, she whispered, "I love you guys."

Eric spoke up, his voice incredibly soft; "We love you, too." Then his voice became deadpan as he ordered, "Now, go to sleep."

Lester swaggered around the stage as he carried the props out to the stage. He had been trying to keep his mind off of the girls he had seen on the way into the amphitheater only a few hours ago. How aroused he felt when he had seen the small outfits they wore to these things. He saw one of the other members of the band run toward him, a guy named Daniel, who only bathed the day of a show. That didn't seem to matter at this point, though, since Daniel was having a shit attack. Lester found himself giggling at that.

"What the hell's so funny?"

"You."

"Lester we don't have time for this shit. Lucifer just had himself a fucking overdose. The medics are getting him to the nearest hospital."

"So, the concert's history."

"Fuck, no!"

"If Lucifer isn't here, how the hell do you expect to run the show?"

"We have a full house out there. I don't know if Lucifer talked to somebody, but in this town we're big news. You're going on as lead vocalist."

"You're serious, aren't you?"

Daniel just kept looking at him with a pissed off expression. He was even more exasperated when Lester perked up.

"Alright, I'll do it. We gotta do one of my songs, though."

"We haven't rehearsed that worth a shit. You should've told us about it so we could put some time in."

"I didn't know if you'd bother even looking at it."

"Well, we're looking at it, now."

He pulled a thin set of sheets from inside one of the amplifiers. "It's alright. I called this piece Death Machine. It's death metal, with a steady quick beat, you got that?"

"Whatever you say, dude. I'll run this by the other guys. Just get your shit together, and put something flashy on."

"Oh, yes, I will."

"Well, hurry up. Go to Lucifer's dressing room and pick something out! I don't care what!"

"I'll be back."

When he came back on stage, Lester wore a black tank top, and a tight pair of leather pants. The audience screamed for him. For one paranoid moment, he felt like they knew who he actually was. The thought made him break out a sweat, although everyone up close that saw it must've thought that he was just getting used to the heat of the stage lights.

He screamed out, "Yeah!" The crowd went wild, and he loved it. He looked down at the foot of the stage, and saw three young girls. He pronged his three fingers and made a gesture that he would see them later. They screamed with delight, and he thought that he had never heard anyone so excited to die.

He looked out at the crowd, and asked them all, "You want a ride?"

They screamed.

"I said, do you want a ride?"

They screamed louder this time, those three girls in front made a grab for his ankles. He almost forgot himself and scowled at them, but he quickly composed himself and screamed back at the crowd.

"Come take a ride, then. Ride with me in my Death Machine."

They all screamed as he took a bow, and gestured to the band. They began to pick up a heavy beat, quick tempo, just as he had asked. He was glad they hadn't tried to change his piece. He wouldn't have killed them for it, but he would surely have made them regret it.

His words came out in a scream as he held the microphone to his mouth, making the feedback fade out as he screeched the first few words.

Crawling through the grinding sand,
I thought of all I left behind,
Charging into the fire, feeling your heavy hand,
Resting on my back and keeping my face to the ground,

Then he lowered his voice to a croak that made him sound like one of his victims, having screamed until their throat was raw. It gave him a bad turn, but his eyes were already glazed as he relived the moment. He would tell them all what he saw. He would show them all, the world through his eyes, and make them love it. They would have no choice in the matter. He would make them see what he wanted them to see. Such power he felt on the stage, and it was like a drug. It would never satisfy him, though. It would never fill him the way his nocturnal life had.

The three girls came backstage later, and they were all well built. However, two of them were with a larger group that was waiting for them outside. He did the best he could with them, and asked for their number. One of them said that they shouldn't since they had a boyfriend, but gave it to him anyway. The other gave him her address, and another time when she would be available. He took her by the shoulders firmly, looking her in the eye, and demanded that she not lie to him. She let out a squeal, and whispered as sensuously as she could, "Oh, yes, master. I will not leave you hanging."

The last one told him that she had hitchhiked to the concert, and hoped to see Lucifer. Inwardly, he growled at that, but held her close. "I can't let you go home, then."

"Why not?"

"I must have you as my own . . . Forever."

"You want me?" Then she looked away from him for a moment; unaware of the large pair of pliers he had behind him. Just then, one of the other girls came back in, and smiled with embarrassment.

"I forgot my jacket back here."

He pulled the girl in his arms closer, and whispered, "I want you to wait for me just down the steps, alright?"

"The ones leading outside?"

"Yeah."

She obediently went where he instructed her to, swaying her hips as she looked seductively back at him, over her shoulder. He winked at her, and watched her descend slowly. As soon as she was gone, he leaned back against the back of an amplifier, and left his pliers inside. Then he went over to the girl as she searched for her jacket.

"Are you sure you left it here?"

"I know I had it on me."

"Let's check out front. It might be out there, sitting on your seat."

"Are you kidding? I wouldn't leave that jacket out there. That thing cost me-"

Daniel came in, holding a suede jacket, "Hey, dude. I found this on one of the seats out there."

Lester looked to the girl, "Is that yours?"

She smiled again, this time completely red, "I'm so sorry."

"It's alright. Anyone could've made that mistake. I'll call you later."

She turned to face him with stars in her eyes, "Really? Hmm . . . ok. I'll tell my boyfriend I'll call him tomorrow night."

He gave her a lurid gaze, his eyes moving to her midriff. "You do that."

She excused herself, and went on her way. As soon as she was gone, he took the pliers from inside the amplifier and put it under his belt. He moved down the stairs to join his victim. He regretted that he could only take one tonight, but he guessed that no one would be asking for her any time soon. It was low risk for him. He led her to a dilapidated shed.

"Is this your place?"

"Yeah. Just let me get the keys so we can get in." He pulled out a set of keys, even though he hadn't needed any of them since the lock was broken. He dropped it on the floor, "Damn it, now I can't see them."

"I'll get them." She bent over to pick up his keys, and never saw his face reach the near state of euphoria as he brought down the heavy end of the pliers onto the back of her neck. He caught her before she crumpled to the ground, and pushed in the door to the shed. He tromped into the shed; carrying her as best he could, and dropped her to the floor. She was muttering something about her father not wanting her to go to the concert, and how she had to run away.

"He was saying there was someone out there. You'll protect me from him, right?"

"Shut up."

"My daddy was really worried."

"Shut up, I said."

"Can you call my daddy? I know he's probably wondering where I am right now."

He pulled out the long tire iron he had hidden in the shed and brought it down on her skull this time. She was still moving, so he hit her again. He continued until she stopped moving. Once she was completely still, he leaned in close to hear her breath, and could feel it coming out weakly. He turned her over so that she lay on her back, and opened her legs so that he could penetrate her. She couldn't scream, but her mouth was wide open as she tried. Lester pulled his belt from its loops, and wrapped it around her neck. He tightened it, strangling her as he penetrated her. Her eyes widened as she looked into his, and she tried to scream again when she saw the black holes looking right back at her.

He leaned in and placed his mouth over hers so he could kiss her. He smiled as her last breath went into him. Even an hour after she was dead, he continued on. He realized that he couldn't bury her around the amphitheater. So, he carried her and took her into his trailer, which he no longer had to share. He had a large trunk for his clothes, or his tools. He threw it all out onto the floor hurriedly, and stuffed her in there. Then, he went outside, and helped the band to haul stakes so they could pull out as soon as possible.

The hitchhiker's name had been Janine Taylor. She was seventeen, and had actually been her father's favorite. She never could get along with her mother very well since she turned twelve. She wanted to go to the Devil's Advocate concert, but that was one thing her father forbade her. She told him she hated him as she stomped out the door, and had thumbed her way to the next state.

Lester actually drove to the woods just outside of her town, without his knowledge of such, one week after he had killed her. He had taken off her clothes, and had her over and over beside a campfire in the woods. He later buried her, while Lucifer was in the hospital recovering. He had played with her head over the week, emulating oral sex, and putting make-up on it so that she looked like a doll. Now, he had become bored with it, and he threw that into the fire as well watching as her clothes became ashes along with the skull. He made sure there was nothing left, using a small shovel to throw dirt over the dying embers of his murderous fire. He returned to the band's car just before dawn, and drove back to the band's campsite.

Lucifer was sitting on his bed, and waiting for him when he got into his trailer. He had been hoping to clean up before anyone in the band noticed that his trailer was a mess.

"Hey, pal. You feeling any better?"

"I'm not here to talk about me, Lester."

"Oh, yeah. I stood in for you, last week. You're not mad about that, are you?"

"I heard the crowd loved you."

"They sure did. I wouldn't mind doing that again, sometime."

"You will, pretty soon. What were you doing last night?"

"I don't see why that would concern you."

"You had someone, didn't you?"

"Doesn't matter."

"Look. I don't care about what you do. If you do it enough, though, the police are going to be looking for the band."

"Now you're telling me what to do?"

"Just try not to get used to this. You can't take a girl in every town. I mean, just try to pace yourself."

"Are you telling me what to do?"

"I'm telling you not to get used to doing it a lot."

"You got a deal. I didn't do anything, though."

"No, you didn't. I never saw you. Get some sleep."

Lester slept very well the whole morning, while Lucifer pulled the band together and finally got everything on the road. Lester barely felt his trailer moving. There was another town in view, and Lester was still not full.

Derek was getting Dave a drink from the mini-bar, even managed to mix a drink for him. Dave, himself, was admiring the rifles on the gun rack, thinking deeply about how to deal with Ryan and Eric. In fact, he was thinking of the best way to do away with the two brothers. That is, a permanent solution that would not be traced back to him.

"These yours?"

"They're my step-dad's."

"Are these service pieces?"

"Nah. They're all hunting rifles. I used to go out with him, sometimes. He can get really crazy, too. We have a few kegs of gunpowder out back. He's even managed to secure some napalm. He pretty much taught me how to make pipe bombs, and crap like that."

"Think you could teach me about it?"

"Sure. What would you want to know?"

"Teach me everything you know."

"Alright. That shouldn't be a problem."

"Cool. Got anything like combat knives, or anything like that?"

"Sure."

"What about pistols, semi-automatics, or even an Uzi?"

"Sure. Can't hunt deer with any of those, though."

"Who says we'll be hunting deer?"

Derek looked over at him as he handed the drink to him, "You're serious?"

"Oh, yeah."

"What do you want to do?"

"I want to make that little shit, the one that's fucking my sister, to pay. I want to get rid of her new friends, too. Her only friend should be me."

Derek realized at that moment that Dave was quite psychotic. It wasn't just a matter of simply scaring the sister's friends. It was his obsession with his sister talking at that moment. He wasn't sure he even knew what creature stood before him. He had been thinking of putting a scare into Ryan by driving onto the sidewalk in front of the little shit, or something like that. Of course, Dave had brought a knife with him that last fight and Derek had to wonder what it was that Dave had intended. Finally, Derek shook his head, and huskily muttered, "Dude, no way."

"That guy, what's his name, he's fucking your ex too, isn't he? I guess having my sister isn't enough for him. Don't you want to make them both pay?"

"You don't know that."

"I can see it in her eyes when she looks at him. She wants to fuck him, but she doesn't want to fuck me."

Derek was trying to hide his disgust, "Well, how do you know they're doing anything?"

"I just do. Besides, there's a way to put all the blame on him. We leave two of these by their house, the old one where he was just looking at it. We tell him that we have to meet him in the gym, and lock him in the equipment room with the guns nearby. He put one of those putty bombs on the lock and time it after we do our thing."

"What will be our thing, Dave?"

"We're going to hunt my sister, and her friends. Then, we'll pin the whole thing on him. I know a guy with the cops, someone in charge that will help, too."

"This whole thing will never work. They can trace the guns back to us, and then we'll be in deep shit."

"Not with this cop in charge, since he cut me a break before."

"He's not likely to cut you a break again."

"He will when he realizes what I'm planning. He wanted me to get rid of some people for him. He would cover it up. This is perfect."

"Well, then. I guess the only one who can stop you is myself. What if I decide not to teach you any of this combat stuff?"

"You will. You want that cunt of yours back, or you want her to be sorry she left you behind. Isn't that what you told me?"

"Well, yeah. Still, this is going another extreme. What would killing her do for me, man?"

"It would show her who the boss is, and you want to get rid of that little shit boyfriend of hers, don't you?"

"Well, now that I think about it. I would've done the same thing in his position, you know?"

Dave mockingly imitated him, and whacked him across the face. "Grow up, shit head. Your ex girlfriend is fucking some country bumpkin dude, and you're going to tell me that you understand him?"

"I don't hate him. Not like you do."

"I don't hate him. I just want him dead for touching my sister. Only I can touch my sister."

"That's sick, dude."

"Think what you like. I want some revenge, though. You're going to teach me everything you know about all this combat shit. We'll set up things to go down a month from now. I'll talk to my contact, who's with the police."

"You want to kill all the new people hanging out with your sister."

"Yeah."

"You want to make it look like a massacre, so you'll kill a few people more besides them."

"Yeah."

"Then, you'll blame the whole thing on my ex's new guy."

"Yeah."

"This'll never work, but I'm guessing you're too crazy to really care about that, huh?"

"So what?"

"Yeah. So, what . . . Let's do it."

As Lester screamed the last lines of his set, he looked over at the two girls who had been looking at him through the whole show. They had been so into it, and they seemed to bounce in their tiny outfits so wonderfully that he hoped his tight pants hadn't made it too obvious.

We trust you,
Hail you as the leader,
We know you care.

You are truth,
Mien Fuehrer

He waited until the last beats erupted from behind, as Daniel finished off with his drum solo. Lester looked down at the two girls as the curtains in the old theatre closed on the band. He gave them both a quick hand signal, telling them he would meet them both outside. When he told the band he'd go outside for a breath, they let him go. Something about him made them want as much distance as they could get from him. He had hoped that they hadn't given that impression on stage. He had hoped that they haven't been giving him odd looks, making everyone know him. He got outside of the theatre, and into a sandy alley way in this seashore town. He hated how the sand was everywhere, around here. He hadn't even gone to the beach, but the strong breezes that comforted him during the concert had carried the sand with them. He now shook his shirt as the two girls approached him.

One of them was already blushing, "Hi,"

"Hi. Is the other girl here?"

"I don't know. I just met her at the concert, but she said she'd be back because she had to use the toilet really bad."

"How spiteful . . . I like that."

"Where are we going?"

"There's a shed by the lake. Do you know it?"

"Yeah. A lot of the kids go there to do weed, or have sex or whatever."

"Or whatever?"

"Yeah. I don't know. Is that where we were going?"

"Do you know a better place?"

"Guess I don't."

"Come on then. I just thought of something."

Unseen by her, he dropped a X-rated greeting card on the floor, telling the other girl to wait for him. He inwardly laughed at how that seemed to keep them waiting for him, somehow. For now, he led this girl to his car, and dropped his keys, "Crap. I can barely see in this light."

"Those stage lights must kill your eyes."

"You got that right. Could you get them?"

She bent over to pick them up. He felt and heard the sickly crunch as he hit her on the back of the head with his crowbar. He had placed it on the space between the windshield and the hood. She hadn't seen it because it had been on the driver's side, and hadn't even noticed when he leaned over to grab it when she was commenting on the stage lights. With one hand, he held her by the waist before she fell to the ground, and used the other hand to open his car door. He stuffed her into the passenger side, and closed the door behind her. He hadn't been able to disable the interior lock device on this car, since it was the band's car. He kept the crowbar with him so he could knock her out in case she woke up while they were traveling. So he did drive, to the hiking area, where he had discovered a small shed for indigents. Still, he decided to use it anyway. He put her over his shoulder, and sat her on the floor of the shaft, using hand-cuffs to bind her to one of the beams. Her mouth was bleeding pretty badly now, and he hoped she hadn't bled on the seat. As he walked back towards his car, he could see drops of blood on the dirt, and realized her mouth had started bleeding when he hefted her over his shoulder.

He nervously tried to look at his reflection in the window, and had noticed that his black shirt was a little darker around the waist, but his leather pants simply looked a little wet. He got back into his car, and found the other girl waiting for him. He told her he wanted to go some place more private, and she commented that he was a little rank.

"Well, I was helping the guys break down."

"Well, ok. If you want, we could go to my place, to do this."

"No, it's ok. I know a great place."

"Oh my god. You're not taking me to the Love Shed, are you?"

"The what?"

"That shed by the beach. Everyone goes there."

"Oh. Oh, no. I've got someplace better."

He led her to his car, and she looked back at him. "Where's the equipment?"

"Oh, that stuff goes into the big trailer out yonder. This is the band's car. They let me use it every so often. Is there a problem?"

"I guess not." She got into the car.

He pulled out of the alleyway, slowly and hoping to knock her out before he joined the back road traffic. He pointed at the garbage can he had knocked over before coming back. "Would you look at that?"

She turned to look at the overturned can as a few cats began to gather around the garbage, "Fucking cats."

His crowbar came up, hitting her squarely on the temple, hard enough for him to hear the crunch. Her head dropped onto his lap, and he began to drive towards the shed in the hiking spot.

When the first girl woke up, she saw Lester looking over at her as he raped his second pick-up. She began to scream and whimper as she watched them. The second girl could only grunt. She was barely recovered from the shock of the blow, and then she felt him forcing his way inside her. Her grunt became an inarticulate scream, and she beat at his chest. She looked at him in the eyes, and she recognized him, "Lester?"

He recognized her, too, "Alley?"

"Oh, god, don't do this."

"I told you to stay away from me."

He pulled his leather pants over, and tied the legs around her neck. He strangled her as he continued to rape her. The other girl could only look on, as he did his ritual of catching his victim's last breath. As soon as he was done with her, he looked up at his first pick-up, and whispered, "Your turn."

He stuffed the two girls in the trunk of the car, and called Lucifer's cell.

"Lester, where the hell are you?"

"Never mind that. Are you guys pulling out?"

"Yeah, we're hauling stakes, dude. Are you coming along?"

"I'll be along later. Listen, where do you think you'll be in say by tomorrow?"

"We'll be at the roadside camp just outside of Cainland."

"Alright. I'll meet you there."

"Lester, have you been like busy tonight?"

"Don't ask."

"Alright. We never talked."

"Thanks, Lucifer."

"Ugh. Don't thank me. Just get your ass moving." He hung up.

He found a rock garden in the desert; some of the stones were as tall as he. He was satisfied, and began to dig. He was able to make a hole that was a good five by five by five, by his rough estimate. He pulled the girls over to the hole, but couldn't bring himself to drop them into the hole, especially Alley. He could barely keep his eyes from watering as he pulled off her clothes. When he finished stripping her down, he dropped her into the hole, and threw dirt over her. He had his way with the other girl, the first pick-up of the night, and then he stripped her down. He started a fire, and threw the clothes into it, watching as Alley was burned out of his life. For that one moment, something happened that he never thought could happen. He began to moan, his whimpering grew into a wail, and he could not enjoy this fire as he tried to watch it through his blurred eyes. How he hated Alley for making him feel anything, for being here this night. He wanted to die, himself, then and there. He dropped the other body into the hole, and through the dirt and tumbleweed in. He finished only two hours later, and as an afterthought, he threw his own shirt into the fire.

Then next morning, he threw the ashes of his fire onto the burial site the next morning. He had seen a medium polished stone not too from where he slept, and placed that gently onto the gravesite. He whispered, "Goodbye." Still, he hunched over the site for a long time, and finally got up. He drove the car, shirtless, and pulling up the hood of the car so he wouldn't get sunburn.

When he joined the band at the roadside stand, he handed Lucifer the keys; "I'm really tired right now. So, I'm just going to sleep for a bit."

Daniel was about to protest, but Lucifer grabbed his shoulder, and turned to Lester, "We'll be going into Cainland in six hours. Can you be ready by then?"

"Definitely."

"Get some sleep then."

As Lester went into his trailer, Daniel complained, "Why does he need to sleep so much, anyway?"

Lucifer looked over at him, and muttered, "Truth be told, I'd prefer to know that he's sleeping, than not know where he went?"

"I'll have to ask him."

"Don't. That's an order. Just let it go. We've got stuff to do, anyway. On this song, do you think we can try a variation on the tempo?"

Lester didn't hear the rest. He could only dream of killing Alley, and it haunted him deeper than the waitress had.

❧

Nancy Damon had been her father's favorite out of her and her four brothers. She had been trying to prove that she could go off, and take care of herself. She had been a track star in high school, and was currently trying to get herself in shape for the next relay race at her school. However, meeting Lester made all of her striving, all that she had accomplished a moot point. Death never gave a person a chance to present credentials. It just came.

Alley Henderson had been going to business school for three years after barely making it out of high school. She had met Lester when she was going to an interview, and the memory of not being able to kill her had tormented him. Or had that somehow given him a chance to liberate himself from the life he was now embracing?

❧

Derek looked over the map that Dave had set up. Being a senior, he could leave campus after his fourth class. It hadn't bothered him before, being so old, and still in high school. Now, having met someone like David, he wondered if he should've pushed himself a little harder. Then, maybe he wouldn't be there, just then, waiting for Dave to join him as soon as the lunch bell sounded. How he hated being there at all, and for once, he actually thought that he shouldn't have tried to pull Becca away from the new guy, He should've actually tried to make peace instead of making such an ass of himself, and making an enemy of Ryan.

He muttered to himself, "Fuck this. I can't do it."

He heard a voice behind him, a sultry female voice, "It's too late to regret. Now, there is only one way out."

He felt a hand squeeze his arm, just above the elbow, and saw a flash of silver as he felt the metal blade come to rest at his neck. He thought he did pretty well to keep himself from panicking, not having pissed his pants.

"I wasn't going to do this. Look. I'm taking off right now."

"You're here. You had the intention of hurting, and destroying."

"Look! I said I'm not going to do it."

"You're right. You certainly won't, now." Scarlette pulled the sword to his throat, and cut him. His hands went up to his neck, and then his pants were soiled. Derek would be here when Dave came for the weapons, but she wanted to prepare something special.

Dave waited for the lunch bell to sound, having been sitting through his classes, and thinking of nothing else but punishing his sister. He so much wanted her back under his control. Now, she was out of reach, and he could not even get near her. Didn't matter, he'd get rid of all of her friends, and when he finally had her at the end of his barrel, he would make her beg, even spare her life if she let things go back to the way they were before. When the bell did sound, he almost fell over, having fallen asleep.

He got up from the desk sluggishly, rubbing his eyes as he stood up. When he stretched, he yawned loudly and trudged out of class. He went to the bathroom for a moment, knowing he would not have time later. He made his way out of the building, and towards the parking lot. When he got there, he would've wet his pants if it weren't for the fact he had gone already. He had been looking for Derek, and cursing the older boy for not coming out to meet him.

"Stupid, lazy ass drunk."

He stopped dead in his tracks when he saw Derek hanging from a tree, opened like a deer hide, and hanging over Dave's SUV, with his head missing. He had been like that for a while. Dave knew this because there had been so much blood already splattered onto his truck. He walked around the truck, and opened the back, his rifles waiting there for him. He grabbed one up, and was about to look down the barrel so he could get a good aim. There was a thud, and he heard a voice from behind him, which startled him. He felt relieved that he hadn't cocked the piece, or risk shooting it, thereby alerting everyone. The voice he heard was the sultry voice he heard in his dream.

"Do you enjoy penetrating your sister?"

He turned around, and saw Scarlette standing there, her sword held out at her side as she propped her shoe on Derek's severed head.

He could only utter a feral growl, but could not move. She kicked the head aside, as if annoyed by it. He watched as she twitched her wrist a little, and turned tail so he could run. He had never run so fast in his life, and as he ran into the halls of the school, he heard screams from all directions.

He pointed the gun in all directions, causing havoc and splitting whole groups of students as he yelled, "I need to find Eric Sandler! Somebody, tell me where he is! Damn it! Tell me now!"

The screams only served to annoy him. He cocked the gun, and began to fire into the crowd, killing seven, and injuring several more. Still, he demanded that everyone tell him where Eric was.

"She's trying to kill me! I need help! You stupid Assholes don't understand that she'll kill me!" More shots, more people died.

Among the injured was one of Eric's teammates from the football team, Rob Sterling. He waited until Dave had moved on to another hallway, and crawled outside.

Eric, Ryan and the rest were having lunch in the courtyard, by the tree. They'd heard shots ring out, and they told the girls to stay down. Rob stumbled through the heavy door, and staggered gratefully towards Eric.

"That guy's killing everyone. He's looking for you, so he didn't get you."

Eric ran to catch Rob before he fell. He eased Rob to the ground, and cradled his head, "Dude, you're hurt, you should've called an ambulance!"

"No!" Rob coughed out blood. Eric rubbed his back until the cough calmed down, and he realized that Rob must've taken a direct hit. As he helped Rob ease through the cough, he heard his friend whisper, "Just had to make sure he didn't find you. Don't let him get you, dude."

"I won't."

"Saturday would've been the first game I didn't ride the ben-" Rob died as Eric held him. He eased his friend to the ground, and they heard a few more shots ring out. He stood up, and looked to Ryan, "You stay here and watch them."

Ryan tried to sound reasonable, even though the anger was in his voice. "What can you do? Whoever he is has a gun."

"He's looking for me. So, I'll find him before he finds me."

Claudia was looking down at Eric's friend, and looked at Ryan. She hoped he wouldn't let his brother go into the building. Becca was already on her cell phone and talking to Damien. He told her to find some cover. She told him she was in the court-yard, and there wasn't much. He grumbled a bit, but was glad she wasn't in the building, he promised her he would get there as soon as he could.

Eric went into the building through the door Rob had come out of. He looked around, seeing that there were a few other students hiding under the stage, some of them trying to stifle their moans and frightened crying. He knelt down, and looked into the crawl space.

"Come in here."

"No. You all stay here, ok? A friend of mine is on his way here. In the mean time, keep under cover."

He stood up, and looked ahead, hearing that insistent voice again. "What are you, Crazy? He'll kill you."

"I'm the one he's looking for. Just stay here, ok?"

He walked off, and found himself exposed. Dave was looking right at him as he walked down the hall, coming out of the west wing doors.

"Eric, you got to help me, man!"

"What are you doing, Dave?"

"She's after me, man! That psycho bitch killed Derek, and now she's after me!"

"Who is? Look, put the gun down, and we can talk, ok?"

"Fuck you, man! I am not putting this down when she's out there!"

"Ok, ok. Listen, now. I want you to calm down. Tell me what happened, and we can talk through this."

"I didn't mean to hurt anyone, man!"

"Dave. People are dead. You killed them. You know Rob?"

"Aww, man. I told him not to play the fucking hero!"

"You made it necessary, by doing all this. Now, come on. Put the gun down, right now."

Allan came from around a corner behind Dave, and treaded stealthily towards David's back. Eric pretended not to notice, just as Allan had hoped.

"Now, Dave, I need to know. Is there anyone else helping you?"

"What the fuck you talking about, asshole? I just told you she's trying to kill me, man! I'm the only one left! Derek's all fucked up! He's fucking dead!"

Allan took that as a signal and put his pistol to Dave's temple, "Drop it, or I'll drop you, I swear to god!"

"Motherfucker!" Dave was about to raise the barrel towards Eric, until he heard Allan cock his gun. He did actually piss his pants, just then, about to drop his rifle. Allan yelled into his ear, "You hold on to that! You put it down slowly, got it?"

Dave did as he was told, and Allan threw Dave to the floor, not too far from the puddle of urine. Allan shoved Dave's face into the floor as he pulled his arms behind him, high on his back, and handcuffed him.

Damien arrived, and helped to secure Dave. He also tried to secure the rifle, picking it up with gloves.

Harry Quartz came in at that point, and had his people swarm the place. He looked down at Allan, who was trying to pull Dave to his feet.

"I'll take it from here."

This time, Damien snapped at him, "No! You are not going to have your people glaze over this one! People are dead!"

"That's no longer your problem. You were able to apprehend the suspect. Now, I can take it from here!"

Allan ignored all of this, and read David his rights.

"Hey, shut up over there! He's my suspect!" He raised his foot to kick Allan, which made him look up at Quartz menacingly.

"This isn't even your jurisdiction!"

"Yeah, he's right. This ain't even your jursisdictor."

Allan dropped Dave's head into the puddle of his own urine. This time, Quartz did kick Allan, who got back up, pulling back a fist. He heard several pistols cock at the same time. All of them were pointed at him, and Damien.

"Like I said. This ain't your jurisdiction." Harry walked over to help Dave up, and pulled him to his feet. "You don't need to worry about this. My boys will do the clean up ops. You guys can go home."

"You'll clean up, alright!"

"I don't know what you're talking about. You've seriously lost it. I mean, getting violent with a suspect in custody. That could be seen as police brutality. What would your people say if they knew?"

Allan wanted to fight Quartz; he no longer cared about the badge. "You son-"

Damien held his shoulder, "Don't. That piece of garbage isn't worth losing our jobs."

"You talking to me?"

"Take it however you like. This round is yours, sir."

"Damien! What the hell!"

Damien looked to Allan, and scowled. Allan subsided, but he wasn't happy about it, either as they watched Quartz walk out of the school with David in custody. Oddly enough, as well, there was no press outside to greet Quartz and his people. That was when they knew that Harry was going to cover the whole incident up. As they watched Harry walk Dave to his car, they saw that Harry undid the cuffs, and let Dave into the back seat. Defeated, they want to check on Becca and the others as Eric walked with them, and told them what he saw.

"Now, what the fuck happened? Why would you go ape-shit like that?"

"There was this girl, and she had killed Derek before I got there."

"So, where is he?"

"She hung him out on a tree, over my truck."

"Stupid kid. You mean, she hanged him."

"That would mean that there would still be a body to hang on a noose. No, this guy was cut up, and set to hang and dry like a deer's hide."

"What a sick bitch."

"I don't care. I'm staying away from her."

"Well, listen. I need you to go after those two guys that were trying to arrest you."

"My fucking pleasure. She might be around, though. I saw her hanging out with one of those cops, or that lawyer friend of theirs. There's no way I'm going to try to go up against her, though."

"Do you want me to charge you for this, or are you going to do what I tell you?"

"Do what you tell me."

"Don't worry about the body, either. I'll deal with it, ok?"

"Yeah, sure."

Harry parked on a residential street, not far from Becca's. "Now, listen. I need you to get rid of those girls, and those two cops, ok?"

"Fine. Can you get me off the charges for what happened at the school?"

"Don't worry about it. We got the insanity defense."

"What the hell are you talking about?"

"You, kid, are one crazy little shit. This is where you get off. Now, do what I told you, ok?"

"What about that crazy bitch?"

"I'll send some of my boys to deal with her, ok?"

"Alright. Can you let me out?"

Harry got out of the car, and opened the door for Dave. "Now, get your ass out there, and do what you have to do."

Dave grunted, and ran off into the dark.

Harry drove along the red light district, hoping to catch someone turning a trick, since he felt so lucid at that point. He saw a tall blonde woman, who looked a lot like Lester's first victim. It was Pam Fanning, or whatever name she had now. He pulled over next to her, and told her, "You're not supposed to be here."

"I know that shit head."

He pulled out his badge, and showed it to her, "I mean it. Get in."

She did. As she settled into the passenger seat, she closed the door behind her. Pam had aged a little; she looked like she was coming off from a high.

"You're in big trouble, you know? There's only one way out of this, you know?"

"What? You want me to do you?"

"I might even pay you, if you're good."

"I'll make it good."

He drove his car up into the woods, and had her for an hour. He then told her he would have to take her in.

"Fucker, you can't just take me in. I just did you!"

"Well, I guess no one would ever know, right? Got any friends that can bail you out?"

"Fuck, no!"

"Right, right."

"I'll just have to tell everyone what kind of cop you are then."

She didn't get much farther than that, because he had pulled his own belt from its loops, and wrapped it twice around her neck. He strangled her, and waited a few moments before he confirmed that she was dead. He went to the road along Route 88, where his son had gone, just before starting his rampage. He saw a cluster of rocks not too far away, and pulled over. He pulled Pam's dead body out of his car, and dragged her over to the cluster. He saw the bones that were resting there, and shook his head.

"You're so fucking sloppy too."

He dug a four by four by four feet hole, dumping the bones in, and then Pam, having stripped her down. He built a fire from the tumbleweed, and some rocks for a cairn. He threw the clothes into the fire, and as he watched the fire burn away the last traces of his crime, he sighed in relief. He promised himself that he would not do it, again. It was only then that he realized that Lester had taken after him, after all.

--13--

Handle without Care

I wished for someone who won't say goodbye
If I knew it would hurt this much,
I would've gone out farther, more than I had allowed myself to go at the time.
I would have allowed myself to drift

If I was so far off shore, why did you call me back?
Why did you pull me in, and make me care, when all I wanted was to drift?

I drifted on the ship I called my life. I can't sail anymore, though for the boat is broken.

That, which was my dreams, is now thoroughly thrashed by the torrent of emotions I felt, while with you. I hang by that which I thought was love, and finding myself stranded on this large shore,
Where I can hear the voices of others nearby, the crowd starts to approach me from far away

I don't want them to come. I want to drift; I want to dream, believing only in that which I treasure.
But that was you, and now you're gone.
So I ask . . . why ask me how I feel.
Why ask if you're only going to say goodbye?

I don't understand how we suddenly come to this to the point where we can't even talk, to the point where "friends" is an unwelcome word, to the point where my words are only like so much noise.

Am I just that? Have I become "just a noise"?
If I've become a Noise . . . what's the point in bringing me here?
If I'm a NOISE, then everyone is listening.
Everyone is listening because when I speak, and all that comes out is my Noise.

I close my eyes and shut my ears, I cover my mouth so that I don't have to speak.
I cover my mouth so that I don't have to make noise.
If I do let me be the only one that hears it, because MY Noise belongs to me.
I want it to belong only to me again.
For all you did was get me through ALL those NON-Existent Hours.

- Songs of Demi
Light of Hope Album

    Scarlette was glad that Ian had already left to join Allan and Damien for breakfast at the Thompson's place. She was happy for him because there was finally a place for him, where he could be himself. She felt that he could only give so much to her, since he barely knew her. He wasn't at all like the animals she had met for the past few months. It was best not to think of them, now. The thoughts of Harold leaning over her as she lay in a drug induced daze, thoughts of her father leaning over her; all came back to haunt her at that moment. She chased the thoughts away. Then she thought of Ryan, about seeing the beginnings of a monster within him. Those thoughts faded as she saw Ryan's older brother, and how wonderful he seemed. Her thoughts began to twist, and she saw Eric holding Melissa, fondling her. She could even imagine him forcing himself on her. She knew that she would have to destroy that monster later. For now, she looked outside, and saw two cops walk up the path to Ian's door. She saw that one of them stayed by the car, and he didn't look like he was particularly enjoying this at all, so she answered the door hoping that was a good sign. She could only wonder how they knew where she was, but she guessed that while she had been stalking Dave, and Derek, one of them might have been doing the same.

"Is there a problem, officers?"

One of them reached out, and grabbed her by the hair, pulling her face to theirs, most unforgivable. The one cop that had grabbed her leaned towards her, and turned to nod at the others.

"This must be her."

Another of them grabbed her by the arm, pulling her out of the house. "Come here, you little bitch." She already was already marking him for death.

The last cop went on to the car to open the door for them all, while the cop that held her had reached lower and grabbed her ass. They saw that she was smiling, and slapped her across the face. "This ain't funny, you little bitch."

"I know what you want, but we need to go someplace private."

"Where is this private place?"

"It's this old house I used to live in."

"Where?"

"I'll give you directions. Wait, it's the old Frankfurt place. You guys want some place private, so you can fuck me, right?"

The two cops that had collected her, looked at each other and laughed, shoving her into the back seat of the car. The third said nothing, and drove as she gave him directions. They found her old house, her first place of residence. The cop that sat with her reached behind her, and pulled her hair down her back.

"What the fuck is this?"

She feigned being in pain, which wasn't that hard. She only had to pant and shed crocodile tears. "It's my old place, seriously. Even my guardian knows."

Satisfied, he loosened his grip, reached up, and shoved her head forward, onto the other seat. She allowed this, letting them feel like they had control. She turned her head to her tormentor, and rasped, "Before I kill you, I'm going to cut your manhood off, and let you suffer a little." The driver seemed to shiver at this, but she pretended not to acknowledge him. She could feel that he was simply disgusted by his two partners, she could see he was straining not to shake his head. Good. That showed he had a lot of will power.

He brought the car to a stop in front of the old Frankfurt house. One of them looked to the driver, and muttered, "You keep a lookout, chicken shit."

The driver nodded furiously, trying to keep the act up, shedding his own crocodile tears. Scarlette applauded him, and realized that he was her reinforcement if her plan went awry. She feigned desperation, allowing them to lead her into the old house. They broke the flimsy door in, and pushed her to the floor. One of them was loosening his belt as he came towards her. She emulated fear, and told them to wait.

"Let me dress for it, at least. I got this whole lingerie set in my old room. It's right there, see?" She pointed frantically at the door behind her. "You can even check the room, and you'll see there aren't any windows."

They indeed looked in, and saw that the room was simply a box, and the only window was a small one, from which a dog would have trouble getting in or out. Satisfied, they told her to hurry up.

She went into the room, and only closed the door slightly, not wanting to arouse suspicion. She opened the closet, and saw her sword leaning against the far right corner, just where she had left it. She pulled it to her, and placed it under her coat, clipping it onto her belt. She decided she was ready, and opened the door wider.

When she went out to greet them, the two cops were in their boxers and tank tops, but they still had their guns on the floor within reach.

"What the hell, why are you still dressed?"

She looked at them both, and seethed, "Animals." She pulled out her sword, and cut off her tormentor's hand before he could get his gun. The other hadn't put his gun down, but her sword went through his neck before he could cock it. He crumpled to the floor, making his head tumble off as the torrent of blood showered her. Her tormentor screamed about his hand, trying to hold the stump as he bled uncontrollably. She grew annoyed with him, and pulled back her sword, only to stab him right through his crotch, cutting him off suddenly.

At that moment, the third came in through the door, and had his gun held up. He looked very brave, she thought. She looked at him a moment and Bobby Kennedy could only look confused as she charged right at him.

She drove her sword into him, just below his ribcage, and whispered, "Well, it seems you're a tad late."

He struggled to breathe, and rasped, "I came here to save you!"

She locked her eyes with his, and demanded, "Where were you when my father raped me, and killed my brother? Where were you when that pig, Harold, had his way with me while I was drugged? Could you help me ever forget that?" She turned the sword forty-five degrees to the right.

He looked at her, his face twisted in confusion as he tried to answer. She never gave him the chance, she simply uttered, "Exactly." She brought the sword up through him; cutting through bone and organ as it came up through his shoulder. His blood showered her as it spurted from him, and she shook with fury. She was now covered in innocent blood. She had known that he was waiting for the moment when the two others would be caught off guard. She knew he would try to save her if she had not been able to get to her sword. She knew that he had planned to save her from the beginning, and yet she could not stop herself from killing him. She had spilled innocent blood.

She shook her head, attempting to rationalize her actions, muttering, "He would've become an animal, himself." Still his eyes remained open as they gave her an accusing glare. She screamed at it, "No! Stop Looking at me! It's not my fault!"

His eyes continued to glare, and she began to cut at his face, thoroughly, until he couldn't be recognized. She realized that the only way she could redeem herself was to destroy another that she knew was a monster. She knew that David would probably be going home around this time. She also found herself thinking about Eric, the way he held Melissa. Only, in Scarlette's mind, he was fondling her. He would want to touch her, and hold her as he penetrated her. He would become a monster. She knew that if she took Eric's life, then Ryan would want to avenge his brother. She thought, she would rather Ryan end her life, since she thought they were alike in many ways. She had killed the old man for taking her brother away. Ryan would do the same. Everything would balance out. She would deal with him later, she decided. She needed only now to deal with David. She ran out of the Frankfurt place, having sheathed her sword, and went on to wait for David in his house.

She went into David's house, having gone in through a window he left open. He might've left it open out of sheer force of habit. He had used it for those occasions when he wanted to sneak out of the house to go to a party or something like that. Now, she would use it to wait for him, in his room. She looked on the floor, using the light of the moon to guide her, and saw a stack of glossy paper on the floor. She picked them up, and found herself looking at the photographs that he had taken of Melissa. Seeing that had convinced her that she surely needed to destroy him. She had also caused David to go on a rampage that ended up killing at least twenty-three students, and injuring forty others. It sickened her that he was still roaming free somehow. She had known he was because she had seen when Harry Quartz let him out of the car a few blocks away from the school.

So, she sat on his bed, covered in blood, and waiting for him. She would hunt the monsters, and hope that her brother had not seen her spill innocent blood.

❧

David walked home after trying to look for Melissa in the Million Dollar District, where she might be hanging out with her friends. He knew that Harry Quartz would be after him if he couldn't do away with the other girls. Still, he couldn't help feeling so fatigued. He needed some time to clear his head, so he went home. When he got to the front door of his house, he found black splotches on the porch step. Then he remembered a vision of Scarlette, and realized he did not want to go in. Somehow, he felt that she might be looking for him. She must've followed him home one day, he figured. He ran off, but his steps were so heavy that Scarlette had come to the window, just in time to see him run down the sidewalk. She knew where he was going, and used a burst of adrenaline to break the window outward, and pursue him. She would not let this monster destroy any more lives. She jumped onto the grass from the second floor, and was able to do a controlled tumble so she would not break anything. At that moment, she had all the skill of a jungle predator. She had become the very animal she was hunting, and she was thrilled.

As he approached his mother's new house, and could see the two cops that had managed to bring him down at the school. They were sitting in the living room, laughing and talking with his mother. He swore to himself that he would kill her, and them. He still wanted to keep Melissa as his pet, however. It still fueled his fantasies the way fire helped pyromaniacs reach their ultimate feeling of euphoria. With that thought in mind, he saw the upstairs room light up.

Ryan and Eric came out to meet him, and David realized that the living room was actually dark. No one was there.

Eric was the first to approach David, "What are you doing here, man?"

"This is the only way, don't you see?"

"What's the only way?"

"The only way I can be with my sister is to kill you guys. You do see that, right?"

Dave reached for a rifle that wasn't there; he had still been pumped up from earlier that day. Then he heard Scarlette's voice behind him, as she whispered, "Do you enjoy penetrating your sister?"

He muttered his own lines, knowing what was coming, "None of your fucking business." He had seen this moment coming in a dream, and felt there was no reason to fight it anymore. For all he knew, Quartz would kill him after he killed the two girls. He really had no other road to go.

She whispered, "Then that means that you, in turn, would like to be penetrated as well." She drove the sword into Dave through his back. He uttered a gurgled scream as he struggled with the sword, and felt Scarlette's firm grip tightening on his shoulder, holding him still. Ryan and Eric watched in shock. They couldn't even bring themselves to move to stop her.

She let him slide off of her sword, as Melissa pulled up the window and looked outside to see what was happening. "Who's out there?"

Scarlette looked up at Melissa, her face blackened by the blood that seemed to have splattered over her. "Just go back to sleep, my dear sweet Melissa. I've just destroyed your monster." She walked towards Ryan and Eric.

"Don't you kill my big brothers, Scarlette! Don't you take them from me!"

Scarlette grew disgusted and spat, "You didn't seem to mind me killing your own flesh and blood, though. You're an animal, too. You want them to fuck you, don't you?"

Melissa's face went pale, as she demanded, "What the hell are you talking about?"

Scarlette continued to walk to Ryan and Eric, as she said, "Let me tell you, though. You only think you want that. You know that one day, one of these boys will want to be inside you. When they do, however, you will feel so violated that you will want to die. I will spare you that pain, and destroy one of them now."

Melissa wasn't listening anymore. She was running down the stairs of her house, and running to the door. When her mother demanded to know what was going on, she snapped, "Mom, there's no time. Just call Damien and Allan right now, and tell them that someone's trying to break in!"

Her mother hurried to the room to get her cell phone, as Melissa woke up Becca, who was sleeping in the spare room by the kitchen. They went out the door and could see that Scarlette was covered in blood. Never mind that Scarlette called Dave and her brothers the monsters, Scarlette looked like one herself as she walked towards them, sword held out at her side. The girls called their names, and that seemed to snap the boys out of their shock.

Scarlette looked to Becca and Melissa, seeing them glare at her, she ranted, "Do not look me like that! I'm trying to save you!"

Melissa looked at Scarlette; "I don't know what happened to you, or who it was that hurt you. You can't punish them for something they didn't do, though."

Scarlette ignored her, feeling full of purpose as she charged Ryan, seeming to give a battle cry that was full of animal pain. As predicted, Eric pushed his brother out of the way, and took the blade into himself. She knew he would do that, the sentimental sap was so predictable. Eric only had time to look over his shoulder, at Ryan, once before he went, and mouthed that he was sorry. Ryan yelled out for his brother, through clenched teeth, "Noo!"

Scarlette pulled the sword out of Eric and threw it to the ground, far away from her. Becca and Melissa went over to help Eric. She then ripped the sheath from her belt, damaging the article of clothing so thoroughly that it came with the sheath. Before anyone could move, Scarlette was on the floor with Ryan, and holding his head in her arms.

"I know, I know. I felt a lot like you when they took my brother away from me."

He looked up at her, through angry tears, and demanded, "Why?"

"Don't you see? You and me are very much alike."

"I will never be like you."

"Yes. Hate me. That is the only way you'll have the strength to destroy me."

Ryan was breathing hard as he struggled to get up, and yet Scarlette's grip was stronger than he had imagined. It almost seemed like she was smothering him as she held his head in her arms. She whispered, "I can't bring myself to face you, weak as you are now. When you are ready, come and find me. Kill me with that sword. When I am ready to die, I will let you find me."

"Why?"

"You'll never know. I don't think of you as important enough to tell you."

"If I don't matter to you, why would you do this?"

"So you can know how I felt when I lost my brother."

"I don't care how you felt, you psychotic-"

"Let's not throw such ugly words. I do find that you are above that, at least."

"I hate you."

She released him, and as she fled, she told him, "Good. Then come and find me when you're ready. Come and kill me."

With that, she was gone, leaving Ryan to crawl towards his brother. "Why did you do that, dude?"

Eric coughed, and managed, "I couldn't let them hurt you, anymore."

"You're doing that now, by leaving."

"I'm not leaving you, bro. I don't even think she hit anything major."

Becca nodded, "We just have to get him to the hospital, quick."

Allan and Damien called out to them, "Are you kids alright?"

When the two saw everything up close, it was all they could to hold their stomachs. Becca looked up at them, "Never mind all this. Get Eric to the Hospital, Now!"

They moved to obey her, and Damien agreed to stay behind as Becca and Ryan helped get Eric into the car.

Damien told Allan to just go, and he was down the street with his siren blaring in the night. He had known that Allan's car had a siren, but he supposed there had been no reason to use it until that point. He looked around at the mess on the ground, picked up the sword with gloved hands, and took it into the house. Then he began to make calls, one to Ian, and another to his friends in the Bureau.

☯

Damien walked into the medical center, and saw that Ryan, and Becca were just waking from their doze in the waiting room. Melissa and her mom had gone to pick up Demi at Allan's house, and were in the waiting room as well.

"How's the kid doing?"

"Well, they had to rush Eric into emergency and opened him up to make sure that he hadn't been hurt in any of his vital organs. He's doing well enough, and should be recovering soon. He's very lucky. What about the mess on the other end?"

"I called in state troopers to handle it. I didn't want Quartz handling any of it. I wanted to make sure we did everything by the book."

"Well, that's good."

"Well . . . Almost by the book. I kept Scarlette's sword out of sight."

"Ugh. Why?"

"I don't know. I thought about what Ian might feel when he saw the prints on it match hers."

Allan was disappointed somewhat, "I see. Are we going to start doing that? Cover up evidence when our friends are involved, or leave out crucial details from our reports?"

"No. This is different. Something made me think that this wasn't our fight."

"Then, whose is it?"

Damien muttered, "It's not our place to finish their grudge. I think we should let him deal with it."

Ryan was awake, and they were startled when he spoke up, "You're right. I'll go after Scarlette, myself. Only I will deal with her." Becca joined him, and held onto him.

Allan inclined his head, his voice gaining intensity as he spoke. "Right. We'll go after Lester, that bastard. We'll drag his ass in, and make sure we expose his father too."

Becca looked around and asked them, "Will that ever be enough?"

They both looked at her, and they were shocked.

She continued on, though, "I'm serious. Will that ever be enough? I think when you find Lester; you should just do away with him. How many people have died because we wanted the system to handle them?"

Allan shook his head, "That's our job, to bring them in, and let the system handle them, or else we end up like Quartz, making up our own version of the law."

"In order to catch your enemy off guard, you have to think like your enemy."

"It's not as simple as that."

Damien placed his hand on Becca and Ryan's shoulders, "I know how you two must feel. I lost a niece to that guy, and I want to do away with him. The moment I do that, however, I will be just as bad. We let the system handle it. In that way, just one person does not have to hold the burden of justice alone. The person that does is bound to see victims everywhere. After a while, they go mad with the warped perspective that everyone is guilty, and no one is innocent."

"I guess that's why people look down on vigilantes?"

Allan conceded, "Their intentions are good."

"However, the road to hell is paved with good intentions."

Becca shook her head, and looked up at Ryan. He was looking at her, and he was glad that she was with him.

"Your brother should be recovering soon. It'll be awhile before he walks, though."

"Will he be able to play football?"

"Yeah. He'll be fine. He got really lucky. You still want to look for Scarlette?"

"You know, she did tell me something about losing her own brother, and trying to make me see her perspective. Thinking on it now, I can't help feeling sorry for her."

Allan shook his head, "Don't go down that road, friend. From what you told me, it seems she has somehow dehumanized you."

"In her eyes, I'm a monster."

Becca added, "Remember that she said that you two were alike in a lot of ways?"

"Don't remind me."

"What I'm saying is, she thinks of herself as a monster."

Allan looked at the two of them, and said, "Then, let's promise ourselves something. Let's make sure that no matter how many dark moments we might encounter that we never forget who we are. That we try to push ourselves to do the right thing, no matter how much it hurts."

Ryan felt angry at that moment, "No matter, who we lose?"

"I lost my girlfriend, Ryan. Ian lost his stepdaughter, and you almost lost your brother. I think we all lost something."

"Now, we have each other though, right?"

Allan smiled, "Yes. So, when you face Scarlette again, remember to go in holding high the badge of courage and justice."

Becca held her boyfriend, and muttered, "I hope for all our sakes, that it will be enough."

Continued . . .

2592504